UNSHEATHED

AN EPIC FANTASY COLLECTION

AUSTIN WORLEY   CHAD VINCENT

CHARLES GRAMLICH   DR. SCOTT SIMERLEIN

G. DEAN MANUEL   ROSS BAXTER

JAY ERICKSON   LIAM HOGAN

STUART THAMAN

ISBN: 978-1-940466-68-2

Hydra Publications
Goshen, Kentucky 40026
www.Hydrapublications.com

"The sword is the axis of the world, and its power is absolute." ~ Charles de Gaulle

CONTENTS

HANGING AT CROSBHOTHAR

AUSTIN WORLEY

Corpses hung from the ancient maple like leaves. Men, women, children, even dogs. Gagging on the stench, Knight-Lieutenant Arlise Dun murmured a prayer to the Mother for each of them. By the time she finished the fifty third prayer, her guts had coiled tight as a rattle snake. *No survivors. Again. No witnesses. Again.* Did the world derive some sort of perverse pleasure from making her job as hard as possible?

Buzzing, like a bumblebee in her ear, distracted Arlise from the dead. No normal human would've noticed, but five years with the Order of Watchers told her what was responsible. *Magic.* The buzzing grew until its source floated into view: a wisp, circling the maple like a lost squirrel. *Figures.* Violent death tended to crack the Wall Between Worlds, letting spirits cross over from the Outerworld. *Even if folk come back, this village will never be the same.*

She turned back to the final body and traced a finger over the wooden plaque nailed to the chest. 'Collaborator' it said in big, blocky letters. That was by far the most common appellation, but not the only one. 'Coward' labeled a balding, gray bearded man in fine furs, presumably Crosbhothar's alderman. 'Invader' marked five men in the sky blue gambesons of the Kingdom of Corhiel, hung just down the bough. A young woman—her face veiled by hair redder than the setting sun—flanked them. 'Harlot,' her plaque read.

Knight-Brother Robert de Vannen strode up to Arlise's side and leaned on his longaxe. "Eoghan One-Ear?"

The squelch of mud under booted feet cut off her reply. A score of blue clad soldiers—twelve spearmen and eight arbalists—marched toward the maple, led by Sir Samahel Ocrin. Evening sunlight gleamed off the Corhiel knight's newfangled plate armor. "Of course it's One-Ear, Watcher." His basinet's visor muffled his voice. "He's the only wood-chopper still fighting this war. The rest know their place."

Arlise rolled her eyes at the slur against Vyspans, but she couldn't dismiss Ocrin's point. King Delran of Vyspa and his vassals might abide by the Peace of Caer Blaidd, but that just made them—and anyone else who wouldn't fight the Corhiel —collaborators in Eoghan's eyes. And collaborators deserved the rope.

Brushing a strand of blonde hair from her eyes, Arlise surveyed the noble-turned-brigand's handiwork again. Dead villagers rocked in a bitter autumn breeze, their nooses creaking like macabre wind chimes. How could someone do this to their own countrymen?

Brother Robert scratched his scraggly beard and winced. "Worse than Vannen ever was." Heartbreak dripped from every word. Especially the name of his homeland.

Before Arlise found any comforting words, Knight-Sister Elain Bowen sloshed up the village's muddy road. Knight-Brother Alexos Comos followed on her heels, an arrow with red fletching nocked against his bowstring. "Lieutenant," the archer began, "we scouted the rest of the village, across the creek, and—"

Elain cut him off, a grin spreading across her tattooed face. "We found two dozen horses hitched around the Mother's Temple." Bouncing on the balls of her feet, the mage tapped her quarterstaff on a root. "You know what this means, Arlise?! We're finally gonna nail this bastard and his whole bloody band!"

Sir Ocrin dismounted with a clatter and rushed over. "One-Ear's here?" He flipped up his visor. "You saw the bloody woodchopper?"

Fiddling with her long black braid, the young woman shrugged. "Well...we didn't find anyone at all besides the horses." Elain stared down, dusted off her gambeson, and scuffed a boot in the dirt. "But who else would stay in a dead village besides the folk who killed it?"

The knight sucked in a breath, and his face turned from pale to a rich burgundy right before Arlise's eyes. "You thought you'd found him, yet you didn't attack?!"

Elain's grin disappeared. "Sir, I know full frontal assaults without support are popular among the nobility back home, but that's not how the Order operates. Watchers rely on each other. Maybe that's why we live longer than you, even though we have to face the arcane every day."

Silence reigned for a full minute. Arlise could've sworn Ocrin's gray mustache twitched with rage. Finally, the Corhiel commander slammed his visor shut and pivoted on his heel. "To the temple!" he barked at his men. "Fast as your sorry legs can carry you!"

Arlise cleared her throat. "Sir Ocrin, we should lead the way. Folk say Eoghan's lover is a powerful blood mage. You aren't immune to such powers and can't nullify normal ma...." She trailed off as Ocrin trudged back to his mount, swung into the saddle, and galloped north. *Figures.* How many times had secular nobles ignored her now? It didn't matter, those assignments always ended the same way. In a word, horribly.

"You'd think he was off to a brothel for the first time or something," Elain mumbled.

Arlise chuckled at the mental image. "He prefers glory and medals, I'd say." *Thank the Mother I'm not like that anymore.* She took a deep breath and repeated her mantra. *The woman I was is dead; I killed her when I took the Order's vows.*

Brother Alexos swept his gaze over the empty thatched cottages around them. "Your commands, Lieutenant?" He tried to mask it, but she caught the anxiety in his voice.

Twisting the gold band around her left ring finger, Arlise tried to cobble a plan together. It would've been nice to survey the temple for any side entrances or windows, but Sir Ocrin's assault made that impossible. "I suppose we're marching in after them." Adjusting her coat of plates, she glanced at the great maple. Crosbhothar's residents still swayed from its branches. "Dispensing a little justice is the least we can do. Armor up."

THE SCENT OF ROAST MUTTON, onion soup, and elder-berries filled the temple's vestibule. How could Eoghan's band sit and feast when death still hung over the village? Arlise pushed the question away and drew her arming sword. Black specks flecked Ferde's pale starmetal blade, making it resemble a night sky in reverse. She raised her roundshield and paused before the sanctuary's enchanted gates. "We've stormed rooms before, so you know the drill. Robert and I will clear the way. Elain, Alexos, stay back and deal with ranged threats."

Arlise slipped off her open-faced helm and pressed an ear against the temple gates. Quiet. Absolutely quiet. She slipped the helmet on again. "I smell a trap, but we don't have any options. Ready, Robert?"

The silent giant braced himself against one gate and nodded.

They pushed in unison. The gates swung open with an unholy groan, revealing the bloodstained battlefield which had once been the temple sanctuary. Without the enchanted gates in the way, Arlise sensed it now. The slithering, crawling sensation which haunted half her nightmares. *Blood magic. Thank the Mother we're immune.*

Sir Ocrin and his soldiers stood motionless only a dozen paces into the sanctuary, locked in place by a mind control spell. A handful of men in ragged tunics swarmed over them like scavenging ants, drawing blades across their helpless prey's throats one by one. Past the slaughter, pews had been pushed off to the room's eight sides, clearing space for trestle tables laden with food. More dirty men and women in tattered clothes gorged themselves on their bounty, either oblivious or numb to the bloodshed.

Near the pulpit stood a starling-haired woman, one bloody hand held high. Katrin the Black, Arlise knew from the wanted posters. At the sight of the Watchers, she raised her uninjured hand. "Halt!"

The ragged bunch butchering Ocrin's soldiers immediately pulled back toward the tables, casting wary glances at the Watchers with every step.

Katrin glared at the black Mother's Eye embroidered on Arlise's coat of plates, then spoke. "More supper guests." She snatched up a tankard from the nearest table and took a swig. "Mead always makes me a little...generous, so I'll extend you an offer. Just this once. Walk away, and you won't end up

like these…," the woman paused, her lips curling as she
waved a hand at Ocrin and his surviving soldiers, "like these
piles of horseshit. I have no quarrel with you, and this isn't
your concern."

Arlise blinked in surprise. The woman's guttural accent
called to mind the rolling plains of home, of the Seven
Marches. Why in the Void was a Marcher all the way across
the sea, in Vyspa, fighting with Eoghan One-Ear's brigands?
She shoved the question away. Answers would come later.
They always did.

Stepping forward, she shook her head. "Blood magic is
very much our concern, especially when you use it to seize
minds. Besides, I hear your lover slaughters patrols and
villages with an enchanted blade. There's more than enough
reason for the Order to be involved." Arlise swept her gaze
over the sanctuary, vainly searching for One-Ear's armored
form. "Where's Eoghan?"

The blood mage stood straighter than a spear, as if the
question were offensive. "I'm not with him anymore. None of
us are. Not after what he's become." She jabbed a bloody
finger at the entrance. "I joined to butcher invaders, not peas-
ants too weak to stand for themselves. Children don't deserve
to hang. Neither does some gal who screwed a couple Corhiel
soldiers. We all make mistakes." Without warning, Katrin's
tone grew frigid. "I told Eoghan we'd stay behind and burn
down Crosbhothar, then rejoin him. Instead, we're supping
here, then riding south. Unless you mean to stop us."

Before she could reply, Alexos leaned close and whispered. "Keep her distracted, Lieutenant. I'll sneak around the
side and put an arrow through Katrin's eye."

That was no empty boast; the memory of Alexos shooting
three apples from a tree in just as many seconds still rang clear.

Never looking back, Arlise nodded sharply and took another step forward. Ocrin's frozen soldiers surrounded her like a forest of men. "Whether we let you go depends on how you answer my questions," she lied. While all eyes lingered on her, Arlise barely caught Brother Alexos' footfalls as he slunk into the shadows.

Katrin's nose wrinkled. "Name these questions."

Arlise bit back a curse. She hadn't thought of any. Her mind scrambled in a dozen different directions. Finally, a logical one came to mind. "Did you use your magic on the villagers outside?"

A long pause. "Yes." Guilt and regret dripped from the lone word. "Only because I thought Eoghan wanted to search the houses for invaders without any problems. And I suppose he did. But when we found those soldiers and the girl in the communal barn, something snapped. His eyes turned all black, and the man I love disappeared. Then the hangings began."

"You just stood there while he murdered the folk you claim to protect? Children?"

Taking another sip from her tankard, the blood mage nodded. "Watcher, you haven't seen Eoghan in one of his rages. Let me tell you, as long as he's fixated on revenge against the Corhiel, no single person can stand against him. Not even me"

That's no excuse. Katrin and her followers bore as much guilt as Eoghan. They'd had the power to act, but refused to use it.

Arlise recalled the folk swaying from Crosbhothar's old maple. The children, the elders, the lives cut short in their prime. That girl with the red hair. Her blood boiled. *I shouldn't have agreed to Alexos' plan.* In that moment, she wanted nothing more than to cut down every last brigand in the temple. To bathe Ferde's starmetal blade in the blood of evil. *Too late. We're committed, like it or not.*

By now, an arrow should've hurtled through the blood mage's eye. Where in the Void had Alexos gotten off to? Becoming aware of the awkward silence filling the sanctuary, Arlise pushed the question away. *Just stall a little longer.* She decided to sate her earlier curiosity. "I know you're a Marcher. How'd you end up here, fighting Vyspa's war?"

Katrin gulped more mead and smiled. "My abilities are in high demand, so I crossed the sea to this isle. The Corhiel came a year later, hungry to control the trade in steel-heart wood and coryphium ore. It struck me as so...crass a reason to kill folk, I decided to fight for my new homeland. When the nobility stabbed us in the back with that damn treaty, I found Eoghan." A lock of midnight black hair fell over one eye. "I'm not sure what this has to do with anything, Watcher. What are you-?"

A bowstring's twang cut her off. The first arrow grazed Katrin's cheek. The second should've buried itself in her eye, but she dodged with an impossible fluidity and ran a finger over the fresh gash. Once again, Arlise sensed the slithering, oily sensation of blood magic.

A shimmering violet bubble enveloped Katrin's form, and the third arrow shattered against it. As its iron head bounced across the temple's marble floor, she giggled. "Perfidy, is it? I have tricks of my own."

Again the air turned oily. Sir Ocrin lurched to life, flanged mace in hand. Candlelight glinted off his plate armor as he jerkily closed in.

Still giggling, Katrin waved at her followers. "Slay them all, invader or Watcher!"

The ring of two dozen drawn blades filled the temple, but Arlise barely heard it over the blood rushing through her ears.

Everything other than the approaching puppet knight died away. Sir Ocrin might be abrasive, but he didn't deserve to die. *Mother, how can I put him down non-lethally?* Plate armor couldn't make a man invincible, but it sure came close. Worse, Katrin's brigands would fall on her at any moment.

As it turned out, Arlise didn't have to save Ocrin. Bellowing, Brother Robert charged past like an enraged aurochs. He ducked a wild swing of the knight's mace and slammed into him with a clatter. Steel crunched as Ocrin hit the marble floor. Hard. Arlise stood, mouth agape, while Robert wrestled the mace away. She hadn't expected the cautious axeman to seize the initiative.

Elain slapped her on the back and rushed forward. "Get Katrin! I'll keep her people off us." Air buzzed with magic as she called forth energy from the Outerworld. The young mage snapped her fingers, and three advancing bandits burst into flames. "Go!" she yelled over their pitiful wails.

Raising her gaze, Arlise searched for the ringleader. She caught Alexos near a pillar, emptying his quiver at their ragged enemies. Four men and women slumped in their supper, red-fletched arrows sunk into their flesh. Three more arrows whistled across the sanctuary, and three more brigands fell.

Unfortunately, Katrin wasn't amongst them. The blood mage clambered over a table and hurried toward the sanctuary's rear, still enveloped in her protective buddle. *You're not escaping. Not today.* Remembering the murdered villagers, Arlise charged.

A screeching bandit met her, sword raised high. Dead children flashed before Arlise's eyes. *Mother mighty, shield me in battle.* She slashed deep and diagonally, from ribs to hip. Falling, his screeches turned to howls. The stench of vacated bowels rose moments later.

Mother merciful, forgive me my sins. Arlise parried another attacker's low thrust, then punched with her round-shield's iron rim. The bandit staggered. She remembered the hanged girl with the red hair and punched again. This time, the man crumpled.

At heavy footfalls, she spun to find a squat, muscular woman lunging. Arlise sidestepped, but not fast enough. Instead of sinking into her groin, a dagger flashed across her hip. She grimaced. *Mother moral, pour out your judgment on the wicked.* Blocking a second thrust with the shield, Arlise smashed her pommel into the woman's temple with all her might. Brains spattered her helm's cheekpiece. The old alderman with the plaque nailed to his chest lingered before her mind's eye.

A fourth enemy fell mid charge, a red-fletched arrow lodged in her throat. *Mother magnanimous, thank you for your blessings.* The air hummed around numbers five, six, and seven. Clutching their heads, all three bandits fell. Torn skin and frost on their lashes betrayed the manner of their death: every last drop of water in their skulls had been frozen by magic.

Though her hip throbbed, Arlise hurdled the nearest table. *By the Prophets I pray.* The stench of blood, sweat, and death mingled with the aroma of mutton, soup, and alcohol. Only a dozen paces separated her from Katrin now. Magic barrier gone, the woman rummaged through baggage piled past the pulpit until she finally drew a short sword. Even from a distance, Arlise recognized it as a katzbalger. A good enough blade for slashing on the battlefield, but not in tight quarters. And not against an armored opponent.

She allowed herself a smirk and stalked forward like a cougar. This would be easy enough. How talented a duelist could some blood mage be?

"I gave you a chance. This isn't my fault." Katrin slashed at her knee.

An obvious strike. Arlise blocked it with her shield, then launched into a flurry of thrusts. High, middle, low, a dozen in total. Astonishingly, the blood mage parried every last probing blow.

She switched to cuts. Their dance drug on. All around them, the cacophony of combat died. Arrows ceased whistling, and the wailing wounded fell silent. Soon, only the clash of blades filled the Mother's temple.

Too solid on the defense, Arlise decided when Katrin countered her sixteenth slash. Had Eoghan taught her sword-play? She shivered at the thought of an even more talented brigand. *I'll need a feint to end this scrap.*

When Katrin edged around her right side, Arlise only halfway matched her footwork. Her roundshield hung a little low, as if exhaustion were taking hold. She caught that glimmer in the bandit's eye. The moment of decision. Katrin's body language flushed with premature triumph.

The vertical slash came exactly as she'd predicted. Arlise hopped back, letting the strongest section of her coat of plates take the blow. Katrin's katzbalger bit deep into the layers of cloth, but didn't even touch the metal underneath. As the short blade withdrew, Arlise sprang her trap.

Ferde's starmetal blade snipped muscle and tendons on the palm side of her wrist. Katrin groaned, eyes wide as her sword clattered to the floor. *No way she can hold a weapon now.* Arlise had meant the blow to sever her sword hand, but she couldn't complain. The fight was over; only a few formalities remained.

She bashed the brigand with her roundshield, sending Katrin reeling into the pile of baggage. Before the mage could stand, Arlise stamped a studded boot against her neck and raised Ferde for the killing blow.

"Stop! Arlise, stop!"

At the sound of Elain's voice, she froze.

"We still don't know where Eoghan is. Bait could draw him out. What better bait is there than a captured lover?"

Dead children flashed before Arlise's eyes. That girl with the red hair. The alderman. The slow, creaking rhythm of corpses dangling from the maple. She wanted to ignore Elain, to bury Ferde up to the hilt in Katrin's body. Make her pay for all of it. But right now, with the mage gasping for breath under her boot, it wouldn't be justice. More like vengeance. And Arlise knew what the Prophets said about that. *"Revenge will drown you in a sea of blood."* By the Void, she'd lived it once. "Fine."

Her brow furrowed as she contemplated their next step. "We'll treat her wounds, then make for Dalkey."

Elain nodded. "They have pillories there. Eoghan's sure to hear about her being held in one." Hazel eyes settled on Katrin. "Should I fetch one of those coryphium collars from the pack mules? I'm sure you don't want her casting spells."

"Of course." After her comrade left, Arlise let Ferde's point hover over one of Katrin's blue eyes. "Don't even think about blood magic."

"I yield," the beaten woman wheezed.

Arlise grunted and glanced toward the entrance, where Sir Ocrin's surviving soldiers remained locked in place. She turned back to the blood mage underfoot. "End your mind control spells."

A nod answered the command, and the crawling, slithering cloud crowding the temple vanished. "See," Katrin wheezed, "I yield."

TOSSING STUDDED LEATHER GAUNTLETS ASIDE, Arlise warmed her hands over the campfire. The hum of magic filled the evening, calling to mind bagpipes. She glanced at the birch where they'd bound their prisoner. Elain knelt over Katrin's wounded arm, casting a healing spell.

Muscle and tendon wove themselves back together, fueled by energy called up from the Outerworld. Arlise marveled at the patience required. *Like watching a master artist at work.* Not that she'd ever tell Elain that. Her best friend already had a high enough opinion of herself.

With only a short line of skin left to regenerate, the humming ceased. "It's best to let the last bit heal on its own," Elain said, winding clean bandages around the prisoner's wrist.

Katrin grunted. "When Eoghan finds and frees me, I'll make sure your death is a quick one. One good swing of a longsword, perhaps."

Rolling her eyes, Elain mopped sweat from her russet brow and sauntered back to the campfire. "What a friendly woman." Her gaze settled on Brother Alexos. "Your turn for guard duty."

While Alexos grumbled, Elain turned to Arlise. "How's that hip wound?"

"As if it never existed. One more reason I'm glad to have you at my back."

The mage blushed and stared up at the blanket of dark clouds. For a long while, only the crackling blaze kept silence at bay.

Sir Ocrin trudged up from where the surviving Corhiel had made their camp, wringing his hands all the while. "I... I'd like to thank all of you for sparing me back at the temple.

It was a risk you didn't have to take." He coughed. "I'll be sure to listen to your advice in the future."

Smiling at his contrition, Arlise nodded. "Good. We may run into more arcane happenings before Eoghan meets his end."

Elain cleared her throat. "Speaking of the arcane, do you think Katrin told the truth?"

"About…?" She frowned. Sometimes, Elain's mind moved so fast she left out important details.

"About Eoghan's eyes turning black before he murdered everyone in Crosbhothar."

Before Arlise could speak, Sir Ocrin leaned in close. "I'm sorry, what do black eyes have to do with magic?" His mustache twitched with every word.

For the first time all evening, Brother Robert looked up from cleaning and sharpening his longaxe. "A sign of demonic possession."

Nodding, Arlise met Ocrin's gaze. "Which would mean Eoghan has become some form of vampire. Or terror, if he has latent magical ability. But going by all the stories and rumors, that doesn't fit. He doesn't consume blood or human flesh. He doesn't use magic, other than the enchantments built into his longsword. He can't be either creature. I say Katrin lied."

Her words rang with confidence, but doubt gnawed her innards. Katrin had no reason to lie about that detail. Uncertainty building, Arlise fiddled with her ring.

Elain shrugged. "Maybe. This may not fit what the books say, but we know they're not necessarily complete. Remember the wendigo?"

From his post beside their prisoner, Brother Alexos groaned. "My ribs sure remember, Sister."

The memory of snapping bones made Arlise wince.

Alexos was lucky to survive that mission. By the Prophets, we all were. She ran fingers over the burn scars along her left jaw, ear, and neck. The Order had also said skin-walkers were just wild tales, but that hadn't stopped one from trying to melt her face off.

Elain continued. "This may not be possession. More like…affliction." She glanced at their prisoner. "Katrin described rages and immense strength during them. There are theories that spirits, demon or not, may lend aid to humans in exchange for feeding on their emotions." Stretching, the young woman's gaze settled on Sir Ocrin. "Were I a gambling woman, I'd say the one Eoghan made a pact with likes the taste of vengeance."

Arlise grimaced. "Then we have to end this fast."

"Why?" A hint of panic crept into Sir Ocrin's voice. "W-what'll happen if we don't?"

She took a deep breath. "Are you familiar with the scriptures? Never mind. I've dealt with creatures of vengeance before. Things always, always spiral out of control. We all saw Crosbhothar. If he's not stopped, dozens of other villages will share its fate. Or worse."

For a few moments, Ocrin regarded her in silence. The scrutiny made Arlise's skin crawl. "You've piqued my curiosity, Knight-Lieutenant."

She sucked in another deep breath as old ghosts came to life. "It's a long, complicated story."

"We have time."

Ocrin didn't take hints very well. *Figures.* On the other hand, Arlise couldn't counter his point. Between the new moon, the heavy cloud cover, and Vyspa's primordial forests, they couldn't accomplish anything productive until dawn. Even the enhanced senses of Watchers wouldn't change that. *I suppose there are worse ways to pass time that dredging up the past.* Still, a tornado of emotions twisted in her gut. "I'll give you the shorter version."

Clearing her throat, Arlise stared into the flickering campfire. "Go back, years before taking my vows. I gave an order. A stupid, poorly worded order. I thought a few dozen innocents caught in the middle would be worth ending a war. And I was wrong."

Visions of the fateful battle at Laufenden flashed before her mind's eye: a pillar of blue flame, air thick with smoke and the clashing of arms, wailing wounded and screaming horses, the scarlet and gray banners of House Dun, and a rain of arrows battering a surging mass of silhouettes. Then dawn revealing the field of corpses—soldier and freeholder alike—full of her company's arrows, the charred skeletons of ruined homes, and a crumbling temple to the Mother. "Terribly, terribly wrong."

The Corhiel knight spoke, scattering the visions. "Doesn't sound wrong to me."

She ground her teeth. "You didn't see the results. You didn't lose family because of me. Lars Fischer, Lance of Kressen, did." Guilt threatened to drown Arlise. *The woman I was is dead; I killed her when I took the Order's vows.* The mantra failed to hold the waves of regret at bay.

Sir Ocrin leaned forward, entranced. "And?"

"He dogged my trail for half a decade. We clashed a few times in my mercenary days, but I didn't learn why Lars cared until after I joined the Watchers." Arlise cradled herself. "My first assignment as a sworn sister in the Order. Lars took a whole caravan hostage, just to draw me out. Killed them one by one until I arrived. Some demon twisted his mind and body, until he became worse than I'd ever been." She shivered at the memories. Humans shouldn't have so many eyes. They shouldn't melt into amorphous blobs at will.

"You struck him down?"

Arlise nodded. "Only after a nightlong scrap. The rarer vampiric forms are…difficult to slay."

Frowning, Sir Ocrin tinkered with his greaves. "This man was possessed by a demon feeding on vengeance? The same sort One-Ear may have a pact with?"

Glancing at their prisoner bound to the birch, she nodded again. "Another reason to hope our trap kills Eoghan in Dalkey. If it doesn't, and Elain's right about the pact, he'll only grow stronger. Perhaps even too strong to stop."

———

ONE HAND on Ferde's hilt, Arlise surveyed the creek's edge. *No boulders. Good.* Her grip on the sword relaxed. No boulders meant no lurkers, and no lurkers meant she could bathe for the first time in three weeks, without fear of some massive amphibian devouring her. Dropping a basket on the bank, Arlise fumbled with her belt buckle, then set about undressing.

Naked, she tiptoed into the water and shivered. Cool, but thanks to the unseasonably warm weather she didn't have to worry about hypothermia. Arlise untied her bun, letting blonde tresses fall to her shoulder blades. Wading deeper, she hummed a bawdy tune she'd forgotten the lyrics to.

It should've been a welcome respite from the pressures of duty, but as she scrubbed filth away, Arlise couldn't stop thinking about the hunt for Eoghan. *A week we've quartered in Dalkey, yet he still hasn't shown.* A week Katrin spent locked in a pillory for all to see. Surely word of it had reached her lover. So why didn't he charge to the rescue?

A hint of despair made her guts tingle. What if he sensed a trap? What if he hit somewhere else? Once again Crosbhothar flashed through her mind. *Fifty-three lost souls.* How many more would die to sate One-Ear's appetite for revenge?

Arlise put the questions out of mind and scrubbed harder. As grime melted away, her gaze lingered on the rings of triangles tattooed around her arms and thighs. One hundred and eighty-seven. One for every innocent killed at Laufenden. That smoldering village filled her mind's eye while her stupid order echoed through her head. *"Capture everyone you can, kill everyone you can't."*

Once more guilt nearly drowned Arlise. She bit her lip until the metallic taste of blood touched her tongue. *If I'd known how many troops the Usurper had, if I'd known we wouldn't be able to hold the villagers prisoner and fight a battle at the same time...* Pushing the familiar thoughts away, she recited her mantra aloud. "The woman I was is dead; I killed her when I took the Order's vows." Every mission, every twisted mage or monster felled by Arlise's hand, was penance for Laufenden. For the one hundred and eight-seven. Proof she'd changed.

Was that why she worried about Eoghan and the trap in Dalkey so much? *If I fail, does that mean-*

Her thoughts scattered as a war cry echoed through the steel-heart trees. It began low and deep before rising into a crescendo. Vyspan, without a doubt. A second cry rose from the north. From Dalkey. *Eoghan!*

Duty drove Arlise back to shore. *No time to dry.* As a third war cry erupted, she snatched her clothes from the basket. Trembling fingers fumbled over trouser laces, and again over bootstraps. Soaked hair clung to her skin like a veil, reminding Arlise of that hung girl from Crosbhothar. *Innocents won't hang today,* she vowed, grabbing Ferde from the muddy bank. *I won't let them.* Stiff fingers meant it took four tries to buckle the belt around her waist.

Instead of another war cry, sounds of battle filled the misty morning. *He took our bait.* She wondered how many troops Eoghan marshaled to free Katrin. Five dozen? Ten? It didn't matter; today's battle would break One-Ear's band. Ripping Ferde from its sheath, Arlise sprinted up the snaky path leading back to Dalkey. Her sopping socks and boots squelched with every step.

A litany of battle calculations and tactics swirled through her brain as Arlise wound her way past ancient steel-heart trees. Their sweet fragrance tickled her nose. Then came a revelation. *I have no armor. Or shield.* How could she fight a battle with her gear tucked under a bed in the alderman's house?

Panic crept into Arlise's flesh. The complete absence of animals—whether singing birds or foraging squirrels—only hastened its spread. They knew what lay ahead, and fled. Yet here she was, running headlong toward the clash. *Mother, Prophets, guide me.*

Writing off the path as too long and twisty, she charged through the underbrush. Thorns and branches clawed at her garments while dead leaves clung to wet skin.

It seemed an eternity, but the forest finally gave way to Dalkey's southern fringes. The wailing of wounded and thud of marching feet drew closer. With the aroma of porridge on the wind, Arlise hurdled a fence and cut between two thatched cottages.

She emerged on a battlefield, panting. Scores of men in greens and browns broke against a thin, sky blue shield wall stretching across the road. Arlise searched for a trace of her fellow Watchers, or Eoghan and his plate armor, but found neither. However, Sir Ocrin stood on the right flank, shouting encouragement as his men began to buckle.

With a swelling battle cry of their own, Dalkey's residents joined the fight. Arrows loosed from rooftops stung the brigands, while cudgels, spears, and pitchforks wreaked havoc in their unarmored ranks. As Arlise watched, the mass of green and brown routed.

Sensing an opportunity, Arlise leapt into the fray. She dodged a desperate slash from one of the first routers and thrust blindly. Ferde parted flesh like warm butter, then ground to a halt as it glanced off bone. Skewered through the throat, the brigand dropped. While he lay gasping in an expanding welter of crimson gore, Arlise pried the heater shield from his arm. She preferred roundshields, but some protection always beat no protection.

She'd barely strapped it on when a towering woman with a flail swung at her skull. Arlise's scavenged shield flicked up to block. The spiked head struck like the Mother's wrath, splintering wood and sending shockwaves up her arm. Clingy strands of hair obscured her vision. Another swing came whistling in before she could strike back. It drove Arlise to her knees and numbed her shield arm.

A final prayer formed on her tongue. As the big bandit picked up momentum for a fatal blow, a flanged mace shattered the woman's cheek with a gut churning crunch. Eyes still wide open, she sagged to the side. In her place stood Sir Ocrin.

While his men pushed on in pursuit of the routers, Ocrin extended a gauntleted hand. "Knight-Lieutenant!" he boomed through his visor. "You live!"

"Only thanks to you," she muttered, letting him pull her up.

"Consider it payback for the temple in Crosbhothar."

Panting, Arlise surveyed the sodden road. Dozens of corpses littered the muck. *All because one man can't accept a war ended.* She stared into the eye slits of Ocrin's helm. "Where are my people?"

The big knight shrugged. "Last I saw they and some villagers held the north road against a few dozen wood-choppers."

Arlise took a step up the road, but Ocrin caught her arm. "Watcher, you should know: Eoghan and a few men on horses skirted the village. Like they wanted a clear path to the green. I'd say they aim to break that damned blood mage out while we're distracted."

Damn. She might have a shield now, but against competent, armored men on horseback Arlise didn't have a prayer. Panic crept back into her flesh. If Katrin escaped... "Come with me."

Ocrin shook his head. "We need to keep the pressure on these woodchoppers or they'll regroup and overwhelm us with sheer numbers. I've already lost half my men."

"In that case," Arlise began, despair tightening her throat, "I'll see what I can do on my own. Mother be with you."

He nodded. "And with you." Then the knight lurched into a clanking run, joining his men in their pursuit.

Alone, every prayer she'd ever learned came to Arlise's lips. Instincts urged her to find Elain and Alexos and Robert first, but duty's pull was stronger. Trudging uphill, she pushed toward Dalkey Green.

Rising fear made the trek pass in a blur. Arlise paid little heed to the muck, the cottages either abandoned or locked up tight, or the unnatural silence. Did she even have a chance at stopping Eoghan? Mother forbid, what if he slew her here? If the trap failed, could anyone hope to slay One-Ear? As more and more fearful questions flickered through Arlise's head, her breath quickened.

All those questions died on Dalkey Green. Seven butchered villagers littered the dead grass, some more whole than others. At the green's far end, Katrin remained locked in her pillory, though a figure in full plate meddled with the lock. *Eoghan.* Two more men in mail circled the pillories on horseback, sweeping their eyes over the village's heart.

Thanks to her enhanced senses, Arlise heard their words. "Milord, we have a guest."

For the first time, Eoghan's soft voice touched her ears. "Deal with it. Quickly."

The horsemen, with only a few yards between them, settled into a trot and aimed straight for Arlise. *Idiots.* Two on one, they could've parted and charged from different directions. It would've been nigh impossible to defend against. She allowed herself a grim smile. *I'll make them pay for that idiocy.*

Their trot became a gallop. Arlise strode forward to meet the charge, taking in the slaughtered villagers. A strand of hair blew into her mouth. Spitting it out, she recalled the folk of Crosbhothar. The dogs, the children, the elders, that red haired girl, all swinging from the maple's boughs. *This is for you.* One deep breath, and Arlise stood ready to meet the onslaught.

They thundered in, only a yard separating their horses. The man on the left raised an axe overhead while the right one held a saber low, parallel to the sole of his boot. *At least they're smart enough to attack from two different positions.* Arlise stood still as a stone wall until the last possible second.

The blows fell simultaneously. Springing to life, Arlise parried the low saber cut and met the axe with her shield. It lodged in the linden wood. Splinters scraped skin, and her shield arm fell numb again.

Instead of making the wise choice and breaking off to draw another weapon, the left rider—struggling to pry his axe free—tugged so hard on the reins his mare reared. Off balance and distracted, he couldn't possibly have avoided Arlise's counterstrike.

Ferde drilled through hauberk and flesh, severing the axeman's spine just below the ribs. As his mare bolted, he tumbled out of the saddle. Arlise turned her attention to the saber wielder.

He slowed to a canter, circling like a hawk. She ground her teeth. *He's just stalling so Eoghan can free Katrin.* And dammit, he was succeeding.

Trying to draw the last horseman in, Arlise turned and strode toward the pillories. Sure enough, hoof beats quickened behind her. She counted them, waiting to turn until the horseman couldn't veer away. Spinning on her heel, she found a frustrated brigand slashing down with all his might.

Arlise lunged, her shield rising to meet the saber cut while also obscuring her own blade. Mail rings burst around Ferde's starmetal tip, and the rider's own momentum gave the thrust more penetrating power. She felt the sword skewer his kidney and burst through the back of the horseman's hauberk. He toppled from the saddle, howling until he hit the earth. Then, the last foe between her and Eoghan One-Ear shuddered and died.

By the time she turned her focus to the pillories, Katrin was free. "You came," Arlise heard the blood mage whisper to her rescuer. "The real you."

Once again, Eoghan's soft tones touched her ears. "I lost it at Crosbhothar. Sorry. It won't happen again." The renegade removed his helmet. "I swear."

Katrin smiled and wrapped him up in a hug. Their lips locked in a passionate kiss.

If she hadn't known them to be callous murderers, Arlise would've found it all heartwarming. As it was, the display only made her more determined to visit justice on them both.

When she closed in on the couple, Katrin broke away from the kiss. "Get me out of this collar, and we'll kill the Watcher together."

Eoghan shook his head. "No." He pointed to his lover's bandaged arm. "I'm not putting you at risk again. Take my horse and ride for the safe house. I'll handle the Watcher personally."

"But-"

"She won't expect what I can do. Go!"

Katrin clambered into the saddle, and Arlise nibbled her lip. The bloodshed in Crosbhothar, the time spent setting this trap in Dalkey, all now rendered pointless. Her gaze settled on Eoghan. *Decapitate the snake, and its body will die.* Hope of ending it all, of bringing justice for Crosbhothar, still lingered.

Eoghan snatched up his helmet and drew his longsword. A new sort of weapon, though she'd seen Mama practice with one a little. Just as the rumors said, lines of a gold-like metal twisted across the blade. *Coryphium enchantments.*

Searching for weak points, Arlise swept her eyes over his elaborately etched armor. *That suit must've cost his entire fortune.* Since she found no weaknesses, it was money well spent. Mail protected every gap between the plates. Only a perfect thrust could hope to hit flesh. Prying open his visor to stab him in the face appeared to be the only available option. How to do that while unarmored, Arlise had no idea.

A low, curious hum radiated from the bandit. Was it just the enchantments in his sword? Some demonic pact, as Elain speculated? Or something worse? "I expected a prim, armored Watcher," Eoghan said. "Not some soaked, bedraggled rat." His voice remained soft even as he sneered at her.

Bristling, Arlise edged closer. "This rat slew three of your men this morning, and three more last week at Crosbhothar. I'm sorry if you find that disappointing."

The mention of Crosbhothar brought a sudden change over Eoghan. His eyes turned all black, and the humming around him grew louder. "Watchers ought to be neutral," he boomed in a far deeper voice, "yet you serve invaders, imprisoned Katrin!"

She shook her head. "You murdered children! Mother help you, Eoghan!"

Twirling his longsword, Eoghan snorted. "The Mother never helped me, but I found someone who will."

That settled it. Elain's guess was right. Taking a moment to steady her breathing, Arlise lunged.

One-Ear danced away, faster than a normal human had any right to, and slashed at her temple. Only her enhanced reflexes allowed Arlise to parry in time. Loose hair obscured her vision, preventing a follow up attack.

Dropping into a low guard, the brigand unleashed a flurry of cuts aimed for her unprotected shins. His longsword disappeared, replaced by a whirling blur. Blocks and parries left Arlise breathless. Thanks to the reach of Eoghan's weapon, she couldn't take back the initiative.

Desperation swelled. *Mother show me the way.* The fight in Crosbhothar's temple leapt to mind. Arlise decided to handle Eoghan in the same way Brother Robert put Sir Ocrin out of that scrap: by tackling him.

A hoarse cry tore from her throat as she charged. They hit the earth with a thud and clatter, blades trapped between them. Unable to wriggle either arm free, Arlise kneed Eoghan in the crotch. A sharp cry escaped his lips. "Not again," he wheezed.

Before she could rip off his helm, a silvery blur smashed into Arlise's mouth. Something cracked, and the taste of blood blossomed. Reeling, she caught a glimpse of Eoghan flicking his wrist. Waves of heat roiled along the length of his steel.

She barely blocked the next two thrusts. Her shield burst into flame under the enchantment's heat. Old memories of Laufenden bubbled to the surface. *No, no, not now.* Arlise hurled the shield at her assailant, hoping to extinguish the fire and the memories.

Eoghan casually batted it away, then flicked his wrist again. The heat waves gave way to frost. He thrust twice more.

Arlise managed to clumsily parry the first strike. Her luck broke on the second one. It sliced across the edge of her right breast and armpit. A yelp escaped her throat, both from the cut itself and the strange prickling that followed, like thousands of needles. *Frostbite, almost.*

Unable to move her arm, a third blow knocked away Ferde. She stumbled backward, tripping over a rock and landing in a mud puddle. Eoghan loomed. "See?! You're naught but a rat." He raised his longsword overhead. Arlise recognized the position from Mama's longsword practices: Vom Tag. Perfect for launching powerful, killing blows. *Mother, Prophets, don't end it like this. I still have so much to atone for.*

A whistle interrupted her plea. Eoghan grunted as a red-fletched arrow slammed into his back. The bodkin penetrated the plate, but didn't appear to actually injure the brigand. Another arrow bounced off the backplate, and when he spun a third buried itself in his breastplate.

Dazed, Arlise's head lolled to the left. She dimly caught the white armor of her comrades.

"Chance spared you today, Watcher." Eoghan spoke in his normal, soft tones again. "Pray we never meet again; only divine intervention will save you if we do."

As Eoghan loped off, darkness gobbled up Arlise's consciousness. The last thing she felt before it engulfed her were Brother Robert's sturdy arms.

———

COLD GLASS PRESSED against her lips, and a sour fluid drug Arlise back to the land of the living. Hacking, she lurched up. *Where am I?* A wood ceiling above, linen sheets up to her waist, a hearth blazing near the bed's foot. *The alderman's house. Dalkey.* The air hung heavy with rot and cleaning alcohol. Her tongue brushed against her front teeth. More specifically, the gap where one should've been. "I'm toothleth," she lisped.

From her bedside, Elain suppressed a giggle. "I'm sorry," she said, setting aside a potion vial, "I shouldn't laugh." All levity drained from her russet face in an instant. "Eoghan busted that fake tooth good. I pulled it. Don't worry, the Order'll buy you a new one, made of the finest Mklarite ivory. I'll put it in myself."

"That's not reassuring. You're not a dentist," Arlise groaned, careful to enunciate her words. Her gaze settled on the vial. "What's that?"

"A little something to accelerate tissue growth. I need to debride that cut Eoghan gave you, then heal it."

Arlise frowned. "You didn't do it already?" Judging by the sun rising through the east window, a day had passed since the battle. *Since Eoghan kicked my ass.*

"I debrided it once, but your flesh froze again. A chunk of the enchantment must've broken off in the wound." Elain gingerly grabbed a scalpel and tweezers. "Lie down."

She stiffly obeyed, mind trying to fill in blank spaces. "What happened after Eoghan escaped?" Just saying it made Arlise angry. *Dalkey should've been the end of it.*

Elain hummed, cutting away bandages. "Alexos tracked them the old fashioned way. Eoghan and his boys are holed up in an abandoned mine as we speak. Sir Ocrin commandeered a Corhiel patrol, and two Vyspan Thanes mustered their rangers. With Katrin free again, Brother Robert's overseeing the whole thing. Just in case of blood magic, you know."

Corhiel, Vyspans, the Order, Eoghan sure made a lot of enemies. A scalpel nipped at her armpit, and Arlise winced. "They haven't launched a final assault yet?"

"No." Tweezers prodded the cut. "With such close quarters, everyone's worried about casualties." Elain paused, mumbling a string of curses. More prodding. "Eoghan knows it too. Last night, he sent an emissary offering trial by combat. To the death. If our champion wins, his whole bloody band surrenders. If he wins, they go free."

While her friend cut away more dead flesh, Arlise bit her lip. "I hope nobody plans on dueling Eoghan." The thought of that murderer escaping again because some cocky little shit took his bait made her stomach roil.

For a long time, Elain said nothing. Just more prodding in the wound. Finally, she spoke up. "I hear Robert's thinking about it. If anyone could win, it's him."

Her throat clenched. Arlise imagined the big man striding into battle with One-Ear, ignorant of the brigand's unnatural speed. All the horrid scenarios made her heart ache. *I can't lose another comrade.* Between her days as a noble, a sell-sword, and a Watcher, the list of fallen friends stretched far too long already.

"Gotcha, you little bugger!" Elain shouted, scattering Arlise's ruminations. As the tweezers pulled away, it felt like someone plucked a sliver of ice from her breast. Then the low buzz of magic permeated the room. She gasped, feeling new muscle bulge and ripple under Elain's bony fingers. After a few minutes, the magic ceased. "There you are, pretty as yesterday."

She snorted at Elain's attempted flirtation. "That's not saying much."

Full of new life, Arlise sat up in bed and ran through her repertoire of cuts and thrusts. *I can fight again.* Thoughts of One-Ear and his challenge surged to the forefront. He had to pay. For Crosbhothar. For Dalkey. For everything. "Take me to this mine Eoghan's besieged in."

The mage recoiled. "No. No! I know your mind. You're not dueling. Right now, Robert's stronger than you. Trust him." She paused. "I can order you to bed, you know. Section 9.3 of the Order's Charter: medical rulings of the ranking healer are final."

Arlise sucked in a breath. "Remember your speculation about a demonic pact? You're right: Eoghan moved faster, hit harder than he should've. But Robert doesn't know about it. He doesn't know how One-Ear fights. I do."

"No! Prophets, you're worse than a mule."

Despite the protest, she caught her friend wavering. "Elain," her voice cracked, "I don't want Robert to die. I know you don't either."

Elain stared at her for a long time, hazel eyes boring into her soul. "Eoghan shredded you once. If he does it again…."

"He won't."

Ambling toward the door, Elain stopped and tossed Arlise

a clean tunic. "If you can put on your armor by yourself, I'll escort you to the mine."

———   ———————

ARMORED PHYSICALLY AND MENTALLY, Arlise strode onto the muddy field. Chants rose with every block of troops she passed.

First came the swelling war cries of Vyspan rangers. Though their longbows wouldn't be needed today, they stood at the ready, dull gambesons making them blend in with the dead landscape.

The ululations of Corhiel men-at-arms followed. Their mail glittered under the noon sun. Arlise noted the sweat beading on their faces. *Just a little longer, boys. Then we can all go home.*

She reached the local commanders next. Thanes whose names she couldn't recall plied her with platitudes. Sir Ocrin clattered over and took her by the hand. "I'm sure you'll win, but we must plan for the worst. If Eoghan emerges victorious, should our forces attack anyway? I mean, the thanes tried talking me out of it, but our numbe—"

Arlise cut him off. "No!" Sweet Mother, why did she even have to say that? If the Corhiel leapt to oath breaking and treachery so quickly, no wonder folk clamored to join Eoghan's band.

The knight bowed and slunk away. "Of course, Knight-Lieutenant."

Her comrades came last, bunched up a hundred yards from the abandoned mine's entrance. As Arlise regarded them, a lump formed in her throat. *This could be the last time we speak.*

"Good luck, Lieutenant," Alexos gruffly offered.

Robert gave her a bashful smile and nod, typical of his selective mutism.

Blinking back tears, Elain leaned on her quarterstaff. "Go gut him, Duny." Arlise cringed at that insufferable nickname. Oblivious to her expression, Elain laid a hand on her round-shield. The air hummed with magic for just a second. "If One-Ear thinks his enchantments will do the heavy lifting, he'll be disappointed."

A second wave of war cries and encouragement rose as Arlise slogged out to the middle of the field and waited.

It seemed an eternity before Eoghan's band poured from the mine shaft like enraged ants. Dirty, poorly armed, poorly armored, and ragged, the brigands milled in a formless mass. Most were boys too young to shave and girls too young to bear children. *How many even want to be part of this anymore?* She imagined they'd signed up with dreams of liberation, not lynching villages of their own countrymen.

An armored figure that could only be Eoghan pushed through the mass, with Katrin trailing him. The rebels gave a weak, unenthusiastic cheer as he trudged toward Arlise.

One-Ear stopped about ten yards away. "I didn't know you had armor, rat." He spoke in soft tones, but the humming aura of magic around him felt stronger. Louder. Eoghan glanced up at the sky. "Do you expect the Mother to intervene? To smite me for you?"

Arlise shook her head. "Nothing so dramatic." She called to mind Laufenden and atonement. Her vows. Her comrades. The maple in Crosbhothar. The innocents swinging from it. A hunger burned in her guts and spread until her whole body tingled. She drew Ferde. "Today, you meet justice."

Chuckling, Eoghan advanced. "Not bloody likely." His voice rang like thunder this time, and a hurricane of magic swirled around the brigand.

She rushed to meet him.

The longsword's reach let Eoghan strike first. A scorching blade smashed against her shield. Thanks to Elain's magic, the wood didn't ignite. Still, her arm fell numb.

Snarling, One-Ear struck again. His thrust glanced off her helm. Colors splashed across Arlise's field of vision. Though stunned, she pressed on. Armor buoyed her confidence. She didn't have to hold back this time.

The clatter of his plates guided her thrust. Steel shrieked under the starmetal blade. Eoghan backpedaled and barely parried the next strike. A sweeping cut rang his helmet like a bell. Six more blows fell, and Arlise smiled as he parried them all. After all, they weren't meant to harm or kill, only to force One-Ear into reflexive thinking.

Arlise pulled back, dropping into the same position she had in the last fight, before her failed attempt at grappling with Eoghan. The same hoarse shout rose from her throat as she charged.

The brigand thrust at where her face ought to be, but his steel sang through empty space. Arlise had already side-stepped to the right, and stabbed the back of his exposed knee. Starmetal scythed through mail and flesh.

Eoghan tried to take a step, but promptly toppled face first into the mud. He ripped off his helmet and reached toward his lines. "The deal is off!" he thundered. "Kill the invaders and their lackeys!"

A curse came to Arlise lips as rebels drew steel. *That cheating—* Her thoughts broke as a guttural command cut through the air.

"Halt!"

She recognized Katrin's voice.

"Save me, love," Eoghan wailed.

The dark haired mage shook her head. "You lied to me. In

Dalkey. When you said you wouldn't lose control again. That was the only reason I rejoined you. But here you are: black eyes and harsh voice." Tears trickled down her cheeks. "My Eoghan is dead. Consumed by…you." Katrin turned her blue eyes on Arlise. "Kill him, Watcher, and I'll surrender our band."

Inhuman, unintelligible jabbering rolled off Eoghan's tongue. Arlise stepped back, circling. Even dying cougars could still deal death.

Leaning on his sword, the brigand managed to push himself up. He lunged at Arlise, eyes and expression wild.

She ducked the flailing slash and stabbed into his open mouth. Wild eyes died as blood turned Ferde's white blade a dark pink. Arlise wrenched the sword free and let him fall. Penance for Laufenden. Justice for Crosbhothar. She should've been overjoyed, but only relief washed over her. *It's over. Finally*

"Watcher," Katrin blubbered through her tears, "I won't ask for mercy for myself. But our folk…some haven't even been in battle yet. If you could intercede for them…."

Arlise cut her off, remembering the youngsters she'd noticed earlier. "Of course." She turned and gazed at Eoghan's corpse. The vengeance-eaten ringleader lay face down in mud turning crimson. *Mother, never let me meet a man like him again.*

SIR OCRIN RODE out to meet her. A hearty laugh made his mustache twitch. "Magnificent, Knight-Lieutenant! Such grace." The Corhiel knight surveyed the tattered rebel band. "I'm thinking about impalement."

"Don't"

He blinked. "Why?"

She thought of citing the Prophetess Clara, about how justice needed to be tempered by mercy, but decided on a more pragmatic argument. "Do you want to create another Eoghan? Because executing children is how you do that."

In an instant, his face turned burgundy. "If you'd seen what they do to captives …"

"For the past few days, I've seen Crosbhothar every time I try to sleep. All those innocents, all those nooses." Arlise pointed to the mass of rebels. "Most of the ones responsible are dead, slain at Dalkey or in Crosbhothar's temple. I know there are many men and women over there who deserve to die. By all means, punish them. But the others don't. Execute them, and you'll sow the seeds of rebellion."

The knight bristled. "Fear of a sharpened stake will keep Vyspa in line."

She shook her head. Was he even listening? "Not if you make the whole country hate you. Then the mere sight of a stake will whip this isle into a frenzy."

"Watcher, this lot killed so many husbands and wives. Mothers and fathers. Sons and daughters. My friends. A lover."

Ocrin's words took her back through the years, to wild days as a mercenary in the Colonies. To being a favorite of Riso's prince. To conspiracies, and blood magic seizing her body. To burning hatred, and five months of bloody vengeance. Arlise felt tiny again. Helpless, just as when her hand disobeyed her mind and drew that blade across Septimus' throat. Her throat clenched so tight she could hardly breathe.

When the memories receded, Arlise spoke softly. "Once, I felt like you. But revenge won't make love to you or kiss you goodnight. It won't share a drink, tell tales, or watch your back. It can't. I learned that the hard way. Revenge can't bring back the dead either. But it will add to the pile. Break out your stakes, and it'll be Vyspan parents, children, spouses, or friends today. Tomorrow, when another man like Eoghan harnesses their fury over your invasion, they'll be Corhiel. And on and on."

Shifting in his saddle, Sir Ocrin didn't say anything for a long while. His impressive mustache twitched. "I see." Another long silence. "There's enough misery in this world. We'll sift out the true monsters, send them to the block. As for the rest…I'll have to consult my commanders but…I think, in the interests of a successful occupation, we can avoid executions."

Arlise smiled. "That's all I ask." As she trudged toward her comrades, an unfamiliar emotion warmed her insides. Satisfaction. Mother willing, today's mercy would break the cycle which had given birth to Eoghan One-Ear and his crimes.

AUSTIN WORLEY

A native of Broken Arrow, Oklahoma, Austin Worley is a poet and writer of all manner of speculative fiction. Aside from "Hanging at Crosbhothar", five of his stories have been published. These are split between Weird Westerns and traditional heroic fantasy.

Weird Westerns:

"Hooves and Tobacco on a Sunday Morning", in *Riding the Dark Frontier: Tales of the Weird West,* tells of a young man's encounter with a tribal legend on his ride to church.

"Acheri", in Issue #2 of Warriors & Wizards magazine, chronicles a tribal priestess forced to confront regret and the monster her daughter has become.

Heroic Fantasy:

"Dusk and Dawn at Laufenden", in *The Devil's Piano*, and "The Order", in Issue #14 of Speculative 66, see Lady Arlise Dun faced with a once in a lifetime chance to end a bloody war. She decides collateral damage is acceptable, but can she accept the consequences?

"Decisions", in *Fifty Flashes*, follows Arlise Dun

shortly after joining the Order of the Watchers. Arlise thinks she's found redemption, but an encounter with a werewolf cub forces her to prove it.

When not writing, Austin is caring for his family, reading, listening to music, or playing video games.

RETRIBUTION BY NIGHT

CHAD VINCENT

Chapter 1

WHIPPING in the late night breeze, the tightly held cloak concealed the monster beneath. It was simply a man but within beat a devil's heart. The cloak masked the figure, the filtered shadow of a tree masked the cloak, the forest concealed the tree, and the near moonless night made the forest nothing but distant, dancing shades.

Aodhan stood in the light of a sliver moon which fingered across his cloak like harp strings. Beneath, he had not given up the brown leather raiment of the druidic mage, not his warm woolens, or his carved staff. His vestige had curdled over time into a murky grime; his clothes had soured into little more than the sooty silhouette of a beggar. New lines of age cragged his eyes alongside healing cuts. A gnarled gash wept above one eye towards an ear. His sorcerous staff now channeled demons where once it was the woodland protector and granted gentle communions between fauna and flora.

"You will allot me this?" Aodhan questioned the night's darkness.

A blackened shape slithered between the trees, neither man nor beast. "You will be given what you desire." The discordant voice sent the hairs rising at the back of Aodhan's neck. "You sell your soul too easily," it mocked.

"I was deceived into believing I had one in the first place." A hand went to the half-healed scar that ran up to his hairline to squelch a pulse of pain.

Glowing just enough to give it shape, a medallion edged forth from a hand that was more translucent energy than substance or flesh. Fearfully, Aodhan grasped it by the furthest dangle of the swinging chain. The light died at his touch. Slipping it into a pocket, he turned away. Giving your back was never a wise move when confronting hell spawn, but it would not meddle with its newest servant, not yet. There were motives too complex, too malicious at work here. Aodhan knew only one. He would raise an army of the dead in order to destroy that which he hated. What he did not know, there was another preparing to assume these domains, his woodland domain, to convert these lands into a dark kingdom. A being that required the place to already be a darkened land, a devastation, a place without the presence of man, and ironically a land without Aodhan as well. Slaves-now slaves were always serviceable.

Aodhan flowed through the trees, as these had been his woods for a long age. There was a secretive place that pulled at his soul as if by ethereal string, a place of death-blood through the ages past. An ancient battleground long forgotten except to the venerable, the likes of Aodhan. The land he sought knew not victors, only the perished, those that had been taken into the bosom of the unmarked grave, the grave of warriors left on the battlefield for the carrion and the passage of time. Brisk steps in the night took him over hills that were choked to all but the skilled and finally down into a thin valley, into the heart of a long copse of old trees he knew well.

The ethereal string dissipated and the medallion glinted forth from the folds. Nervous fingers rubbed it down as if scratching behind a dog's ears. Equally nervous eyes searched the ground for a mark. His feet took him in clandestine circles. He came across it with his toe rather than his eyes. The tip of an ancient cairn stared from the tall grass to gape up at the failing moon. The foundation stone was immovable and sunk deep into the earth long before Aodhan, long before even the nameless battle of ages past. Five more stones sat one atop another, all flat, each smaller than the last, an ageless landmark. The topmost, with a dew puddled indention, sat well below his knees in the night's grasses that painted his pant legs wet with droplets. His memory recalled no such waymark, here or anywhere within the forest, his forest. Yet, here it was. For all the darkness of night, it was now strong in his mind. The inky sky spared little moonlight, but he could count its measure, every curve and stony scar without effort, as a blind man discerns the layout of a new face.

Nervous fingers filled the hole with the medallion. Tiny rivers edged out and wet his fingertips. Unseen runes began hinting at existence, twinkling into life. Some internal perception spoke of something imminent. Something sojourned that way, barred not by time or essence or the laws of man. Behind these interdimensional travelers there was another, lurking deep within shadows. Something wanted to corrupt this land, or wanted the land to have been corrupt. It wanted a garrison ready to command the moment it arrived. What it was, he did not really know. Only that it was evil. But for now, he could only see his own hatred growing into existence. The confusing revulsion for those that hurt him, strong. That was enough for now. It was all he could know.

The ground began to churn as he felt their presence take shape. One bony arm thrust into the night air, then another. The scene became terrifying, but again, bewilderment and disgust for his enemies kept him rooted to see his task through. A skeleton pulled itself forth from the depths of the ground. No flesh. Nothing to encumber its path, Aodhan's path in the end. Five, then eight, then twelve, stood motionless, eerily motionless and stared into the void with rotted, blank faces. Soon he was surrounded by over twenty time-ragged remains, the grove became unnerving to every sense. More came. In the end, more than thirty skeletons stood stagnant beside trees and in small openings near upturned bushes, heavy mountains of dirt, and dislodged stones. They were nothing but bone, clumps of trickling dirt, and dripping flakes of tangled and trapped weeds. Roots of all sort dangled through ribs, wrists, and legs. Clods of soil broke apart from beneath one skeleton's scapula. Another's skull was riddled with spilling pebbles as it composed itself to stand. All were awakened and all perfectly still. Somehow, he wished they would breathe, cough, or do something that could indicate life. The nothingness so frightening, he was terrified into immobility, not daring to respire or blink. The battle lost was with his bladder.

They all moved at once, like a well-trained squad given a single, silent order. Each turned towards some celestial beacon, the direction of the outpost called Frelig. Aodhan did not realize it quite yet, as his nerves were gone. He could only focus on suppressing his own fear. One stepped out, then another. Like rivulets of rain seeking lower ground, they streamed through the trees in terrifying, unhurried lines of nomadic death. He followed on numb legs through the fog of his mind.

They were not fast, but steady, constant travelers. The trek was soundless except for feet on the night's dew peppered paths. Time took them ever closer. Persistence brought them. Crossing the stream at the base of the hill, they edged closer to sleeping Frelig, the outpost-village which was the epicenter of his hate, their destination for utter destruction.

Soldiers would soon wake with the sun, but only four night guards patrolled the walls and gate, of which two were asleep. None heard the splash or slogging steps that mired through the last of the trees before open ground. Aodhan followed an uncomfortable distance behind, conflicting with the fear of the ambulatory army of bones but wanting to see the destruction they would bring on what he considered his fanatic enemy.

Chapter 2

SIX HEAVY LADEN wagons lulled and ebbed into garrison Myre, half a day before the cloaked figure ever sought the medallion from malevolent hands during the night. Myre was the last outpost, the last stretch of walled safety on the wilderness highway before reaching Frelig late the same evening. The iron gates shut with a metallic whine and sealed tight beneath a midday sun. Warriors regressed into laborers to re-strap the wagons, check hitches, and grease the wheels. Horses had to be exchanged and a hasty meal would be provided for drivers and security.

Captain Brennan stepped off the side of the lead wagon, overlaid in mail plates backed by a thin coat of quilted linens. All this was wrestled over a thin, ringed shirt. His helm was steel, the insignia of the King's Proctor heat-pressed on the brow beneath a plume of black horse hair. Beneath, the smaller stamps of the scales of justice circled the leather coif that kept the steel from cutting an edge into his head. The swinging pommel of his sword bore the same. His shoulders were wide, widespread enough to have carried the burden of leadership over his own outpost this last year, which he planned to return to this very night.

As he hit the dirt, a line of pilgrims passed near. Each raised a chant of remorse for their weary spirits, traveled lamentations that had seen too many byways but not enough meat and cheese. One turned in slow-motion, a meager bowl of coins outstretched beneath a plea for alms. Captain Brennan dribbled in a worthless coin he fumbled from a pouch, just enough to keep both of them moving. The stranger bowed, then touched his head and heart. A return bow fanned his road-worthy stench, yet he crinkled his nose and winced his eyes at the full parade of stink percolated by grateful unwashed bodies. The bowed man was a fool, but the young can be fool-hearted and all too often naive in their idealism. It was a trial of life for the fledglings, a discovery of self. Brennan pitied and envied him at the same time. There was a time when he too had to figure out his place in the world, but was saved by the sword, a mistress that offered herself to him in salvation. His was a bloody salvation. Still, there was sympathy for these young nomads.

"Get that swarthy line of chattel out of here," a voice cried.

To his right, a club swung down on the bowed man's head. He fell into a crumpled heap. The coins spread at his

feet as the bowl wheeled down the broken thoroughfare in an
ever tightened spiral. Lightning instincts took the form of
defense which pulled Brennan's arms and fists up in a
pugilist's posture. One hand was ready to jab, the other close
to his chin to block or cross. Anger welled in him at the
crushing of one man's spirit, the crushed skull that fell at his
feet. The dirty man may have been a bothersome fool, but he
was still a man.

Captain Brennan reacted in an instant, to the dominant
stance and offending club that unwisely dared to not move
away. A quick-step forward and a set of knuckles found the
soldier's jaw like a magnet pulling at an iron ball. The man's
body went limp, his knees wobbled like grass in the breeze
before giving in. Even as the flaccid head and body sagged
towards the dirt, a second set of hard-skinned knuckles
caught the other side of the man's cheek bone. What would
have been a face-plant turned into an elongated sprawl.

With their man down, two grunts stepped forward with
murderous lust, swinging their own watchman clubs about
their waists. Dust mummified Brennan in a shroud, hiding
rank, but you can't hide the eyes. Not those eyes, the eyes of
a fearless hunter, an apex predator that finds everything in the
jungle its plaything. He turned to face the two louts as if they
were little more than mice caught by their tails.

"Captain Brennan! Get your calloused carcass over here!"
a heavy voice of authority bawled out from a near door.

At the mention of his name the two men wilted. They
tarnished. Even their hair sagged, as if they were but a
painting with liquid thinner doused across the canvas.

"You were supposed to be here this morning. Are these
big city riggers slacking on their runs?" The loud man was
built like a mule, just as long-faced and undauntedly obsti-
nate. His bald head bore a scar from cranium to chin. Ten

different stories had made their rounds about that scar, from a scalded lover's revenge, to catching a spike from a charging cavalier. It was widely believed that he started the lover story himself but none ever questioned in his presence.

"Commandant," Brennan nodded. His face was still a granite cliff that overhung the ocean. "Still some snows up high coming from the south," he said, not slackening his posture an ounce to further taunt the two scared dogs skulking away. As their tails rounded the corner, he helped the man off the ground, breaking his speech not at all. "We are cutting our stay down to however long it takes to change horses to make up time so we don't have long," he grunted, his last words came out across a souring face as the numbed man lifted into his grasp and closer to his nose, too close.

Benevolent words that had been distant murmurs started to materialize in his mind, coming closer, directed at him. He realized that three of the pilgrims, while each helped take a limb in support of their fellow spiritual traveler, were also giving thanks and appreciations in fervor at his kindness to their adept friend. A fourth pious itinerant tied a little trinket onto his sword sheath and then a second bauble on leather cord braided through the holes of his hilt. The carved zig-zag of a lightning bolt cast in bronze, though crude, may have been the man's prized possessions, but he gave it up without question or hesitation.

That harsh voice broke the air once again. "I want you back here for the Tenfold Festival. I'm to the city for the week and you are in my charge. Brennan," his eyes grew serious, even across the distance, "you're the only man I trust." The commandant suggested this in a 'you will' manner of speaking.

Before he could think of a way to avoid or even circumventive a decline, the lead driver rushed past with a wad of biscuit in his mouth. "Load 'em up," he mumbled through flying crumbs and thrust a brick of baked bread into his hands.

Chapter 3

THE STATION of Frelig sat atop a hill, surrounding itself with close fit wooden barricades from the very timberland it bordered. Torchlight flashed through the night about the gate, the only giveaway of activity from the stillness inside. One man girded himself behind the walls, heavy boots marching monotonously under the flickering light at intervals to suppress the sleep that mightily overcomes one in the tranquil dark hours of very early morning.

The outpost had originated as a group of herdsman's huts, pens, and slapped-to barns further down near the stream at the base of the hill. They had been gone years now, the area too wild for free roaming herds. The sheep and cattle were nothing but sport and food for trolls, goblins, and other nasty, natural hunters. None lasted beyond two summers. Even the rugged shepherds met cook fire ends. Their homes and pens made the very the kindling for the cauldron's blaze. A single trader had found a way to thrive. Just after the mutton and beef played out, the place had become a layover point connecting two distant trade houses. With money and trade came the soldiers. Together, the part outpost, part warehouse, part settlement provided wares, sent scouts through the area for mapping, and afforded security forces to assure safe passage for the many incoming and outgoing caravans.

SERGEANT ARMSTRONG STEPPED up to the barrel and grabbed the other man's hand. His meaty paw seized the other as a grizzly bear would lock its jaws onto a spawning fish. A third patron draped his hands over theirs, and with the word 'GO!' the two men grunted into a contest over the barrel, itself given to groans of protest. Their hands locked in wrestling combat for dominance to press the other down. Blood vessels strained and throbbed in exaggerated masks, muscles cinched in a quivering contest of strength and stamina. Men cheered about the half empty warehouse turned backroom pub. Amidst the hoots and jeers, all was silent to the ears of the two locked in battle.

"Now rookie," Armstrong hissed, "you will know," he exhaled quick strained breaths, "why I am called...Arm-Strong." His father's name was Agnew, but the ink dried on his enlistment papers eternally Armstrong.

His bicep flexed into a heavy stone swell that put a strain on the fibrous shirt he wore whenever he was not sporting the insignia daubed full plate armor of the realm. The exposed forearm rippled from a rutted highway into a coursework of pulsing veins and a roadmap of bulging, sinewy muscle. All this pressed down on the other man until his arm bent to the back of his hand, winning Armstrong the challenge.

Silver and lesser coins exchanged hands, but not much as most knew whom to bet on.

"Good shot, boy. I've had weaker opponents," Armstrong cuffed the loser, preparing to tip his tankard of ale to wet his parched pipes.

The other man smiled through a wringing of pain, almost appreciative of such direct camaraderie. Two fellow grunts stepped up and slapped his back with drunken smiles.

"No harm losing to me, boy," Sergeant Armstrong threw out with a haughty but companionable grin.

"Yeah," said another one of Armstrong's lackeys, "don't mess with The Arm." He laughed, staggered a bit with the exaggerated jostle of his wide shoulders and wide belly.

A second man stepped up, ale in one hand and throwing his other around Armstrong. "Mess with The Arm and you might get the club," he said as he tipped to one side, shaking a fist that had nothing to do with any reference to a club.

The slobbery reference was nothing less than a paean to Sergeant Armstrong's having dealt with a local hero turned troublemaker not four days past. The nature's mage, some forest prophet of some indigenous repute, had been harassing the outpost for months to change their travel lanes. The ratty character had finally gotten his just deserves.

"I was telling this moron for the last time that no way, no how, is anything changing," the fist-pumper retold his patchy version to the three newcomers. "Then," he gave a snorting laugh, "Sergeant here gives him a few whacks on the head." He erupted into spitting laughter, spilling a foamy slosh onto his compatriot, who didn't notice as he too was laughing his fifth drink across the floor. "No one, I mean no one turns their back on Sergeant Armstrong."

Armstrong puffed out his sculpted chest through the threadbare shirt. The man exuded a strength and dominance that comes with the air of commanding men in battle. He was a man that led from the front, issued commands while swinging his sword, stood beside his men as enemies charged. A great leader, but an abysmal person. Though a braggart, often a liar, and intentionally socially crude, all the men looked up to him. But his was a rough troop. Most men were staying away from civilization for various reasons or just did not play well with others. "Three of the King's campaigns," he jutted out his chin as well, "and two frontier crusades, no man should turn their back on me, or their front for that matter."

Chapter 4

ONLY ONE MAN gave objection to walling off the land, digging ruts into the beautiful landscape, the plunder of trees, and hunting animals for food and even more often sport. That obstacle was Aodhan. For most of his long lifetime the wild territory had been his prophetic charge, but after multiple confrontations with the influx of workers, and soldiers in due course, it had finally come to a head. The pleas and parlays may have turned into an inevitable quarrel, but the beating dealt out at the hand of Sergeant Armstrong and his men four days ago was inexcusable.

"Oi, on comes the fool," one man announced over his shoulder, a quiver hidden deep in his voice. The others laughed, a little too nervous or embellished for the cruelty of the jest.

Five men-at-arms stood at the east gate, having just slid it open and shut for one of the incoming caravans. As they milled behind the wooden entry each held onto uncomfortable stares. Aodhan approached up the hill with an intent stride, despite the incline. Bravery leaked from five souls like the quick drip of a leaky hand pump as the visage of the magical warden brought up different fearful daydreams of conjured flames, attacking trees, and exploding stones for each beating heart beneath links of chain mail. Their bullying facade hid not the true fear within.

Aodhan made the gates with no sign of fatigue. "Allow my passage," was all he said.

The gate opened and all five flowed into positions with spears and lances at a sharp angle per Sergeant Armstrong's command. "We're not," a stammer slipped the man's lips, "we're not to allow passage, but to keep you here." His power of speech was peaked and shrill as if his words were a question rather than an order.

"Put me off no longer. Your refuse litters the stream below, glass bottles, broken barrels, and the stink drifts on the winds ..." but his voice was replaced by the sound of a cracking tree limb giving its bulk over to a windy day.

Aodhan's eyes amplified into saucers. His body twisted in a slow-motion whirlpool that brought him to the ground in a snaking twirl. Landing limp, his head bounced concentrically off the rutted hardpack. Before any could react, Sergeant Armstrong brought his blackened baton down on Aodhan's head a second time, gashing above his eye and into his hairline. Aodhan's body reeled in such a peculiar way that its limp contortion caused the soldiers to become revulsed, as many find the writhing of a headless snake a horrid nauseation within their own twisted fears. One soldier kicked out in fear-fueled disgust. One by one, the others followed as the masses often do in times of distress.

"Stop! He's had enough," Armstrong declared in his authoritative tone. They left him there to bleed out on the road. One man lingered on outside gate duty to watch Aodhan's eventual zombie-like retreat.

After that ill-fated meeting with Armstrong's club, Aodhan crawled and eventually limped in a blurred stupor back to his protected shelter to mend the bashed dent and profuse bleeding gouge at the back of his skull. In such a state, his magical mending was faulty at best, which caused his already angered thoughts to wander further from sanity.

Over the next few days he healed in his pain. Through warped and blurred thoughts he turned his back on the natural world and sent forth all his focus onto hate for the near hundred troops and merchant's men that were the blight making up the pulsing heart of Frelig. A once sensible man with a most compassionate heart, he was slushing through a muddled mind, often confused and infused with loathing. Hate consumed his heart and his mind. Enmity replaced his breath. Odium flicked his lips like a snake's tongue. Nature was no longer his divination, but black art dabbling and an abhorrence of all things man. In it all, he even reserved some hate for himself.

IN THE FLICKERING LIGHT, the gate guard was not asleep, but neither was he fully awake. Forms exited the trees but an uphill charge away. It was too dark and his eyes were too heavy. To his fortune, he was on the inside of the wall, for as they grew near, their arms stretched out to rend flesh from the living. The man's head fell forward as a nod was caught sneaking up on him. With a snap, his head jerked up in struggle with slumber. Jerking out a deep sigh and staring through bleary eyes, he looked around to see if any were near enough to catch him dozing on duty. Head turning, he saw them, shadowy forms pressed towards the wall. Eyes wide, a gasp clung to the sides of his throat and a waking coma overtook him. One hand knocked across the gate, rousing the man to his fear-infused reality.

"Alarm! Alarm!" the man finally shouted as full consciousness returned to him.

His view fell between heavy oaken slats, taking in broken images of long dead warriors at the gate and pawing along the walls. Behind him, another guard dashed from the shadows and signaled the outpost with the clang of a large triangular dinner bell. Sleepily, men spilled forth from barracks, lethargic and confused. Some fell into their training, other just fell. The skeletal hands raked on the wood, digging in, rutting the heavy planks.

"Too slow," Aodhan said in frustration from the darkness along the edge of the trees.

He may have given up his druidic ways, but decades of practicing magic had not left him. Hands raised in a pattern, words spilled forth. The wooden planks began to soften, then regressed into weighty slabs of pulpy mud. The skeletal hands no longer caused mere furrows. Globs fell away, holes widened before fearful eyes. Whole sections bent and dripped away, many touched only by gravity. The undead creatures would be through in but a few terrifying moments.

Twenty soldiers, many underdressed for battle, stood a line of spear points to the oncoming army. Ahead of the precarious phalanx, the skeleton's bony charge was a slow approach, but instilled an abysmal fear. The men lunged with spears dancing between ribs, glancing off skulls, and generally giving little resistance to the fleshless onslaught. Most men dropped their useless impalements as the enemy slid towards them, nominally unscathed. A few fear-slick men slunk backwards into the night, embracing their cowardice. Those with swords drew them and entered into melee. More retreated, having not a weapon to fight with since their spears were discarded or intertwined within a skeleton's bones like another useless limb. Others fell in behind, just in time to watch their fellows fall before the dead army. One bony arm was severed, but the other hand took its attacker's throat. Another filched deep troughs into a nightshirt. Others were bitten, hands broke living bones, but all staggered forward to send fear-choked nightmares into the chaos of men.

Skeletons filtered in disarray throughout the small warehouse outpost. Captain Brennan, red-eyed from his return trip that very evening, left the armory with sixteen of his lieutenants, sergeants-at-arms, and men-at-arms. Each was outfitted for battle, straps at half hasp and boots being pulled on.

They stepped into the streets, thrust into combat before having reached the center. The only two other officers, both lieutenants alongside three men-at-arms, dove into a wall of trudging skeletons. Though well organized, the two officers fell to sheer numbers. Hands drug them down and tore them apart. Their bodies wilted into lifeless heaps, the plate armor reverberated like church bells when bony feet gave chase to the three men-at-arms falling back in rank. One daring soldier stepped up to send two skeletons to the road on brittle pegs, legs shattered with a single swing of his massive sword. The battle was organized by anarchy.

Captain Brennan severed the spine at the neck of one skeleton separated from its brethren by its selfish drive to seek out his death. The grime speckled head rolled downhill until stopping in a cart rutted puddle. With a slight pant in his voice, he ordered his remaining men to flank alongside at his right as another swarm broke through a street filled with screaming warehouse workers. Another swordsman fell to the clutching talons as the flock of bones passed in flight.

In the bustle, Brennan hauled one man back to stand beside him. That man was his best sergeant, one of the gruffest, meanest criminals out in the wilds. Sergeant Armstrong. Some said he was part ogre, others said part guard dog. He was smelly, rude, and overall unpleasant, exactly the shoulder you wanted rubbing yours in a fight.

Four brave soldiers endeavored to hold their end of the line to that same flock of bones, falling to clinching nails and gnawing, aged projections. Each man fell in order, crumpling beneath the tide. As they fell to the nightmare, the next five warriors drew up shoulder to shoulder, a well-oiled machine of thrusting steel points behind a wall of shields. They had no time to afford any greater tactic, but training and experience brought them together into an instant hedge of thorns.

Even a hedge of thorns could fall to the sickle. That sickle came in the form of some ten pairs of grasping bony hooks and mold encrusted teeth. Two men were pulled from the middle, their shields drug down. Torsos followed the momentum. With a hole in the ranks, there was not enough defense to stop the spread of the calcified plague. The corpses were marched over with the grace that an old cow would give to garden tethers seeking out new greens.

The skeletal mass moved in unison, crashing into the last three warriors. Bones broke, severed, and crunched, but the horde slowed not a stroke. Two men fell in an instant, flesh stripped off in shreds. The last swordsman to Brennan's left bent under a slow dance towards the dirt.

"Sergeant Armstrong, follow me," he commanded above the din of his dying men.

Finding a gap, the Captain pulled Armstrong behind. A plan formulated at its fringes, and they trudged off with intent towards the barracks with its central tower. As the tower was only one level higher than the ground, it offered only a menial sight of the town but good low level views that gave lines of sight down every lane.

The tower rested butting to the end of the barracks, unmanned since the alarm sent everyone into the necromantic streets. The two men diverted down a side alley as they spied four skeletons rounding on them. Neither man was anything short of a cold blooded killer, but rushing skeletons made one weigh options otherwise rarely considered. Reaching the barracks, Captain Brennan pressed through a side door and caught himself in time before slamming it behind on his sergeant. His disgruntled face spoke volumes, but other necessities were dancing about his helmet rack. For one, survival, or at least fighting against better odds.

The tower was at the barrack's far end, and both men felt the emptiness of the room compared to the electricity outside. The smell of encrusted footmen soured their nostrils and gave them a moment's pause, but it was nothing of which they were not accustomed. In an instance, they were at the stairs, up to the top, and looking out over the chaotic street and beyond.

"There," Captain Brennan roared over an accusatory finger. Being a veteran of more than just the battlefield, he knew that creatures such as those coming against him would have a puppet master. Turning, he rushed back down the tower with the intention of cutting off the head of the snake.

Chapter 5

LOPING UP THE HILL, Aodhan wished to learn more than just screams and the sounds of battle that gave inklings of outcome. Having left the edge of the trees, he unintentionally gave himself away. He approached the broken gate and walls, exhausted from running up hill, huffing in large gasps of air. Mud still dripped down in clumps from wooden edges down onto splintered ends. The ground had been upturned into a mire by the onslaught of hardened feet pressed through the shattered gate, the likes of which hadn't been seen since the herders were here with their many hooved animals. A crash just inside the gate drew his attention.

"There he is," Captain Brennan said.

Sergeant Armstrong looked up from having crushed yet another skeleton with a studded mace from behind a round shield. "You," he bellowed, his voice the growl of an angry mongrel.

Aodhan nearly shrieked the same, having recognized the man behind the shield through a fanning cloud of emotion. It was one of the men that attacked him the last time he propositioned the outpost to take up new routes around his territories. At first, fear began to well within, but after a short memory of the pain of that day, anger seethed into its place.

"Eliminate this enemy," Captain Brennan said through gnashed teeth.

Armstrong dutifully sized up his foe, a sergeant loyal to his captain, and took a stance just inside the opening that was once the gate. Here, his enemy must come to him, stepping over debris and handing him a free shot at the fool yet again. The old trooper had more than a few tricks shunted up his sleeve.

Aodhan didn't quite know the specifics, but he knew if he stepped through that doorway his head would be broken worse than before. Instead, he readied his staff and settled into his own effective but unorthodox fighting stance. He did not wish to taste the man's malice ever again but wished to deliver his own.

"We seem to be at an impasse," Sergeant Armstrong smiled through a wicked turn at the edge of his lips, then slackened a bit, giving less bend to his knees. "If you were to allow me safe passage, I will meet you on the outside."

Aodhan considered, then stepped backwards four large steps. "Come on, but beware. You do not have a gang of monkeys knocking me around before you come at me from behind with a cudgel." A memory bolted through his wound, thrummed about his skull, and gave a slight throb of commemoration.

"I didn't need them. It was just funny to hear the hollow thump of your dismal head." Armstrong stepped through, ready to pounce. Never did the eyes stray from their intended quarry.

That will be your downfall. Aodhan thought to himself, knowing he'd fought more goblins, trolls, giant serpents, and so many more creatures than some soldiers would see in a lifetime. Coming at him five on one while he tried to keep a civil tongue was the tip of the scale which defeated him, not his lack of fight. That and a heavy tipped club from behind.

Armstrong feinted in with a sharp lunge and retreated back stiff-armed to test the man's defenses. The tactic also gave away his reluctance to strike, which Aodhan saw right through. Aodhan followed in, but facing a tight, veteran defense he too slid back. They circled like carrion birds. Sergeant Armstrong drove in with his shield and immediately brought down an overhand blow with his mace. Aodhan's staff pressed on the shield, then rose to deflect that malicious mace head. Secretly, he winced at the pained memory. With Aodhan's middle exposed, Sergeant Armstrong smashed in on unprotected ribs with the flat of the shield.

A loud 'SNAP!' broke through the air. Armstrong's arm bent awkward and terrible at the elbow behind the shield. Before he could retract, Aodhan's instincts, honed in decades of fighting, brought his staff snaking down and around to the barely exposed bend. The incursion was hard and fluid. Without a pause in the arcing trajectory, the hardwood staff crested on around and hammered through towards the man's ear at the engraved edge of his helmet. Speechless, legs buckled beneath the blow, face contorted, his broken arm flailed at an irregular angle as he slumped into a pile on the churned earth. His right ear bled mercilessly beneath the dent in his helm.

Captain Brennan skulked up behind Aodhan, having just watched his sergeant fall to the ground like a pile of old clothes. A blackjack in his hand, he swung hard. The hard-centered implement was usually meant for drunken rabble or to persuade a close-mouthed prisoner, and this late eve it sent one more troublemaker into unconsciousness. It would not do to be known as a back stabber, not the intrepid Captain Brennan of the Frelig Grey Cloaks. Yet it would impress to have taken the woodland witchdoctor without harm after he just devastated the outpost's hardest mercenary. Send him in chains back to the warehouse, then the city, the caravans safe to travel through the forest once again, safe from supernatural interferences.

Chapter 6

BLACKNESS OVERTOOK AODHAN. While his consciousness sank, his dispositions rose. Falling towards the ground, his mouth began to swell. His hands evolved into stubby fingers and long claws. Black fur sprouted from every follicle, and his body bulked of massive muscles without sympathy. By the time he met the ground, he was already prepared to rise again on thick arms, now a large, humanoid deformity of a black bear. The idea of unconsciousness was impossible to the nature of existence that rested within the heart of such a degenerated omnivore.

"Roawrr!" Aodhan bellowed, semi-conscious behind the angry teeth of salvation.

"No, you foul shifter," Captain Brennan bawled in attest by his drawn sword, "time to die."

Aodhan circled, not like a man, but like a hungry bear on all fours. The puny morsel circled as well. The fool may have known the dance of distance from a spear or a blade, but not the claw and wild lunge of Ursa. Aodhan did just that. He lunged in with a deftness that defied the bulky muscles and squat legs. Both claws slashed in, one high, one low. With a desperate swing the sword caught the first, a callous wound. No defense would come close to the lower rake, which gashed through metal as if it were the skin of any other animal. The claw channeled rivers into the thigh. Not only was it swift, but it hooked into the flesh and drew the whole leg right into rows of thirsty teeth. Captain Brennan turned upside down, dropping his sword in the dirt beside his dignity. A rough shake was nothing for the jaws, head, and neck of a bear-thing clutching such a limp bundle. The ravenous shaking and gnashing of teeth turned the man from a commander of warriors to a voiceless chunk of steak sending a light shower of blood across the ground.

Captain Brennan was not dead, but the cavernous lesions, the punctured flesh, and the mangled leg sang a song of prediction. Aodhan hopped on three limbs beneath the wall, a wounded bear's limp. One front paw dripped the Captain's blood, but the retracted paw dripped blood of his own. He licked it, cleaning and closing the wound as best could be done with nature's nectar. Finally, he was free to ravage the town clean. His animal ears keen, he found few expressions of man, risen in terror or in charge. Few indeed. The skeletons had fulfilled their obligation or were close to completion.

A single man turned the corner, headed down the wide, dirt-packed street away from Aodhan. Three skeletons gave pursuit. Two more rounded a corner and sent the despairing man into their arms of eternal slumber. The skin rendered and a shrieking wail died in his throat. At his end, no other mortal noise filled the city. They were all dead. Every man.

Three labored hops forward, Aodhan smiled a long row of teeth in triumph. His revenge was complete. Looking to the side, he saw that horses, mules, and oxen had been slain. A pair of hunting dogs splayed lifeless near an open pen, unfortunate fatalities. All were sad casualties of war for the greater good.

Four skeletons exited an alleyway ahead and turned his way. Six more filtered from storage houses and side streets, emerged as if called back to their graves. They no longer saw the one that raised them from eternal slumber, the protected one, only a wounded bear. Every step a trundle towards their disguised master. Many had damaged legs, missing arms, and even one off-kilter skull. Impaired or not, they returned to him, or rather emerged on him. Pride and conquest swelled his oversized cavity of a chest in the shadow of victory. Yet, never before had they shown any loyalty, nor fealty. Doubt slowly began to show across his muzzle, for they had no faces in which to read. Their bodies took up the mobbed plea of the masses. Apprehension flushed to overshadow his thoughts. Near half the spine-chilling company had endured to culmination in the street. His mind clouded, what reason had they to return to him?

With one paw still withdrawn, he skipped aside from the ruined city gate. *Obviously they are but returning to their eternal slumber,* he considered inside his bear-like consciousness, *their entrance will also be their retreat.* With a giant sigh and a huff, he took a tired and wounded seat in the dirt at the corner of the closest building. The bear form sat with such resemblance to the man that a friend might have noticed, except for the paw licking.

Skeletons swarmed. Their task was nearly complete. Only one living form remained. Aodhan rose as the first few skeletons edged his way rather than exiting out the shattered gate. A snort and low roar of contempt left the man-bear's lips. The pain in his arm subsided to the chemical release as the conflict became evident.

Two stepped near, white palms and bones raked towards him. A broken, legless fiend slithered towards him in staggered steps from the side. He tracked each and every one with a predator's observance, moving mind and body as one to defend. A swipe shattered ribs and spine, sending bone fragment floating through the air like soiled snowflakes. Grabbing the second, his wounded claw pulled in the head to his open jaw. With a loud crunch, he shattered the skull as easily as a clay bowl fragments across a tiled floor. Dirty white shards and splinters rained down from his maw as he instinctually chewed the crunching morsels into bits.

Shouldered together tight, four sets of bones shuffled before him. Behind, another small pack ambled ever nearer. Aodhan swung both mighty paws and hopped backward, a wince for his painful arm. Two fell to wreckage, another broke just below the skull, useless. The last stepped forward without emotion. He anticipated the precise moment, as his claws must deliver immediate death. More followed on its heels. With a flash, his good paw lifted one leg, flung it away, sending the body to the ground as if shot from a catapult. A massive downward strike of paw and pad sent pieces of skull bone to the sides like a smashed egg shell. Another crowd approached, pressed, solemn and apathetic.

Fostering an anger erupting from deep inside, he roared and flailed precise arcs with lighting quick reflexes. The close knit crowd erupted into broken bones. All were shredded before him. With the splintering of the last he grimaced at his wounded paw. The half skeleton scooting along the ground finally made his leg, reached out, and received twin hammer fists raining down to turn the crawling relic into dust. With this last victory, with no skeletons within sight, he sighed.

Pain erupted between his shoulders. Something pierced him from behind. Disbelief supplanted the anger across his black eyes and snout. A blade punctured and retreated backwards out the wound through matted fur and laid open flesh. Aodhan witnessed the blade perforate through the skin in the front of his chest and felt it as it slid backwards through his body like an escaping snake through a rat hole. He looked down then away, confused. The hand on the long blade… was Captain Brennan.

Chapter 7

IT WAS NOT CAPTAIN BRENNAN, not as he had been. A blackness, an errant composure had replaced those eyes. The lips smiled, knowing that the blade had nicked the man-bear's heart with its thrust. That smile, no longer the smile of a mere man. Serenity washed over Captain Brennan's lips, his teeth, as if he were grinding on a mouthful of pure willpower.

"My Condolences. You played your hand the best you could," the man suggested. His face, even in the near moonless night, had the vacant, pasty pallor of the nearly deceased. One ragged hip was torn, a manifold of channels. Though the mangled leg seemed to stand without problem. "I had no idea you were powerful enough to raise an army such as this. By the will of Ultha Tah, your spirit has travelled far to stoop to such tricks," he made an attempt, if not exaggerated, of druidic gestures to the four corners across his chest, but his lips were taught from exerting his mind over the pain, yet, part of him was still full of disgust. He was not usually a man of insult, but he had just witnessed the complete desecration of every man under his command. Even his hunting dogs were dead.

"You," Aodhan growled, a deflation of life with each breath, "are not, are not, who are you?"

A most triumphant smile moved across the dry, gray lips. "This post was mine, no thanks to you, but your time seems to be leeching away." His smile widened, now a bridge of execution as he gazed down at the growing pool of blood. "You see, I am…"

Aodhan's ears were closing too fast for him to hear. Falling forward, he stirred only in flashes of memory. The world closed, then winked into a forever passage of oblivion. All melted away like the inevitable transient of seasons. With his eyes skyward, he saw only the amused spirits of many beautiful trees come to collect his soul. Bear lips smiled, at least the best they could. A final huff passed through those loose lips, an exhalation in death. He took the trail through the ethereal forest towards eternal bliss. The large, fur clad body nestled against the world, he would never rise again.

Brennan fell to one knee, the internal fire fading as he too was bleeding enough to water the royal lawns. "…Brennan, Captain Brennan. Commander of the Grey Cloaks," his voice wavered, "sometimes warrior, sometimes vagabond, haha," he laughed towards the lifeless body of his bearish foe in a confessional. "Sometimes even I wonder what is to be my lot in life."

A skeleton tripped over Aodhan's bulk, but Brennan had no more stamina and could do little more than move his eyes to take in the scene. There was no strength left to fight. The anger that riddled his veins had departed alongside a small pool of blood at his heel. His mind succumbed to the exhaustion that tranced him in place, awaiting the approaching enemy without fear.

Hands reached out for his face, his skin.

As the end reached for his flesh, a concussive fire erupted in the middle of the street. Skeletons fell as if spiritually dispersed, released from their enslavement. Numbed seraphim escaping to their own heavens or hells while sets of bone fell as if an invisible rope were cut from atop each head. Brennan fell as well, but for him the jolt gave him life, a surge of preservation that one only finds deep within the depths of a man and played out when all energies have been exhumed, all but pure resolve has been exhausted.

The smell of sulfur and decay permeated the air. Smoke swirled in a tight dust devil, its gray huffs etching towards the sky and slowed to a diluted thick mist. The initial brightness lit the night in an unnatural flare of resonation that left blinding flashes behind his eyelids. As vision returned, it revealed a lithe figure, darkened in the blur.

"What have we here?" the figure asked. His hand cupped around his chin, one claw-like nail tapped a hollow tune on a snaggled fang hanging down past its lower lip. "I could have sworn that all were dead." Its nose jerked in pulses, drawing in air over a sneer. "No, you are still alive, even if only a little. No matter, I will have the pleasure of sending you off myself. Captain Brennan."

Beneath the folds of his grey cloak, Brennan griped the sheathed hilt of his sword with one hand and fingered the sap as his energies drained. The creature's devious eyes licked over him like a snake's tongue, cold, but unable to read the growing strength hidden deep within a pocket of survival.

"Do you know why I have come? Why I am here?" the demonic visitor paused to usher in a smirk and clasped its hands before it began again. "These lands are scarred…and mine." The last was given to a theatrical sarcasm. "Have been for far longer than you could comprehend," it hissed, "I am…" but it did not get to finish.

Brennan interrupted the cruel beast, "You are nothing more than an imp, a gargoyle fell from its perch." The slap of words held sharp edges, much for the insult and more for having cut off its soliloquy.

"You impotent fool," it susurrated, taking a step to close the distance and tear at him with brutish hate. Cloven hooves clapped forward, hands outstretched.

Captain Brennan waited for the nether creature to approach. When it was close enough for the smell to have twisted into taste, he tossed the sap up towards its face. The dark fiend lurched backwards, hands raised to defy the implement. In the same instant, Brennan drew his sword and arced upward. A glow emanated along its length, manifesting at the holy lightning bolt trinket wrapped into the cross-guard. His sword cut deep into the exposed middle of hairy flesh that should have been impervious to an ordinary blade. The creature bayed as its torso gashed open. The worldly transformation had given it substance, skin, organs, and bones. Entrails spilled out into the dust of the road. Ribs gave pardon to the opposing force.

A look of concern eroded down its face, mouth wide open in astonishment at the odd sensation of pain, the newness of torn tissues, the internal moved to become external, all effected by steel and gravity. How easily it all fell from its body. The world closed in through a blackness that charged around its eyes, circled inward in its vision like some kind of hypnosis. The burn spread outward as vision gave retreat.

A single thought passed into its mind, *Bested by a tavern trick and a bauble.*

Innards slowed their unraveling descent and a hellish plasma eviscerated forth in the place of blood. Hands grasped to stop the outflow but with no more success than if it were clutching at a tide of spilled milk. The skin wrinkled into sickly excess across its torso while the body shriveled down in size, but it did not stop with the emptied cavity. Its head pulled down, the neck lost in the folded depths of skin wrapped about its shoulders, joints bowed as if muscles were turned to jelly, and the spine curved forward as a slow felled tree would bend beneath its own weight born on by the axe. Without the use of its mortal body, the hell-spawn had no choice but to return to its perdition.

Captain Brennan sheathed his sword with the last of his waning strength. A grimace danced across his face at the pain in his leg while the once intimidating foe liquefied into a jelli-fying, felled carcass. Though the depraved lacerations at his hip and leg looked cruel, they were little more than a field of bleeding perforations hidden behind torn leather, vaguely snout shaped, and less actual severed muscle and flesh. He pulled a flask from beneath his armor, took a swig, and then sprinkled it over his bleeding hip and thigh. The sting ran up his leg as it heated down towards his stomach.

It was not his first encounter with monstrosities, and due to a little celestial influence, it would not be his last. He contorted a smile, which was a lie shrouded within the sting and throb of his side. Pushing off, he stood to take in his surroundings. A hard-blown hiss of agony escaped his lips. As it subsided, long trained instincts drew his eyes across every surface in quick glances to ensure there were no more enemies hidden throughout or plainly sneaking up on him. Satisfied, he strained to recognize much of the devastated place. Skulls, bodies, severed limbs, ribcages, dented pieces of armor, bone shards, and broken weapons were strewn across the street and walkways. This once quiet outpost now settled into an eerie silence. Even the night had given up on sound.

The front gate was churned globs of mud waiting for the morning sun to turn them into bricks. Building fronts had torn doorways and broken shutters. Far away, a wall burned in the livery at an upturned lantern that was just starting to feed into a charge of hay. The smoke gave off a signal to the world: 'Death rules here.'

A sigh escaped Captain Brennan's lips in two words, "Now what?"

CHAD VINCENT

Chad Vincent is a teacher in rural Missouri. He lives in a small town with his wife, 3 kids, 3 dogs, and two rogue cats that refuse to officially join the family. His work can be found in *Trembling With Fear* and the anthology *9 Tales Told in the Dark #21,* Silhouette Press *Here Comes Everyone,* Anti-Matter Magazine, *Whispers of the Apoc* anthology, and Hydra Publications' fantasy anthology *Unsheathed.*

WHERE ALL THE SOULS ARE HOLLOW

CHARLES GRIMLICH

Out of choking dust and black smoke
came a warrior with eyes
like broken blades.
Wherever he journeyed,
war followed.
None could say why.
The survivors called him Krieg.

I. Need

THE SAND-LOPERS WERE three in number and had been following the man for three days. Hunger rode them but they were patient. In the broiling desert, the stranger would become prey. At first the human's trail across the dunes ran arrow-straight, with each stride matching precisely the one before. On day two the first misstep happened, a gouge in the sand where a boot slid. Another mistake followed. Gradually, the heels began to drag, the sand whispering beneath them. By day three, the man staggered.

The lopers recognized the signs. With thin black tongues lolling to cool their tawny bodies, the beasts sped themselves to the pace that gave them their name. Their four muscular legs, atop wide, flat paws, covered the ground rapidly. Saliva began to sting their mouths.

The man's track now meandered up one dune and down the next. At places it looked like he'd fallen. Where the dunes faded into a wasteland of wind-blasted rocks, the beasts caught up. The man lay collapsed against a boulder, his body bent at an unnatural angle. Only the absence of desert vultures convinced the pack that he still lived.

One beast's pantherish body shook with hunger. He was youngest of the three, driven by want and not as cautious as his companions. His lipless mouth opened on a needful whimper, revealing triple, saber-like canines protruding from the upper jaw. He rushed the human. Another beast, anxious for his share of meat, followed quickly. The last creature, a brindle-hided she, stayed a few lengths behind the others. She was the biggest and most experienced of the pack. She didn't care if others had the kill; she would have the bulk of the meal.

The first beast reached the man; it hesitated only a moment. The human's chin rested on its chest. The head was turned so the eyes could barely be seen. One hand lay limp in the fellow's lap. The fingers of the other were buried in sand. A rind of throat revealed itself at the juncture of the prey's neck and the leather jerkin covering his chest. Saber teeth gleaming, the loper lunged for that flesh, where a pulse beat.

As the loper attacked, so did the human. One hand leaped up, locked onto the throat of the charging beast. The second hand came free of the sand, revealing the gleam-shine of a knife that plunged into the creature's chest to split the breastbone and find the throbbing heart.

The man surged to his feet as his second enemy leaped. He slung the corpse of the first beast away, and hurled himself to meet his new foe. Both were fast. The warrior was faster. He slashed with his broad-bladed knife, and the honed edge caught the creature behind the bulge of the hard skull, severing the spinal cord. Paralyzed, the creature dropped to earth.

With her mouth open in a red snarl, the last loper froze as a killer's gaze turned toward her. Saliva dripped from her scissor-like teeth to carve tiny holes in the sand beneath her. The man smiled, revealing teeth every bit as white, if not nearly so sharp.

The She backed up a step. She wasn't exactly afraid, but she understood that her pack had been tricked. And she knew from experience that humans could strike from a distance her own fangs could never cross.

"Wise," the warrior said, his voice dry and gravel-rough. "More patience might have brought me down in truth."

The loper shook her broad head, almost as if she understood and disagreed. Then she skirted the scene and headed off in search of easier meat. The man turned to the first loper he'd killed. Puncturing its throat, he drank his fill of bitter blood. He then cut the body open and felt the stomach and upper intestine. They still contained some mixture of water and partially digested food. He tied them off at either end with twine and sliced them free to lie on the sand.

Though he had the means to make fire, there was no fuel to keep one burning. He ate the beast's heart and liver raw, then peeled off the hide. He knifed away a few strips of meat to chew as he traveled. After sipping from his makeshift gut-canteen, he stuffed it and generous portions of loper meat into the hide to carry.

Finally, the man known as Krieg turned to the second beast. It lived, though paralyzed from the neck down. Krieg bound the creature's muzzle with twine, hoisting it over his shoulder for when he needed fresh meat. Taking up his previous route, he probed deeper into the desert. His chances of crossing it alive had just improved.

II. Armor

KRIEG LAY at the edge of a desert valley and studied the terrain ahead. The sun was rising behind him, annihilating the shadows that had owned the place moments before. Morning light painted pleasant warmth on his back after the night's chill. It was temporary. The heat would grow. But, perhaps, he would not be in the sun for long.

The valley before him ran narrow and rocky, with cliffs rising high and rough to either side. A dusty trail scored the center of the valley, ending before a wall that spanned from ridge to ridge. The wall stood some twenty feet high, with two taller walls rising behind it. Stone steps led to the top of the first wall. This must be the place he sought. Nothing else around smacked of human habitation.

Discerning no way to approach the wall unseen, Krieg rose and stepped into the open. He'd taken off his chainmail while crossing the desert but donned it again and stalked down the path before him. Sand dribbled from his mail and leathers; he paid no attention. The dawn wind soughed around him, smelling only of dust.

Reaching the foot of the steps unchallenged, Krieg did not

pause. Only at the top did he halt. The wall was as thick as it was tall. Though scoured by wind and sand, its granite blocks seemed as solid as earth itself.

The second wall was taller and thicker, set back from the first by thirty paces or so. Krieg could see no way to reach it. He *could* see that he was not alone on the wall. Near his feet, lying flat within a large bluish glyph of a twelve-pointed star, rested a plate-armored form almost seven feet tall. The glyph was faded, the armor tarnished. Krieg could not tell if anything wore the armor. If so, it wasn't human.

With padding, a human's upper body might have fit into the breastplate of the suit, although it was almost triangular. But the legs were too long relative to the body, and the arms too short. Where gauntlets should cover hands there was instead a sword blade on the right side and a shield shaped like a six-petal flower on the left. Strangest of all gleamed the helmet, which was far narrower than a human helm should be, and sharply tapered from front to back.

Krieg used a dagger to pry at the helm's visor. It popped open to reveal nothing but emptiness within. He studied that emptiness a moment, then straightened and sheathed his knife. He stepped to the inner edge of the wall and looked over. A thirty foot drop greeted him. At the bottom, stretching to the next wall, spread a dense carpet of metal spikes. He could see no way past them.

A scraping brought Krieg's head around. The empty suit of armor had risen from its bed. It lunged toward him, sword extended to steal his life.

III. Threat

KRIEG HAD no time to draw his axe. He seemed to hesitate,

as if unsure what to do. But it was no hesitation, only calculation. Like a glittering bolt of lightning, the sword came stabbing. At the last possible moment, Krieg thrust his right arm up and out while swaying the rest of his body to the left. The sword passed between Krieg's body and his arm, and he snapped the arm down to imprison the weapon against his mail. Instantly, he twisted his torso halfway around, jerking his armored attacker off balance.

A human enemy might have released the sword's hilt to avoid what happened next. Whatever force animated the armor could not. The sword was part of it, and the leverage that Krieg's twisting motion exerted dragged the thing to the lip of the wall. It teetered on the edge. Krieg felt its weight grow heavy on the trapped blade as it strove for purchase; he lifted his arm.

The armored shape fell backward, crashed onto iron spikes that tore it open. Dispassionately, Krieg studied the rent form as it struggled to escape impalement. Cyan sparks flamed. The bitter whiff of heated copper accompanied the sparks. Then the fiery discharges died away. The form stilled.

Another sound drew Krieg's attention. From the midpoint of the wall where he stood, a metal ramp extruded. It stretched out and up toward the second wall. He started toward it, then paused as two more armored forms appeared atop that wall. They were shorter and far more slender than the thing he'd just fought. They carried weapons in gauntleted hands.

The ramp touched the top of the second wall, locking itself to stone. The armored figures stood to either side of it, weapons ready. A puff of air passed through Krieg's lips—perhaps the faintest of sighs. He drew his axe.

IV: Battle

THE SUN BLAZED the sky white. Its heat hammered Krieg. When it became clear that his new enemies were not going to advance toward him across the bridge, Krieg advanced toward them. The steel span gave slightly beneath his weight, and though it was narrow he did not glance down. His gaze studied his foes, particularly their weapons. They looked like tridents, but the middle prong was much longer than the others.

Krieg had seen sai before; such weapons were primarily for blocking and bludgeoning. The prongs were not typically sharpened. The middle prong of the new weapon resembled an awl, with the tip tapered to punch through plate armor. It would work just as well on his chain mail.

As Krieg approached within ten feet of the armored forms, they crouched in preparation for attack or defense. Their positions made it impossible to exit the bridge without leaving himself vulnerable. The sag of the metal span also meant he'd have to attack uphill against a defended point. Krieg approved of his enemies' strategy. He did not stop walking. The axe swung back and forth at his side.

Eight feet.

Six feet.

Four.

Krieg took one more step, spun off that heel ad snapped the axe around to let it fly. The weapon's heavy crescent blades smashed one armored form in the chest, crushing plate steel and hurling the thing from its feet. The handle struck the other foe in the head, staggering it. Krieg's hands leaped to his belt and ripped free a set of long knives. He launched himself across the last slice of bridge. As his boots slapped down atop the solid wall, the standing foe twisted back to face him and tried to raise its weapons to block his attack.

Too late. Krieg was too close. His right-hand knife struck upward with all the power of his shoulder behind it. The blade's tip rasped across the enemy's gorget and punched into the helm above. The whole helmet tore free with a metallic shriek and spun away in a shower of purple sparks. The body fell backward with a clank. Only the stench of burned copper spilled out.

The foe with the crushed chest wasn't finished. It strove to rise. Krieg plucked it up as if it weighed no more than a feather and hurled it into the pit of spikes below the wall. The spikes ripped it in half, revealing nothing inside. As Krieg stared down at his torn enemy, he had one thought:

Automatons.

Krieg's black axe glinted on the nearby stones. He scooped it up just as a familiar grating sound stung his ears. A metal ramp pushed out from the second wall, reaching toward the third. Looking up, Krieg saw what awaited.

V: Tableaux

WHERE THE STEEL ramp touched the third wall, three armored forms stood. Each was as big as the first one he'd fought. Two carried pikes that far outreached his axe. The third held only a dagger, but it lay pressed to the neck of a young boy who looked human and no more than eight or nine years old.

Krieg studied the scene, stalking to the new bridge and starting up. As he reached halfway, the boy spoke:

"Wait," he said.

Krieg kept coming.

"They'll kill me!" the boy shouted.

The armored thing holding the dagger pressed it harder against the boy's throat. A droplet of blood rolled down the youth's pale skin.

Krieg stopped walking.

The boy's face was contorted with fear; his small body shook.

"Thank...you," he murmured. "Please don't come any farther or they'll kill me."

"Who are you?" Krieg asked.

"Stimon. We were traveling. My family. With a small caravan. We got separated. Lost. Ended up here." Tears dripped down the boy's face. "My father and mother. My sisters. Dead now. I'm all alone."

Krieg nodded. "How long?"

The boy hesitated. Then, "A few months. Maybe a year. They keep me in a dark place. Most of the time."

"Why?"

"I don't know their reasons."

Again Krieg nodded.

Against his white face, the boy's lips gleamed a sullen red. They trembled.

"If you drop your weapons over the wall," he said. "They won't kill me."

"How do you know?"

"I...hear them. In my head. When they want me to, I hear their thoughts."

Krieg held his axe out at shoulder height, over the long drop off the bridge.

The boy smiled.

VI: Choice

KRIEG LET GO of the axe.

The boy shrieked with glee.

Krieg thrust out with his boot, hooked the falling weapon behind its crescent blades, and kicked it back up into the air. His hands caught the axe's haft as he charged forward along the bridge. The armored form holding the dagger had just started to relax and straighten. The automatons with the pikes had eased their grips. With his weapon regained, Krieg came in among them.

He brought the axe slicing upward from low on his right side. The pike-wielding foe to the boy's left had no chance. The fearful twin blades of dark steel hooked in beneath the thing's chest plate and carved upward. Metal shrieked; purple sparks exploded. The thing collapsed to its knees, leaving two automatons for Krieg to deal with.

The boy yelped in surprise and turned to run. Krieg snatched for him, hooking a finger in the youth's linen shirt. The dagger-wielding automaton seized Krieg's arm in a crushing grip. The boy tore free. The automaton slashed its dagger at Krieg's head, and Krieg dropped his own weapon to catch the thing's arm, halting the tip of the blade an inch from his eye. The thing was strong, immensely so. But it could not force the dagger closer to the man; nor could the man force it away.

Krieg shifted his weight and smashed a kick into his foe's chest. The blow hammered it backward, breaking the hold on his wrist. The thing stumbled into the third automaton, which was looking for an opening to use its pike. For a moment, both enemies were off balance. Krieg took up his axe.

The third wall butted against the dome of a big, round metal building that looked like a soup tureen. The boy raced up the side of the dome toward a hatch at the top. Krieg had questions for the child but in his way stood the last two automatons.

Krieg's lips curled. He stalked forward, the axe vibrating with the intensity of his grip. The dagger-wielding automaton dropped its weapon and shook its metal arm. The gauntleted hand folded back and a sword slid out from the wrist, locking into place with a click. The thing slashed the blade at Krieg and the man blocked with his axe's haft. He smashed a boot into the armored knee and saw it give way as the thing fell heavily.

The other automaton thrust with its pike. Krieg swayed aside, but not quickly enough. The steel tip of the weapon burst the links of chain mail above his left hip, spraying shards of metal and droplets of blood into the air.

Krieg grunted. But his axe was already swinging. The blow struck the automaton just below the shoulder, severing the arm that controlled the pike. The axe drove on into the thing's side, sending it careening over the wall into the spike pit below. Not waiting to see the thing land, Krieg spun back to face his other foe. It had regained its feet and lunged toward him with its sword out. Krieg twisted to avoid the blow. Steel scraped across his chain mail but did not cut through.

The pommel of the black axe was a knob of solid iron. Krieg punched it into the side of the automaton's helm. Sparks flew. The helmet's cheek plate caved inward. The helm itself twisted to one side. Krieg brought the axe up, over, and down. Steel cleaved steel, splitting the automaton from head to waist. Tendrils of purple and cyan fire licked the air like fingers of lightning. Krieg's nostrils tingled. The automaton collapsed, twitched, and lay still.

Krieg glanced around. The first automaton he'd axed was still kneeling upright but not moving. He kicked it so that it tumbled onto its back like a dead turtle. Whatever had animated it was gone. Alone on the wall, the human warrior glanced down at his side where he'd been struck. The pike had gouged through his mail and taken meat with it. Blood dripped slowly from the wound but no bone shown through.

Ignoring the injury, as he'd ignored many before, Krieg started up the side of the domed building after the boy who had disappeared. At the top was the hatch-like structure he'd seen. It appeared to be an ingress into the building but would not open to a hard yank. As he was about to fetch one of the automaton weapons to use as a pry-bar, he noticed a small hole in the hatch's center. It looked like a twelve-pointed star. Krieg hooked a finger through a loop of leather encircling his neck. Hanging from the loop was a brass nail as long as his thumb. The head was a twelve-pointed star.

VII: Key

KRIEG INSERTED the nail into the hole in the hatch. A vibration rumbled through the metal beneath his feet. The hatch cracked into a dozen pieces that slid away to reveal a glass cylinder full of bright blue light extending down into the building. A staircase spiraled down the inside of the cylinder. Hanging the key back around his neck, Krieg sheathed his axe and started down the stairs. The steps were narrow, unsuited to a grown man's feet. Krieg turned sideways to navigate them. The boy was nowhere to be seen.

Fifteen feet down, Krieg spied another hatch. He expected to need his key again but this one folded away as he approached. He passed into a dimly lit area. The sides of the cylinder fell away, and he descended through a shadowy expanse with transparent blue walls glowing all around.

Through those walls he glimpsed dozens of bodies floating upright in some kind of liquid.

The bodies were human, mostly females, all adults. Many races were represented. All had shaved heads. Most of the females looked pregnant. The figures' eyes were closed and at first Krieg thought them dead. Closer study revealed chests that rose and fell. Sporadic bubbles of air bled from the nostrils. He did not know how they remained upright without visible support. Neither could he understand how they breathed in such an environment.

The reason he'd made the long journey to this place would likely be found in that room. He could see no access to it. Seeking a portal, he moved on, soon coming to a floor and another hatch. This one opened too as he approached, and he passed into a chamber even stranger than the last. The stairway ended and he stepped off onto a polished metal floor.

Blue light suffused the chamber which was perhaps thirty feet across but which stretched high into the shadows above. A large metallic slab stood in the center. It might have been an altar except that it was tilted at an acute angle. Faint runes inscribed its surface. He imagined that they had meaning, but though he'd seen many languages he did not recognize this one.

Scattered about were chairs too slender for an adult human. Beside them stood small metallic tables with more of the unusual runes written on them. Embedded in the wall behind the strange slab gleamed what appeared to be an oval window. Shifting lights of pearl, mauve, and ocher flitted there. Krieg sensed more meaning in the motion of the lights. It occurred to him that the room was the building's heart, where decisions were made and executed, though he could not say why it felt that way.

The walls to either side of the glowing window were transparent. Here, too, were bodies. These did not float in liquid, however. They stood in ranks like statues painted with the colors of living flesh. Their eyes were shut but they breathed. All were children of various ages.

A sound impinged on Krieg's awareness. Ever since he'd entered the building there'd been a faint, resonant hum. The new sound was different, like the wailing of a distant voice in the dark. It seemed to originate within the slab. Krieg approached that structure. The runes dimmed and brightened in some intricate pattern. The pattern wove around a triangle of three small holes that perforated the metal, each shaped like a twelve-pointed star. Once again Krieg reached for the leather loop around his neck. He drew it off, with the brass key dangling. A soft voice halted him as he leaned over the holes.

"Please don't do that."

He turned. A green-eyed girl child with a sweet face and dusky skin had come from somewhere—though he'd heard no door open or close. She appeared to be a couple of years older than the boy from outside. Linen of many layers and colors gowned her. Sets of tiny cymbals, called zills, clasped her fingers. From a silver chain around her neck dangled a bronze key like his.

"Keys are to be used," Krieg replied.

"Even if it destroys the innocent?"

Krieg shook his head slightly. "I don't know what you are, but you're no innocent."

"I'm only a child."

"No," Krieg said.

The girl's lips curled back over teeth that glistened with saliva. A low hiss sizzled from her mouth. She snapped her fingers and the cymbals on her hands clashed and jangled.

Krieg glimpsed movement at the edge of his vision and let his gaze be drawn to the walls and the children standing in rows behind them. Their eyes were open now, focused on him. Knives filled their hands.

Krieg unsheathed his axe. "Do not imagine that because you have the semblance of youth that I won't slaughter you all," he said to the girl.

A smirk remolded the girl's features from sweet to vicious. Again her finger cymbals clashed. Hidden doors in the walls slid back and children poured into the room. Twenty. Thirty. More. Their knives glittered; their mouths frothed with hate.

Krieg placed his back against the slab, his axe in front of him. A memory came, unsummoned—a memory of a distant time, of true innocence. Darkness blazed in Krieg's pupils. He snarled.

VIII: Berserk

THE GIRL POINTED AT KRIEG. "Kill him!" she shouted at the others. "Knife him apart!"

The children attacked, the bigger ones at the vanguard.

Krieg roared. The sound exploded from his throat in an almost physical wave that punched into the mass of children. The ones at the front froze; the ones behind piled against them. For a moment, utter confusion reigned.

Krieg charged. He lowered his shoulder, smashing into the children at the front of the horde. It was like a bull charging a field of wheat. Small bodies went flying. Children cried out; many turned to flee. Krieg trampled through them until he found himself in the clear.

The girl with the zills stood there with eyes wide. Her

finger still pointed in his direction. Before she could move, Krieg snatched her under one arm and locked her helplessly against his side. The doors that had admitted the other children were still open. Krieg leaped through one, into a corridor that curved out of sight ahead. He raced along it. The girl struggled but could do nothing against the man's strength. When she tried to bite, her teeth ground on links of armor. She shrieked then. He cuffed her cheek and she fell silent.

So far there was no pursuit. Krieg expected it soon. He watched for some way out of the corridor and found it. Bolted to one wall, a narrow ladder extended up into the shadows. Krieg sheathed his axe and went up, finding himself in an alcove from which a tunnel extended back into the wall. He crouched there, putting the girl down for a moment while he tore the ladder loose from its perch.

When he turned back, the girl was scrambling down the tunnel. He caught her by an ankle, yanking her toward him. She kicked at him and he caught her other leg and twisted her onto her belly. His knee pressed into her back so she couldn't move; he clamped a hand over her mouth to stifle a scream.

From below came the sound of running feet, small feet. Only after they passed did the girl's struggles subside. Krieg released her mouth. He pulled the zills from her fingers, then yanked her into a sitting position across from him. Thoughts of calling for help crossed her eyes like flights of sparrows.

"Scream again, I'll snap your neck," he told her calmly.

The girl glared at him but made no sound.

"What is this place?" Krieg asked after a moment.

"Your tomb," the girl snapped.

Krieg flashed a faint smile. "Mine becomes yours. What is this…place?"

The girl shrugged, but added: "It's home. To me. I don't know what you're asking."

"I was looking for a ruin. Some place that might house bandits. This is no such place."

The girl fingered the brass key on her necklace. Her gaze studied the similar key hanging around Krieg's neck. She pointed.

"But you have *that*. Surely you know this place."

Krieg shook his head.

"Then how?"

Krieg considered. "An old man," he said after a moment. "His granddaughter was taken from a caravan in this desert. A survivor of the raid found the key. He gave it to the man, who gave it to me."

Krieg watched the girl as he spoke. Her eyes widened. Her surprise seemed genuine. "That should not have happened," she said.

"The lost key? Or the survivors?"

She glared. "Neither."

Krieg did not pursue further questions. He pulled the girl toward him and clamped a hand over her mouth. Her linen dress had long sleeves; Krieg ripped them off. The girl had barely begun to struggle when he pushed her away again and quickly tied the two sleeves together to create a makeshift rope.

"Ankle," he demanded.

In shock, the girl stuck her leg out. Krieg grasped her ankle and tethered one end of his rope around it. The other end he kept in his hand.

"Down the tunnel ahead of me," he ordered. "Crawl!"

IX: Exploration

THE TUNNEL WAS narrow for Krieg but he squeezed

through. Soon they came to a new corridor. It was empty. A ladder descended. Krieg scooped up the girl and climbed down. He untethered her ankle but retied the leash to her wrist.

"Which way?" he asked.

The girl started to the left and Krieg yanked her back and headed to the right, parallel to the direction they'd come from. A few hundred paces brought them to a hatch that closed the way. It opened when Krieg pushed the girl in front of it. Beyond the portal waited a long, wide room, with metal tables down the center and recesses cut into the walls. Both tables and recesses were populated with automatons. They were inactive. For the moment.

The automatons on the tables were in various stages of being assembled or disassembled. One lay face down and Krieg stopped to inspect it. He noticed something he'd not seen before. A small hole with twelve points exited the back of the armored helmet. Krieg nodded to himself, then turned to look at the girl. She paid no attention to either him or the automatons but seemed to be listening for something.

The boy, Stimon, had spoken of "hearing thoughts." If that's what the girl was trying to do, Krieg couldn't do much about it other than kill her. He wasn't ready for that yet. Best to keep moving.

Krieg tugged the girl behind him as he continued through the room and out a hatch on the far side. Another large room opened before them. This one brought Krieg to instant stillness. It was a map area, but not for maps of any lands he'd ever seen. In the center squatted a large glass sphere. Glowing clusters of what he recognized as stars floated within it, thousands of them. A few resembled constellations he recognized—the dragon, the snake, the hawk. Most were unknown.

The girl seemed indifferent to the sphere. Krieg pushed on. The next room was the one he sought.

X: Goal

THE ROOM that he entered with the girl was large and circular. Half a dozen paces beyond the door stood a long metal table surrounded by child-sized chairs. The rest of the area was filled with a huge, transparent tank of bluish liquid. He'd seen the tank when he entered the building. From here, though, he had a better view of the people floating in it. He counted ten women for every man. The women looked pregnant, but even the men had oddly swollen abdomens.

Krieg had come for the granddaughter of a man he knew. If she lived, she must be here. But he'd known her only as a child, and she was grown now. He'd hoped to still recognize her gale-green eyes and her dark hair so tightly curled. But all the eyes were closed and the heads shaved. Then—he recognized a mole on one woman's neck.

Krieg pressed his hand to the tank. It was glass, cool to the touch. He turned to the girl.

"Free them!"

She laughed bitingly. "Fool!" she exclaimed.

A frown creased the warrior's face. "Why a fool?"

She thrust a hand toward the people. "Can you not see?"

Krieg studied the floaters. He did see. Stitched scars crisscrossed their bodies and wove through their scalps. Except for the bellies, they all looked shrunken, including the heads. They might still be breathing but they weren't completely alive any longer.

"What did you take?" he asked.

The girl shrugged. "Anything that wasn't needed."

"To breed?"

"Yes."

"Your kind."

She chuckled; an odd rattle burbled in her throat. "Not completely unaware, perhaps," she said.

"What are you?"

"A child. One you have tormented."

Krieg shook his head. "No human child."

"Human. Yes. Human and more. And…the last thing you'll ever see."

The door opened. A flood of children poured in. They carried knives. At their head scampered the boy, Stimon, whom Krieg had seen outside. He, too, wore a twelve-pointed brass key around his neck.

Behind the children came a dozen automatons, armed and armored. They stopped between Krieg and the only way out; their weapons flashed in the dim light. Stimon locked the exit hatch, then gave Krieg a look that crawled with smugness.

Krieg clasped the back of the girl's slender neck with one big hand.

"Killing me won't stop them," the girl snapped. "Whether I die does not matter. Whether all of us in this room die does not matter. There will be more. Enough to take your world."

"It only matters that *you* die, warrior," Stimon added with a giggle.

Krieg twined his fingers through the girl's necklace, the one holding her key. With a sudden twist, he broke the links and yanked the key away. The girl shrieked as she realized what had happened. She spun toward Krieg, grabbing for the necklace. He shoved her roughly away, sending her stumbling into the others who faced him.

Then he drew his axe one more time.

XI: War

"TEAR HIM DOWN!" the girl commanded.

The automatons started forward, their armor clashing. The children hung back, waiting to use their knives but half afraid of the man who'd trampled them before. Krieg raised his axe, spun and hacked the twin-bladed weapon savagely into the chamber full of liquid and people.

Fragments of glass sprayed outward, glinting like diamonds. Cracks spidered away from the impact point. A small chunk clanged on the floor. The automatons paused. Krieg did not. Again, he hacked his heavy axe into the tank. More glass shards broke free. A stream of blue water hissed though a tiny hole. The hole grew. Chiming filled the room as the cracks in the chamber widened. The glass bulged.

Krieg sheathed his axe and grabbed onto the nearby metal table. It was anchored to the floor. The automatons had recovered from their surprise and were pushing toward him, their weapons readied.

The tank ruptured; glass exploded outward from the weight behind it. Churning with bodies, a deluge of water stormed the room. The surge swept over Krieg but did not wash him away; he held on to the table, muscles cording under his mail.

The automatons had nothing to hold on to. Water struck like a hammer, smashing them into the wall behind them. They made no sound, but the children screamed as the flood battered them as well. The huge wave of liquid hit the back of the room, rebounded. Krieg hung on as it washed over him again. A shrieking child hurtled past, then another. He waited. The girl swept by, then the boy, Stimon. Krieg grabbed Stimon, tore the key from his neck, and released him again.

An automaton reached the table. It slashed its sword arm

at Krieg. But the force of the flood had lessened. Krieg let go his grip, turned and leaped through the gaping hole in the tank. He splashed through fallen bodies and ankle-deep water to the far side of the chamber. There, he looked down on the room he'd judged to be the building's heart, where a tilted metal slab awaited with three holes for three keys.

Raising his axe, Krieg focused his strength into one blow. The glass wall shattered and Krieg leaped through, landing in a crouch only steps away from the metal slab he sought. Knowing the automatons would be after him, he lunged forward and stabbed the girl's and Stimon's keys into two of the holes. Incised runes all across the slab bloomed with light and began to blink.

"No!" the girl screamed from above.

Metal clashed as automatons began dropping into the room after Krieg. He didn't look. Instead, he jerked the key from around his own neck and thrust it into the remaining hole. Then he put the slab between himself and his enemies.

A sudden rumbling jolted the room like an earthquake. As dust spurted from floor and walls, Krieg grabbed hold of the slab to avoid being thrown down. The automatons were not so lucky. The five who'd followed him staggered wildly as the floor juddered beneath them.

From the corner of his eye, Krieg saw the glowing "window" at the front of the room turn inky black. Emerald patterns began dancing across it. Krieg recognized them as charts. Instinct guided him. He pressed one blinking shape on the slab. A single emerald pattern solidified on the window. A metallic voice began to bark from the air. The words were unrecognizable but sounded like a count. The rumbling intensified. A high-pitched keening began to build.

The girl screamed again. "No!"

The boy's plea joined hers. "Get them out. Get them out! The ship. Buried. It can't take off."

The closest automaton thrust itself toward Krieg. It wasn't after him, though. It fumbled to pull the keys from their holes. Krieg swept his axe across, snapping off the keys, leaving the heads buried in the slab. The shrieking coming from the boy and girl then did not sound human. It howled with despair. The automatons froze, as if their purpose was lost. Krieg pushed past them, lunging into the stairwell he'd climbed down to get here. He started up.

For a moment, Krieg's gaze met that of the two children who were not children. He glimpsed their real natures. Their eyes bulged, then popped free of the sockets containing them. On black, snail-like necks, those orbs stretched and quested toward him. At the same time, the mouths opened. From between the still-human lips, tongues like the tails of rats writhed.

Krieg did not tarry. He pushed faster up the stairwell but it was a tight fit and the world shook violently. He had to brace every step. Smoke coiled around him, yellow and stinking. A crackling sound drew his attention. It wasn't fire. The bodies of the men from the great tank no longer lay still where they'd fallen. They convulsed. Distended abdomens split wide. Black and yellow antennae poked free, like those of wasps. Heads and thoraxes followed. On thrumming wings, dozens of hornet-like monsters the size of a man's thigh took the air. They came for him.

Krieg sped his pace. The hatch to the outside lay just above him. He reached it as the stairwell began to echo with the snarl of wings. Krieg shoved up on the hatch. It didn't move. The jarring of the building must have jammed it.

The warrior threw his weight against the portal. It creaked, shuddered, resisted. Now, Krieg exerted his full strength. Muscles coiled and rippled across his shoulders and down his arms. The metal step beneath his boots began to bend. The hatch's resistance gave. It flew open with a clang.

Thrusting his way through the opening, Krieg spared one glance back down the stairwell. Out of smoke and blue light, a dozen flying shapes materialized. This close, they looked more like winged scorpions than wasps. Stingers coiled over their backs, dripping green rheum. Krieg slammed the hatch before they could reach him. The portal jolted as meaty bodies pummeled it from the other side. Krieg smiled. For a moment.

The hatch began to lift.

XII: Ending

BLACK, clawed feelers swept from beneath the rising hatch. The humming of wings intensified. In another instant, the doorway would be thrown open; the monsters inside would be free. Krieg stomped the portal down, cutting off the feelers. His axe pounded once, twice, three times into the hatch. The metal caved in, jamming tight. Nothing would open it now.

The ground still shook; the tremors spread. Krieg did not run but did not dawdle either. He recrossed the stone walls and took the desert trail he'd followed to get here. Only at the edge of the valley where the quaking was centered did he turn to look. Smoke and lurid flame rose around the structure he'd escaped. The boy, Stimon, had called it a "ship." Whatever ocean such a ship had sailed, Krieg did not think its shores lay on earth.

The flames intensified and purple arcs of lightning began to stroke the air and ground. Slowly, the heart of the valley sank into the depths. Soon, nothing was left but a glowing hole. Still, Krieg watched. When the watching stopped, he would have to leave. Far across the desert, an old man waited for word of his granddaughter. Unpleasant or not, that word must be given.

Krieg spat into the valley and turned away.

CHARLES GRAMLICH

Charles Gramlich grew up on an Arkansas farm but lives now among the pines in southern Louisiana. He is the author of the Talera series of Sword and Planet Adventures, and has several collections of his short stories released from Wildside press—Bitter Steel (heroic fantasy), Midnight in Rosary (vampires), and In the Language of Scorpions (horror). He has also published westerns, children's stories, and poetry. His westerns appear under the name Tyler Boone. Charles's work is available on line from Amazon, Barnes & Noble, and Wildside Press. He is on Facebook as Charles Gramlich and welcomes new friends. He blogs at: http://charlesgramlich.blogspot.com

SWITCH BLADE

DR SCOTT SIMERLEIN

"A TRAGIC MISUSE."

Chop-chop-chop-chop-chop-

"A dis*grace*ful conversion."

-chop-chop-chop-chop-chop-

"A ludicrous waste!"

-chop-chop-chop-chop-SWIPE!

Ragna Riggle looked up with heavy-lidded eyes and growled, "Are you quite through, Rooter Regal?"

Rooter Regal, Esq., a gnome of considerable repute in the Humdrungle community, wisely stayed his disparaging tongue. Wisely, because he abruptly found the point of Ragna's enormous sword hovering beneath his upturned nose.

"This sword," said she, "was my father's pride and joy, as you well know. It was left to me when he and Mama passed, and it shall stay with me until *I* pass."

The blade returned to its task of dismembering rutabagas on the wooden table standing between sword-owner and sword-coveter. It sliced neatly through the vegetable victim, savaging it to bits with a few deft flicks of Ragna's slender wrist. Rooter was taken aback at how expertly the tiny gnomette manipulated the outsized blade. *That sword's even more unusual than I realized*, he thought. Peering over his shoulder at the cluttered dirt floor behind him, Rooter managed a wary step backward before risking further conversation.

"I appreciate your feelings, Ragna, but I can't ignore a travesty when I see one. By the Five Elements, you've reduced Vic, here, to the service of a common kitchen knife! I can give you a dozen such utensils—fashioned in silver, if you wish—if only you would allow me to liberate that magnificent blade from its piteous existence."

Another *SWIPE!* sent the chunks of rutabaga tumbling off the end of the table. Not one piece missed its target—a large iron pot on the floor.

"Trade Vic to you so it might be used in battle?" she asked quietly. A mighty clang filled the room as she rapped the broad side of the sword against the table's worn edge. "You know that we Riggles are strict pacifists."

Rooter's instincts of self-preservation had forced him to jump back—right into a basket of soggy mishamash mushrooms. Keeping a wary eye on Ragna, he bent to brush phosphorescent fungus fragments from his squirrel-hide shoes. From his crouched position, he risked a retort.

"If your father was such a pacifist, why would he forge a sword in the first place? And to human scale, no less?"

Ragna lifted the elegant weapon as high as the earthen ceiling would allow. She turned it in her grasp, studying its edges as they gleamed in the firelight.

"Have you never heard a fisher-gnome tell of throwing back his prize catch?" she asked. "Some things are accomplished for the joy of the craft—with no expectation of utility."

"Still, craftwork as fine as *that* could buy you and your

siblings much security," Rooter pressed. "And that sorry saber cries for a taste of something more substantial than rutabagas and potatoes. If not a living foe, at least a bit of dead meat." He sighed theatrically. "Eight humdrunglings growing up in this burrow under your care and not a morsel of swampkunk meat on the table. A shame, that's what it is."

Ragna's eyes lit upon the trader-gnome. "Not only are the members of this household strict pacifists, Rooter Regal, but strict vegetarians as well."

"Unnatural's all I can say. No, I'll say this, too: a sword so wondrous can't remain unknown outside these parts indefinitely."

Ragna's ire was rekindled. "What are you insinuating?"

"Nothing, nothing," he assured her with haste. "It is only that I fear the next one to call regarding Vic, here, might not do so offering payment."

"Begone, Rooter Regal!" Ragna ordered. "Vic is not for sale! And if you know what is good for you, you shall cease your crusade to acquire it!"

Rooter made a little bow and backed up the packed-dirt stairs, leaving glowing footprints all the way. He lifted the flap-hatch of the burrow and emerged into early autumn sunlight. The leaves were just beginning to change, and there was a distinct bite of the approaching winter chilling the air. Adjusting his moleskin cloak with a tug, he set off on the half-mile walk home, to a handsome above-ground cottage convenient to his every need. His dealings with humans had taught him one thing: no self-respecting being should ever reduce himself to cohabitating with earthworms and subterranean hackerpedes. Why his Humdrungle brethren persisted in such an unsanitary and degrading practice puzzled him to no end.

A shrill whistle drew Rooter's steed from its nearby den.

The snorkack was a fright to behold—taller than Rooter's own twenty inches, with crumpled horns snaking over its bristly neck and sufficient malice in its blazing orange eyes to set any sensible gnome a-quiver under his pointed cap. The beast gave a bellowing yowl, baring its double-row of serrated teeth which had undoubtedly torn apart more fluffer-bunnies and dillyhogs than it was healthy to think about.

Rooter grinned as he regarded his frightful mount. From early gnomelinghood, he had shown an alarming penchant for dominating and domesticating all manner of terrifying beasts. Crumple-horned snorkacks, ring-tailed wereweasels, snaggle-fanged zingbats—he held them all in thrall. Clicking his tongue sharply, Rooter enjoyed watching his command smother the vicious snorkack's will. The beast knew who was boss.

Rooter gripped one of the snorkacks's gnarled horns and swung himself onto its back. The sword called Vic had remained underground long enough. While Rooter himself would never stoop to thievery, he wasn't opposed to arranging a change in ownership. And he knew precisely who that new owner ought to be.

CHAUNCEY DU SHAYNE was a royal disappointment.

From the day of his birth, Chauncey lacked the robust nature of his cousins, the princes. At the age when most human babies were taking their first steps, Chauncey had yet to be seen sitting up. When he began to walk at the age of three, it was with an awkward, loping gait unbefitting a member of the noble class. Chauncey's parents responded to the harsh scrutiny of the king's court by keeping their toddling son behind closed doors.

Now eleven, Chauncey's limbs had taken a fair bit of length, but they remained as ghoulishly thin and weak as ever. Prince Emmett, the cruelest and eldest of the king's three strapping sons, was heard to remark that if the skinny boy were to stand still too long, guests at the castle might mistake him for a coatrack.

Though physically impaired, Chauncey possessed a keen mind and a burning desire to prove himself worthy of his heritage. His concerned parents lamented the trait, thinking it easier if the boy would only accept his limitations. But such was not in the boy's nature.

So it came to pass that Chauncey would watch his older cousins as they engaged in their knightly training. Hungrily, he studied their exercises and drills, committing to memory every elegant move his own body balked at performing.

"Excellent, Your Highnesses!" cried Sir Percival one blustery autumn afternoon as the princes practiced their parries and thrusts. "Your father would be so proud. Three master swordsmen in the making, and all in His Majesty's own family!"

The master-at-arms in charge of the prince's training was given to excesses of praise, but the flattery was not having the desired effect on Prince Fabian, the middle son. Having just been handily disarmed by his older brother, Fabian snatched up his errant sword and dashed it to the flagstones at the obsequious knight's boots.

"This is rubbish!" he declared, his black bangs clinging to his sweaty forehead. "You're the fourth sparring instructor Father has appointed us this year, and you're as big a toady as any of them! If I am ever to defeat this buffoon of a brother of mine, I need *critique*, man, not compliments!"

"Oi!" Prince Emmett protested as he strode forward. "Just who are you calling a buffoon?"

"Sorry, Em, but these so-called knights are worthless. Well, worthless to you and me, at least. Geoff is still more rubbish than this kiss-up is."

"'Ere, now," the youngest prince chimed in. "I can knock your block off with one blow, I can."

"Only if your hands are empty," Prince Fabian taunted. "Put a sword in one, and you look like a chamber maid beating a tapestry, what?"

"You placed your right foot wrong."

Four heads turned to look at Chauncey sitting on an oak bench across the courtyard. The boy knew speaking was ill-advised, but he'd had his fill of the querulous trio.

Fabian, as usual, was the first to recover. "Did you speak, Twig?"

Chauncey ignored the barb. "Yes. I said you placed your right foot wrong in that Moulinet attack. Threw off your balance, it did. That's why you lost your sword."

Indignant fury inflated Prince Fabian, propelling him toward his seated cousin. But Prince Emmett interceded, preventing the assault with a firm hand on his hot-headed brother's shoulder.

"Now you're an expert on swordplay, is it?" Emmett sneered. He pointed his broadsword in the direction of Fabian's discarded one. "Pick it up."

Chauncey swallowed hard and looked for Sir Percivall for help. The sycophantic knight had disappeared.

"Go on. Pick it up," Prince Emmett ordered again. "You weren't so shy a moment ago."

Trapped, Chauncey did as the prince bade. He stumbled over a flagstone on his way to the sword which set Fabian and Geoffrey to snickering. Emmett did not laugh but fetched a silver cup from the princes' tray of refreshments. With a flourish, he balanced it on top of his head.

"And now, Sir Chauncey shall demonstrate his superior skill with Fabian's sword by displacing this cup from my princely crown."

Chauncey stopped short. "Oh, E-Emmett, I don't think—"

"*What* did you just call me? Is that any way to address your future king?"

"Oh. No. No, Your Highness," Chauncey corrected, gazing up at the much taller boy. Emmett was fifteen and already the size of a full-grown man. Above his hard, hazel eyes, the wind stirred his chestnut hair, partially obscuring Chauncey's glittering silver target.

"Well, come on," the prince barked. "Lift that sword and have done with it."

"I . . . can't, Your Highness," Chauncey said desperately.

"Sure you can. Look, I'm not even armed. Show us your sword-wielding prowess. Or is that blade too much for you? Should I send Geoffrey for something lighter? A *twig*, perhaps?"

The two younger princes guffawed, and even Emmett cracked a sardonic grin. Such mockery rarely stirred Chauncey's ire, but something shifted in him that day. All the injustices and humiliations he had been made to suffer over the years galvanized his bow-string musculature, empowering him to heft the massive sword. Up, up it went till it reached the level of his surprised cousin's face. But Chauncey's goal could not be actualized by his enfeebled flesh. The blade could climb no higher; it would not reach the cup.

As his trembling muscles succumbed to the sword's weight, a blast of wind tore through the courtyard. Chauncey squeezed his eyes shut at the rush of cold air.

"Knave!" he heard Emmett cry. Chauncey cracked open a bleary eye to see a rivulet of red rolling down the crown prince's contorted visage.

"You *dare* strike your monarch's son! Do you have any idea what you've done?"

For a horrible moment, Chauncey feared he had blinded the prince's left eye. Wiping the tears from his own, he was relieved to find his foe had only sustained a minor laceration to the cheek.

Suddenly, the younger brothers ambushed Chauncey, savage as a pair of blunderelk protecting their calves. The fisticuffs were cut off by a bellowing command from Emmett.

"Desist! A traitor like this warrants a more fulsome punishment for bloodying his prince. I shall have satisfaction . . . and have it in the form of a duel!"

With that, the princely troika stormed out of the courtyard, leaving Chauncey cowering on the flagstones, dazed and confused. He hadn't struck Emmett—not intentionally, at least. Lifting the heavy weapon had required a Herculean effort; he'd had no strength left to bring it to bear. And yet, here he was, accused of attacking the king's favored son.

"Now, *this* is a sticky wicket," came a high-pitched voice from behind him. "Thank the Five Elements, your gnomely godfather is on the job."

"MR. ROOTER?"

"Shhh."

"Mr. Rooter?"

"Zip it, kid."

"But, Mr. Rooter, please. I have a question."

"Nope. You don't. I distinctly remember answering all of your questions on the way here."

"But I didn't think of this one before, Mr. Rooter."

"*Keep your voice down!*" the gnome admonished in a

tense whisper. "And it's just plain 'Rooter,' for the ten-thou-sandth time."

The sound of chitterbugs tuning up for their evening concert punctuated the silence between them. Rooter peered through the jawjackle bush at the line of illumination that marked Ragna Riggle's flap-hatch. Soon all would be dark, and they could proceed.

"I still have a question, Mr. Rooter."

"Gah!" the trader-gnome cried, allowing the branch he was holding to snap back into its natural position. He glared up at the cross-legged boy. "What is it about the concept of a stakeout that you don't understand?"

The boy's eyes slid to the side. "It just occurred to me that if you're my gnomely godfather, why don't you use a spell to get the sword?"

"Because that's how *fairy* godfathers work, Chauncey. Gnomely magic is more sophisticated and subtle."

"Which is a fancy way of saying it's lame," the skinny boy mumbled.

"What? What did you say?"

"Me? I didn't say anything. We're being quiet, remember? This is a stakeout."

Rooter frowned at his pet human. When the trader-gnome first decided to challenge himself by domesticating a spec-imen from this most odious race, Chauncey had seemed the ideal candidate—weak, vulnerable, isolated, eager to please. Years of manipulation and cunning went into brainwashing the boy to think that Rooter was his personal magical play-mate who appeared as a reward for mindless obedience. Little Chauncey grew to trust his special friend so fiercely that he happily took part in whatever larcenous scheme the gnome cooked up. This secured Rooter a steady supply of human artifacts to offer his clientele.

But presently, something was amiss. It had taken every scrap of Rooter's persuasive powers to hook the boy into his latest caper. Chauncey's uncharacteristic reticence had puzzled Rooter as he herded the uncooperative boy out of the castle. It wasn't until this very moment that the answer came. The Chauncey sitting beside him now was far lankier than the one Rooter remembered. How long had it been since their last encounter? Too long, it seemed, for Rooter's pet had developed an annoying habit of thinking for himself.

"So you want me to get the sword marked 'Vic' out of that burrow and bring it here," Chauncey whispered, startling his master out of his musings.

"Huh? Oh, yes," the gnome harrumphed. "We've been over this a dozen times, lad. The sword is kept hanging on the wall opposite the staircase. With those long arms of yours, you should be able to reach right in and pluck it off its hooks."

"Why can't *you* get it, Mr. Rooter? You know exactly where it is."

Rooter rolled his eyes. "Because Ragna's got a state-of-the-art gnome security system. If I try to put a toe in there without permission, I'll get blasted with hexes."

"But it's safe for me?"

"Yes. You're not a gnome, so the hexes won't stick to you. Oop! She's doused the lights."

The duo sat in the gathering gloom listening to the rise and fall of the chittersong. Rooter wiped his sweating forehead with the sleeve of his brown tunic. *Almost there,* he told himself.

"Stealing's wrong, Mr. Rooter."

"By Terra's bowels, kid! You're having a crisis of conscience now? It's not stealing if you intend to bring the item back. Besides, it's a *human* sword trapped in a gnome's burrow. It doesn't belong there."

"So I'm really just borrowing it for you?"

"Not for me, Chauncey. For yourself," the gnome corrected. "You need it for your duel, remember? You can't swing a normal sword, but Vic is special. It's light as a feather. Probably because it's charmed."

"And once Vic has won my duel for me, we'll bring it right back."

"*Yes.* Now, are you ready?"

The human boy hesitated.

"Couldn't we just ask the owner to *lend* us Vic?"

"*Ga-a-a-ah!*"

Rooter's frustrated explosion drove Chauncey out of the bushes. Not yet recovered from his exhausting trek from the castle, the boy's gait was even more ungainly than usual, making a stealthy approach impossible. Nevertheless, he managed to haul his various body parts to the hatch and crook a single finger through its iron ring handle.

Chauncey's first pull on the little door didn't budge it; his second barely produced a gap. Jamming his toes into the crack, he used his free hand to rub at his aching shoulder muscles.

"Get *on* with it!" the gnome hissed from the shrubbery.

Chauncey ignored Rooter's impatient squeaking. Concentrating hard, he willed the soreness in his muscles to give way to a tingling tension. Then he exhaled slowly and unleashed a coordinated burst of strength. The flap-hatch door swung up and over on its hinges, landing with a thud on the grassy earth beyond. He looked skeptically at the hole the door had revealed.

"I can't fit down *there*," he whispered to Rooter.

"You don't have to," came the reply. "Just reach in and pull the sword out."

Chauncey knelt with difficulty. Mindful of security hexes, he tentatively poked a hand into the unlit aperture.

"You'll never find it like *that*," Rooter scoffed. "Go in up to your shoulder and reach over to the right."

Chauncey twisted his lip in a combination of irritation and foreboding. Easing himself to his stomach, he scooted forward far enough to insert his entire right arm into the hole. Sweeping it back and forth, he felt a wall to the left and stairs below, but only open space to the right.

"It's not there," he reported.

"Yes, it is. Ragna hangs it up every night. You have to go deeper!"

Groaning, the boy shifted his position to admit his other arm and head into the aperture. This maneuver did nothing to improve things visually—it was pitch black inside—but it did augment the experience with a sour, rooty smell carried on dank air. On the plus side, wedging his upper body into the hole did make it impossible to hear the gnome's petulant yammering.

Casting about in the dark space, Chauncey found himself stretching further and further in search of the sword. Just as he was talking himself into giving up, his hand struck something cold and hard. His fingers were puzzling out the shape of a sword's hilt when a pair of high-pitched screams pierced his ears.

Phosphorescent fungus light filled the cramped space with an eerie greenish illumination. It revealed two tiny figures clutching one another at the base of the stairs as they wailed hysterically. Chauncey recoiled and struggled to back out of the hole, but it was no use. He was stuck.

The light took on an orange hue. A slightly larger figure holding a small lantern charged into the scene.

"Ridna, Redna, get behind me!"

Chauncey now got a proper view of the defender of the household. It was a gnomette, not quite out of her teens. What had Rooter called her? *Ragna*, he remembered. The creature's brown nightclothes certainly seemed to fit her name, being raggedy to Chauncey's noble eye, but her attire was the least of his concerns at the moment. She was advancing up the stairs with a wickedly sharp paring knife extended before her.

"Wait! Wait!" Chauncey cried, throwing his hands between the weapon and his face. "This was a bad idea. I admit it. I'm really sorry."

"Oh, you'll be sorry soon enough, thief," the gnomette growled.

"Me? A thief? Oh, no," the boy wheedled. "Well, not technically, anyway. Everything's still here. See?"

"Intruder, then," the wild-haired minikin revised. "Doesn't matter. Either way, you're dead." She climbed another step.

"Hold on! You seem like a reasonable person. Can't we talk about this?" Chauncey flashed her a weak smile.

Ragna paused to regard him. "Nope," she stated flatly, and she thrust her knife straight at his nose.

Chauncey's thin left forearm bore the brunt of the attack as he flicked his elbow to knock the charging gnomette off the open staircase. While she worked to right herself, he grasped the hilt of the sword named Vic. Summoning all the strength he could, the boy jerked the blade up off its wall pegs. He'd forgotten Mr. Rooter's warning that it would be light. The excessive upward force embedded the tip of the sword in the dirt ceiling.

Loosened soil sprinkled the gnomette. She was back on her feet, screeching and waving her hands.

"Stop, human! You can't wield that sword! It's forbid—"

But Chauncey's adrenaline was pumping. A yank freed the sword from the ceiling, again with more force than necessary. The blade came down out of control, right onto the gnomette's—

Knife. Ragna had curled up, throwing her own weapon over her head in a defensive posture. Vic's edge collided with its smaller counterpart.

Curiously, Chauncey then lost track of . . . everything. He must have closed his eyes, for he could see nothing at that moment. A distinct impression of tumbling forward overwhelmed him—an impossible movement, of course, considering the tight spot he'd gotten himself into. The caterwauling chorus—which had grown to half a dozen gnomeling voices —was cut off. For a terrifying moment, he was blind, deaf, and disconnected from his body and surroundings.

Then his senses were back . . . but *wrong*.

The panicked screaming recommenced, but Chauncey no longer felt the confining stricture of the flap-hatch opening. His arms were over his head instead of in front of it, and an oppressive weight was pressing down on him. But it was when he opened his eyes that things got *really* peculiar.

He wasn't stuck in the hole anymore. Except that he was.

The weight from overhead faltered a bit, and Chauncey seized the opportunity to pivot out from under it. A strong, elegant spin, performed by his body with power and practiced ease.

But it wasn't his body.

It was the gnomette's.

A rush of realization battered Chauncey's brain. At the same time, a strangled squeak from the top of the stairs made him turn. Chauncey gasped as he found himself staring up at his own, enormous, horrified face.

His scream joined those of the gnomelings around him.

———

"IDIOT HUMAN!" Ragna groused for the hundredth time as she placed one gigantic human foot in front of the other. "I told you not to use the sword!"

The boy called Chauncey looked up at Ragna with the face she saw in the looking-glass each morning. "Well, you didn't leave me much choice, did you? I was trying to negotiate, but you were too keen on lopping off my nose."

"Actually, I was aiming for your eyes."

"Well, it's a good thing you failed. Otherwise, you wouldn't be seeing much right now, would you?"

"What is *wrong* with this body of yours, boy?" Ragna ranted. "Not only am I getting a nosebleed way up here, but I can hardly make it move. These muscles are about as useful as—"

"A sword that can't be used in combat?" Chauncey scoffed. "How stupid is that?"

"Don't you call my father's masterwork 'stupid!' We Riggles don't believe in violence, so he had a spell cast over it."

"If your father wasn't violent, why would he forge a sword? Why not a chalice . . . or maybe a nice chamber pot?"

"Hear, hear!" a third voice cheered.

"You stay out of this, Rooter Regal," Ragna hissed. "If you weren't so obsessed with acquiring Vic, we wouldn't be in this mess! I swear if I had the strength to lift these pathetic excuses for legs high enough, I'd stomp both of you flat."

"Ah, but then you'd never get back into your own body," Rooter pointed out gaily. "It's rather poetic, yes? Enchant a sword so that, if it's used, it puts each combatant into the other's body. That promotes pacifism, doesn't it? If you keep fighting, you risk killing your own body. Then where are you?"

"Can it, Rooter." Ragna shifted her gaze to the other gnomish body before her. "You. Human. Give me that sword."

"My name is Chauncey du Shayne," he said over his shoulder, "and I'm the king's nephew, Miss Riggle. You'd do better to show me a little respect. And there's no point crossing weapons again. We tried that already. It didn't switch us back."

Ragna took several huge steps to get in front of her glib traveling companions. "Look, human, you'd better not be getting any ideas. I want my body back, and the sooner, the better. It was awful sleeping on the ground outside my burrow last night. No human-sized beds for miles around!"

Chauncey stared up at the towering gnomette. "You think *I* want to stay like this? How would I explain it to my parents? Not to mention it stinks having legs this short. How do you gnomes ever get anywhere? Ugh, and the worst thing is . . ." He paused to let a shudder of revulsion pass. ". . . I'm a *girl*."

"You know," Rooter interjected, "there's a certain irony in that, too—"

"Shut up, Rooter Regal!" Ragna and Chauncey cried in unison.

For a time, the only sound the trio made was the swishing of dried leaves stirred by their feet. The agitated thoughts swirling in Ragna's mind eventually forced her to break the relative silence.

"I sure hope this fairy character you're taking us to see knows how to fix this, Rooter."

"Tsk, tsk," the gnome replied. "I can tell by the inflection in your voice that you're misunderstanding my colleague's nature. He's not an F-A-I-R-Y with wings. He's an *F-E-R-R-I-E*."

"What are you babbling about?"

"Chauncey, my lad, have you made a study of Latin since last we met?"

"Yes, sir. All royals do."

"Then perhaps you can enlighten Miss Riggle."

Chauncey cleared his throat. "I think what Mr. Rooter means is his friend is an expert in metal-urging."

"Metallurgy?" Ragna asked.

"No. Metal-*urging*. In Latin, *ferrum* means iron. So, this kind of *Ferrie* can coax the secrets out of metals like iron or steel. Being a Ferrie is a skill, not a species."

"Coax the secrets out how?"

"By getting the metal to speak, I think. Isn't that right, Mr. Rooter?"

"You'll see soon enough. We've arrived."

A few more paces brought the threesome out of the forest to the edge of a sunlit ravine. Rooter gave a melodic whistle that carried over the gurgling of the river coursing far below. The sound of beating wings followed. Ragna in her human-boy body cried out and lost her footing as an enormous shape rose out of the ravine.

"A dragon!" Chauncey exclaimed.

"Sorry. Not enough legs for that," the beast said genially as it landed on the only two it possessed. The colossal serpent stood on them like a man, folding its resplendent, purple wings behind its back.

"A wyvern," Chauncey said, correcting himself. "They're even rarer! I never thought I'd see one."

"Well, now you have," the wyvern said with a wink. The magnificent monster turned its reptilian eyes on the trader-gnome. "It's been a long time, hasn't it, Rooter? What have you brought to tempt me this time?"

"No trinkets today, I'm afraid," Rooter apologized. "Just a humble request, Herald.ewralHer"

Ragna suddenly found her voice. "Harold? What kind of a name is that for a wyvern?"

Rooter sighed. "H-*E*-R-*A*-L-D, Ragna. Honestly! Did you get stung by a misspelling bee?"

Herald added, "We wyverns symbolize heraldry, human."

"I'm not a human," Ragna snapped. "I'm a gnomette."

"Oh?" The two-legged dragon scrutinized Ragna in her human shell. "Ah, I see. The old *corpus inverso* trick. Not an easy one to pull off between species. I imagine you folks want to know how to undo this."

"Yes," Rooter confirmed. "It happened during a fight involving this sword."

The wyvern took the weapon from Chauncey, commenting, "That must make *you* the human. Figures. Your kind is always taken with mine."

"Yes, sir."

"Now, let us see," Herald announced, clutching Vic in his talon and examining it closely. "'Vic.' Surely there's more to its name. You wouldn't happen to know it, perchance?"

Ragna spoke up. "No. My father made it, and we've only ever called it Vic."

"It's difficult to urge a sword without knowing its full name, but I shall do my best."

The wyvern drove the blade into the rocky soil and regarded it silently for some time. Then he began to whisper in a language Ragna had never heard before. Minutes passed, and nothing seemed to happen. Then the sword picked up a sudden sheen that was not due to the sunlight.

"So that's it," the wyvern breathed. He lifted his head to address the trio. "I tried every name I could think of that begins with Vic, but I never thought this one would work."

"What is it?" Ragna prompted.

"*Vicarius*," Herald replied. "An ancient name of power. Small wonder it could switch your spirits so readily. I daresay the magic harnessed in this sword could do much more."

"Well, we just want things back the way they were," Ragna said bluntly.

"That presents a challenge," the wyvern responded. "Allow me to channel the sword's voice so you may hear."

The great beast closed its eyes, and ringing metallic words issued from its lips.

I, Vicarius, champion peace.
    My charge: bloodshed cease!
    He who wields me in haste
    Shall find himself displaced,
    Though no corporeal pair
    My curse, twice, shall bear.
    A conundrum to undo
    From a foe's point of view.

RAGNA FROWNED as she worked out the cryptic verse's meaning. "*No corporeal pair . . . twice shall bear. . . .* Hack-erpedes! Chauncey and I really *can't* use Vic to switch back."

"So it would seem," Rooter agreed.

"But I don't want to spend the rest of my life in a crippled human boy's body! I've got eight brothers and sisters to take care of. I can't do it like this! There has to be a way to fix this."

"Most fascinating," Herald cooed, ignoring the others. "The magic imbuing this sword borders on the preternatural. Typically, I'm immune to such enchantments, but I wonder . . ."

Without warning, the wyvern swung the sword at Chauncey. In Ragna's lithe gnome body, he managed an impressive evasive maneuver, but the serpent was too quick. The flat of the sword struck Chauncey in the back.

And suddenly, it wasn't Chauncey in Ragna's body anymore. Ragna, still trapped in human form, could tell by the new glint of the eyes. That, plus her gnomish body was ogling its hands in abject amazement. The wyvern's body, for its part, was fanning its wings and stumbling about in a frenzy.

"So *this* is what it's like to be humanoid," Ragna's mouth said as she stared on in horror. "I must say I'm slightly disappointed."

"Are you *mad?*" Ragna shouted down at her gnome body, now occupied by the wyvern's spirit. "We can't switch you back!" She turned to the purple serpent body. "Chauncey? Are you in there?"

A gout of flame spewed from the wyvern's maw, singeing Rooter Regal's curly black beard. As the gnome yelped and frantically patted out the flames, the monster spoke.

"Oh. Sorry, Mr. Rooter. Yes, Ragna, I'm in here. By the Elements, I thought *your* body was strong, but this one positively vibrates with power."

"Egad!" Rooter cried through smoking facial hair. "We're going to need nametags if this keeps up!"

"Oh, it's funny, is it?" Ragna growled. "It was your greed

that got us into this mess! Where's that sword? We'll see if you're still laughing when I get through with you."

"Temper, temper, Ragna," Herald broke in. "If you want this body back, I suggest you channel your aggression into the conundrum at hand."

"Conundrum?" Ragna asked. "You mean like a riddle?"

"More like a logic puzzle," Herald replied.

"But Vic said we can't use its magic to switch us back," Chauncey put in.

"Is that what it said?" asked Herald with a smirk.

"No," Ragna said, realization dawning. "It said a corporeal pair—the same two physical bodies—can't use it twice."

"So, we can't switch back," Chauncey insisted.

"Wait! Look what's happened," Ragna went on. "You were in my body, and now you're in Herald's."

"So?"

"Herald's body and mine have been switched. So have mine and yours. *But yours and Herald's haven't yet.* I'm in your body, so if you strike me with Vic . . ."

"You'll be in here, and I'll have *my* body back!" Chauncey cried with an errant puff of dragon smoke. "Then you and Herald can use the sword, and everybody'll be back to normal!"

"A neat solution but for one fatal flaw," the wyvern interjected. "In that scenario, Ragna, now in my body, and I, still in hers, couldn't make the switch."

"Why not?" Chauncey asked.

"Because my body and Ragna's were involved in the switch that landed you in my body and me in hers. That pairing is used up, according to Vic's rules."

"Oh," Chauncey sighed. "Couldn't we do the first switch anyway? This wyvern body is awfully hard to control. No offense, Herald."

"None taken. But I advise we strategize before we act. We can't go flipflopping bodies higgledy-piggledy. Without a solid plan as to how to return everyone to his or her proper place, we could blunder our way into a predicament we cannot remedy."

"You're right," Ragna said as she sat on a rock. "But let's hurry, okay? I've never been away from Ridna and Redna and all the rest of my siblings for so long."

Rooter stepped up to Ragna and placed his small hand on her human knee. "They'll be fine," he reassured her. "I left my steed with them, remember? Snorkacks are excellent watch-beasts."

"May I propose we move this thinking party into my lair?" Herald offered.

Ragna gave the gnome-wrapped carnivore a shrewd look. "You know, normally, when a dragon invites someone into its lair, he'd be a fool to accept."

"Indeed," the wyvern replied, "but I *am* rather innocuous in this form."

"Innocuous?" Ragna huffed. "I'll have you know I fought off a pack of wereweasels in that form!"

"And I thank you for that comforting bit of knowledge, but as I am new to the whole arms-and-hands thing, I'd feel more at ease in my den."

Rooter peered into the ravine. "I assume your lair's down there. How do we reach it?"

"The craggy cliff walls should provide ample footholds for our gnomish feet. Even Ragna's larger human ones should have little trouble finding purchase."

"What about me?" Chauncey asked, his wings flexing uncertainly.

Herald looked up at him and blinked. "Naturally, I assumed you would fly down."

"Me? Fly?" Chauncey squeaked in as much as a wyvern could. "Nothing natural about that!"

"Oh, there's nothing to it," Herald said. "You don't even have to fly, truly. From here, it's more of a glide."

"No way," Chauncey said, his spiked purple tail thrashing nervously. "I'm staying up here where it's safe."

For a creature unused to having hands, Herald placed them on Ragna's hips quite effectively. "Don't be such a coward, boy! You're a wyvern, king of the air currents!"

"Forget it."

Herald sighed. "Very well. I'll ride down on your back and give you guidance, okay?"

Three minutes later, Herald was regretting the offer.

"Left! Bank to the left, boy! You're heading straight for that cliff! Oh, my claws and scales! That's too much. Even it out, or you'll flip us!"

"AAAAAAAAAAAAAA!!!"

"Stop panicking, Chauncey. Find the thermals rising from the river. Use them. Spread your wings out, boy. No, no! Pulling them in like that will make you plummet like

a . . . EEEYAAAA!"

Schwizz! Chauncey's right wing skimmed the river's surface, but a frantic volley of wingbeats somehow kept the hapless duo from splashing down.

"The cave!" Herald cried. "Aim for the cave!"

Chauncey spotted his target. In a desperate maneuver, he built up speed, tucked his wings and talons in tight—

And belly-flopped through the aperture onto the rocky floor, tossing Herald head-over-heels across the cavern into a tangle of tattered cloth and pelts.

"Chauncey! Herald!" Ragna called as she scrabbled down the rock wall using Vic for support. She surveyed the scene. "Where's my body?"

Herald poked his head up out of his nest, pain etched on his face. "Here. And I'm fine, thanks for asking. Lucky thing we wyverns don't fancy gold and gemstones for our bedding." He paused to reflect. "You know, I never *did* understand that."

Secure that her body was safe, Ragna scanned the dimly lit chamber. Stepping over to a horizontal fissure in the rock, she pulled a distinctly out-of-place object from the shadows. A delicate melody reverberated off the stone walls.

"Music boxes?" she asked in disbelief. "You hoard music boxes instead of jewels?"

Herald put his nose in the air. "*Collect*," he said priggishly. "I *collect* music boxes. It's a much nicer word than 'hoard,' don't you think? And now you can put that one back. Just so. There's a good girl."

"I'm his supplier," Rooter Regal added proudly as he sauntered through the entrance. "Chauncey's gotten me a dozen from the castle, and every one of them has ended up here."

"Riveting," Ragna said sarcastically. "If we ever want to tour the collection, we know who to call. In other news, I've worked out how to fix this mess."

Herald clambered out of his bed. "By all means, Ragna, share your solution with us."

"Simple, really. Four switches, and it's done."

"Which are . . . ?"

"One," she began, ticking off the step with a human finger, "I switch with Chauncey. That gets him back into his body straight away."

"I like this plan already," the boy-turned-wyvern said.

"Two," Ragna continued, adding another finger, "Herald switches bodies with Rooter."

"Felonious fungi!" the trader-gnome exclaimed. "You

want *me* to set up camp in *your* body, Ragna? Ha! I'll be staying put in my own skin, thank you very much."

Ragna snarled at the recalcitrant gnome. "Listen, toad-stool, *you* started this. You can do your part to end it."

"Keep your problem to yourselves, that's what I say."

"We can't set things right without a fourth person!"

"Pity, because there is no way in Terra's green pastures—"

Chauncey emitted a roar accompanied by a cloud of black smoke that set Rooter Regal coughing. As the trader-gnome hacked the soot from his lungs, he glared in outrage at his pet human.

"Let her finish," the boy ordered.

"Thank you, Chauncey," Ragna said. "Step three is Herald switching with me. That will put him back into *his* body. At that point, I'll be in Rooter's body, and he in mine, so one more switch, and we're there."

"Except I won't allow it," Rooter managed to rasp.

Ragna lifted Vic menacingly. "In about three seconds, you won't have any choice in the—"

"Halt!" Herald shouted.

Ragna looked sharply at the dragon-in-gnome's-clothing.

"We agreed that we wouldn't do *any* switching until the logic puzzle is solved—"

"And it isn't!" cried Rooter Regal. He rounded on Ragna. "That last switch involves your body and mine, and they were already swapped in the second step of your plan!"

Ragna's brow furrowed in confusion. "Wait. What?" She reviewed the steps in her head. Then she turned to the wyvern trapped in her body. "Is that right, Herald?"

"I'm afraid it is," he confirmed. "When I switch with Rooter, I'm in here." He indicated Ragna's body by sweeping both hands grandly down it. Catching Chauncey's eye, he

whispered, "Always wanted to do that. But you need hands."
He repeated the gesture.

"Argh! There *has* to be a way to do this," Ragna
proclaimed with gritted teeth, "and by the High Gnome's
Giblets, *nobody's* going anywhere till we figure out how!"

WHAT ENSUED WAS A HIGHLY unsatisfactory evening, to
Ragna's way of thinking. She spent hours shuttling bodies
and spirits about in a mental shell game. Every time she felt
the glimmer of victory, Herald snuffed it with a gentle slap of
logic. Otherwise, the wyvern was curiously devoid of inspira-
tion. And since Chauncey had all he could handle reining in
his wyvern body and Rooter Regal had divorced himself of
the whole affair, the disgruntled gnomette was left to do all
the cerebral calisthenics. By the time the moon Lunira joined
its sister stars in their celestial dance, the weariness in
Ragna's feeble human musculature had seeped into her mind
and stolen her off to sleep.

Dawn's light jerked Ragna awake. "By Terra, I've got it!"
she crowed at the body stirring beside her. The wyvern's
intelligence animated the body's gnomish eyes which, under
normal circumstances, Ragna could never see without the aid
of a looking-glass.

"I thought we might need five or even six people, but it
really *can* be done with just us four!" she explained. "First, I
switch with Rooter. Then I switch with you. That puts me
back into my body and you in Rooter's. At this point, Rooter's spirit will be in Chauncey's body, and the sword hasn't
made the human-wyvern switch yet. Do that, and Chauncey's
back in *his* body. That leaves us with Rooter in your body and
you still in his, and for the life of me, I can't recall Vic ever

making *that* swap. So, one more switcheroo, and *presto*! Everyone goes home happy."

Ragna's triumphant expression melted as the wyvern stared at her blankly.

"What? Oh, go on. Tell me I'm wrong," she challenged.

"No, no. Your logic is sound," Herald confirmed.

Ragna regarded him suspiciously.

"You've known about this all along," she accused.

An impish smile overtook the wyvern's gnomish face. "Took me all of ten seconds to puzzle it out," he admitted. "Took you, what? Eleven hours? That's fast, for a hominid. Jolly good show."

"You wily little wyrm!" Ragna exclaimed. "You've been holding out on us!"

"But doesn't it feel good to have worked it out for yourself?"

"Wily *and* condescending! Let's get this over with." Ragna scanned the cavern.

"Rooter? . . . Rooter, where are you?"

"Appears as if he's gone," Herald reported.

"Gone? That dastardly snake!" Ragna inhaled slowly to quell her anger. "Doesn't matter. It doesn't have to be him. We just have to find a trustworthy fourth person and get this done."

"I'm afraid you *will* need a bit more than that," the wyvern contradicted.

"Argh! *More* complications? What else do we need?"

"The sword. I think you'll find Rooter took it with him."

"WHY DID I let you talk me into this?" cried Ragna Riggle, as wyvern wings beat around her. "Chauncey can't fly!"

"Actually, he's doing well for a second-timer," Herald observed. "*Too* well, I fear."

Chauncey ignored them both, concentrating on directing the great wyvern body's flight. As they soared over the winding course of the River Gush, the boy enjoyed a power-rush. Never had he felt such confidence in the abilities of his own body. It made him giddy to think he was so big and powerful that he could transport his old body as if it were a scrap of parchment. Human beings were so *tiny* in the grand scheme of things.

Upon Herald's assessment, Ragna released her death-grip on the sinuous neck before her and sat up. A very rumpled Herald emerged from beneath her hunched torso.

"Holy homunculi," she commented to her riding companion. "He really *does* seem in control. He practically killed both of you with that crash landing yesterday."

"My coaching skills are legendary," Herald quipped, but Ragna sensed consternation in his voice.

"Just curious, Chauncey, ol' boy," he inquired in full voice, "but where are we going, precisely? I'd barely urged the word 'downstream' out of Mr. Regal's compass, and *whoosh!* You whisked us away."

They felt a discontented thrumming emanate from Chauncey's cavernous chest. "Lucky thing you used Rooter's pack for a pillow, Ragna. That dungheap probably didn't even realize he was leaving his metal compass in the hands of a *Ferrie* as he made off with Vic.

"To answer your question, we're heading toward my uncle's castle. I'm betting that *traitor*-gnome has contacts there."

"Sorry. Curious again," Herald said. "How are you planning to get in? Castle guards don't generally take kindly to barnstorming dragons, even if they happen to be the king's kin."

"I figured we'd catch Rooter before he reached the castle —that's it, up ahead. I've been trying to spot him, but it looks like—What's that? Hang on, everybody. I'm doubling back."

Ragna reaffixed herself to Chauncey's scaly neck as he banked hard to circle a clearing just outside the castle grounds. His hyper-acute dragon eyes had picked up a flash of light from a rock formation at the edge of the meadow. A second pass revealed a small, bearded figure.

"*R-r-r-rooter*," Chauncey growled.

"Now, now. Don't do anything rash," Herald advised as the wing muscles beneath him tensed alarmingly.

Only Chauncey's deep regard for the wyvern held him back. "This might be our only chance to get Vic back, sir," he said.

"We must assess the situation before we act."

A rush of impatience weakened Chauncey's self-restraint. "Ragna? Your thoughts?"

The gnomette inside Chauncey's human body didn't hesitate. "I vote for 'rash.' *Hee-yah!*"

Ragna's double heel prod spurred Chauncey into a dive. They closed in on the oblivious gnome.

Thurrrrr-ip! Thurrrrr-ip! A pair of stout crossbow bolts pierced Chauncey's left wing. Searing pain disrupted the dive-and-snatch operation as the injured wing retracted. Chauncey tried to correct his course, but he slammed belly-first into the treeline, snapping row upon row of centuries-old canfa trees. Their massive trunks toppled upon the crumpled form of the dragon.

"Ha, ha!" came a jubilant cry.

"Brought the beast down, we did!"

"All hail the Princes Three! All hail!"

"Something told me crossbow practice was the thing today! Thank the Elements we each had a bolt left. But only two found their mark, so only *two* princes should be hailed. Emmett and me."

"'Ere now," Prince Geoffrey protested. "My bolt flew true! 'Twas one of you louts what missed!"

"You dare besmirch the marksmanship of the crown prince?" Prince Fabian challenged. "Or that of the next in line to the throne?"

"Birthin' order ain't got nothing to do with archery," the youngest prince fired back. "Everyone in the kingdom knows *that* talent skipped over my brothers."

"Why, you impudent—"

A whistle silenced the bickering princes. All three turned to glare at Rooter Regal standing on a rock a short distance away. The extra height the rock afforded him made it possible to jab the point of the sword called Vic into the earth beside him.

"I *do* apologize for interrupting, but that's a real, live wyvern over there. Emphasis on the word *live*. It would be advisable to vacate the area immediately."

"Who are you to give us orders, minikin?" Fabian seethed. "We are princes of the Order—"

He forfeited the remainder of the sentence as his elder brother elbowed him aside.

"We'll not be going anywhere until our transaction's complete," Emmett said dangerously. "I know you, gnome. You tease; you renege. Today you brought me here with the promise of a wondrous feather-light sword. That's *exactly* what I am leaving with."

The prince moved to snatch Vic from Rooter's tiny hands, but the trader-gnome jerked the prize away.

"Sire, I would gladly relinquish this magnificent blade to you, but there *is* the little matter of payment. . . ."

"You shall be paid when I have inspected the goods, mudkin."

Emmett grabbed again for the sword, but Rooter foiled him by leaping to a higher rock.

"Apologies, Highness, but my business is cash-up-front. I assume you have the gold on your person?"

"You assume . . . *wrong!*"

The prince feigned a third grab to distract from the left hook Rooter never saw coming. The fifteen-year-old human's fist connected with Rooter's like-sized head, launching the gnome into the air. He landed with a thud on a rotting log, fifteen feet away.

"Deals made with vermin like you are meaningless," Emmett spat as he picked up Vic and tested its heft with a few practice slashes. "You may consider your payment the pitiful excuse of a life I leave you. Now, begone, lest I rethink my generos—"

A cry cut the prince's rant short. Ragna, in Chauncey du Shayne's beleaguered human body, made a charge from the wreckage caused the wyvern's crash landing. She managed four lunging steps before her spindly legs gave out. The royal threesome guffawed at her collapse, and before Ragna could rally her feeble limbs, Fabian and Geoffrey were upon her.

"What are *you* doing out here, Twig?" Emmett sneered at his wobbly assailant. "I thought you were too delicate to venture out of the castle. Here I was, planning to exert myself by lugging my brand-new sword all the way back there just to teach you a lesson. You've spared me that trouble! I *was* going to carve all four letters of your nickname into your hide in recompense for this gash you inflicted on me, but now I am thinking just the first two will suffice." He raised the sword, an evil glint in his eye. "See how fair-minded your future king can be?"

"You *really* do not want to do that, sonny," a new voice warned.

Emmett's muscular arm froze with Vic aloft as he turned to glare at his newest foe.

"A *girl* mudkin? Are you kidding me?"

"Were I actually a female or a gnome, I might be insult- ed," Herald articulated using Ragna's mouth, "but in light of the fact that you are woefully ill-informed of the present situ- ation, I shall overlook your vulgarity and ignorance."

"Whu--uh?" Emmett stammered as he struggled to process the wyvern's meaning. "Ignorance? I'm not the stupid one here! Stand down, or you'll be the first to taste my blade! I have a duel to resolve with this stick-boy, here."

Herald scoffed. "The term 'duel' rarely applies when it's three-on-one and the one is unarmed. Besides, you've got the wrong 'one' entirely."

The crown prince drew an irritated breath in through his nostrils. "Clarify the gibberish you're spewing, or I shall sever your tongue!"

"Lovely," Herald commented. "I simply mean to say that the stick-boy your henchmen are restraining isn't really Chauncey at all."

Prince Emmett stared. "Then just who is it?"

"Ragna Riggle," said Ragna through Chauncey's lips. "Under normal circumstances, I look like *that*." She nodded her head in Herald's direction. "Chauncey is currently residing in a slightly more formidable form."

She flicked her head toward the wyvern's body, stirring weakly now, but still pinned to the ground by a pile of tree trunks. Herald, still in Ragna's body, made a histrionic show of shushing her as the three princes looked on. *That's over-*

the-top, even for Herald, she thought. *What's that wily wyvern cooking up?*

"Either you two are smoking luna-weed, or something peculiar is going on here," Emmett said slowly.

Suddenly, he had Ragna by the throat. Leaning in close, he hissed, "Tell me what I'm missing here, or you'll never tell anyone anything again."

"No! Don't tell him *any*thing, dear Ragna!" Herald cried.

The melodrama in his voice led Ragna to believe she should do the exact opposite. "Using the sword . . . switches . . . people," she croaked.

Emmett's eyes filled with malevolent wonder.

"You're saying that if I strike someone with this sword, we'll switch bodies?" he asked, squeezing Ragna's throat harder. When she nodded, he continued, "That's ridiculous. And yet . . ."

Releasing Ragna, the prince paced over to the immobilized wyvern. Climbing onto the beast's breast, he stared into its eyes.

"Are you . . . Chauncey du Shayne?"

The prince rose a few inches as his cousin drew breath to answer him.

"Yes, Emmett. It's me. The sword is cursed."

To Chauncey's horror, Emmett raised his weapon anew.

"Then slaying you will either satisfy our duel and make me a hero for ridding the world of a despicable dragon, or . . . it will make *me* into a dragon. I'd be the most fearsome monarch the world has ever known!"

"Emmett, no!" Chauncey pleaded. "Listen to yourself!"

The prince fixed him with a savage look.

"Is that any way to address your future king?"

Chauncey gasped as his cousin cocked his handsome head and grinned.

"This   is   a   win-win   for   me,"   he   said   coldly.
"Good-bye, *Twig*."

The blow brought the tumbling sensation Chauncey had
experienced twice before. Abruptly, he was back in human
form, holding Vic in both hands. Before he himself could
even consider striking a blow against Emmett, Ragna yelled,
"To me, Chauncey!"

Enraptured by their big brother's power play, Fabian and
Geoffrey had released their captive. Ragna, still in
Chauncey's body, snatched the sword from the air and swung
it at Fabian. She purposefully dropped the sword on contact
so it would not be in the hand of her foe when she tumbled
into his body. Scooping up the discarded weapon, she then
turned on the very dismayed Geoffrey. A simple lunge and
strike propelled her into the youngest prince's body. Again
she scooped up Vic, and again she fell on Fabian, now housed
in his skinny cousin's body. She struck, thereby reclaiming
Chauncey's body. Stepping back, she smirked at the royal
brothers, now each staring out of the wrong eyes and into his
own. Shrieking more shrilly than pubescent blunderelk in
heat, they fled into the woods.

"Well played," Herald commented from the sidelines.

"Two down," Ragna reported. "Don't go anywhere. I'll be
wanting that body back presently. But first . . ." She looked
toward the decomposing log. "Rooter, you vile scoundrel!
You're next!"

The dazed gnome couldn't protest after his rude
encounter with Emmett's fist. A firm tap with the sword, and
Ragna found herself in Rooter's concussed brain.

Herald stepped in. *Whack*, and he traded one gnomish
body for another. Ignoring Ragna's cries of glee at having her
rightful body back, he crouched by Chauncey's, which now
contained a disoriented Rooter Regal.

"Come on!" he urged. "Time for you to be a wyvern."

He and Ragna half-dragged the gnome's lanky human frame toward the still-prostrate Emmett. But as they closed in, the dragon-prince let loose a mighty roar and a spray of raging fire. The hobbling threesome circumvented the blast and approached from the only angle the serpentine head could not defend.

His muscles erupting with power, Emmett, the mighty wyvern, finally hauled himself free of his arboreal prison. The seductive puissance of his new form intoxicated his mind. Bridling this overwhelming vitality required every ounce of resolve the boy could muster. He roared at the glory of it all and brought his colossal head to bear on the pathetic little party converging on his great taloned feet. Stoking the dragon fire within him, he drew a gargantuan breath and—

Bink!

The sword's magic jerked the diabolical prince out of his stupendous, vigorous form—

And deposited him into his cousin's scrawny, debilitated body.

Even as Prince Emmett opened Chauncey's mouth to bellow in protest, quick-thinking Herald shot his gnomish hand out to pluck Vic from Emmett's. "Here's looking at you," Herald said, saluting the scandalized prince before striking his rightful body's talon with the sword.

"Ah!" the wyvern sighed as the world became tiny again. "There really is no place like home!"

As Ragna and Rooter (in their own bodies) and Chauncey and Emmett (in each other's) looked on, the colossal beast crinkled his scaly snout.

"Euch!" he cried in revulsion. "Just how many of you little rodents have been scurrying around inside me? I need an exterminator!"

Ragna laughed, forgetting that beside her stood the former dragon-prince. The boy tried to take advantage of the lapse, but his exhausted muscles couldn't lift his feet high enough to crush her. Instead, the effort only served to tip Emmett onto his backside. His cries of fury made the wyvern's roll call a challenge to hear.

"Okay, where is everybody now? All in the appropriate bodies except Chauncey and the one having the tantrum?"

They confirmed it was so.

Ragna asked, "What about Chauncey and Emmett? Can they switch back or not? I've kind of lost track."

Chauncey, Ragna, and Rooter scratched their heads as they tried to sort through the battery of body swaps accomplished in the previous five minutes.

"Oh, let me make this easy," Herald proposed.

HOWMPF! The wyvern consumed Prince Emmett in a single gigantic bite.

"Herald!" Chauncey exclaimed in shock. "That's my body! And my cousin!"

"I've had a hankering to eat one of you bipeds ever since yesterday," the beast admitted. "But I must admit I'm slightly disappointed. You might have provided me a bit more meat and a bit less bone, Chauncey." He let out a titanic, tree-shaking, bird-scattering belch. "Oof! Healthy meat *never* repeats on you like that. I'm no physician, but I think your body's days were numbered."

"But, *Herald*," Chauncey moaned. "The crown prince! How could you?"

The wyvern leaned down to look the boy in the eye.

"*You* are the crown prince now. Better start acting like it."

Chauncey's look of bewilderment marred Emmett's comely visage far more than the tiny wound he'd inflicted upon it just two days before. As the boy flexed his bulging biceps to touch the scab, a smile spread over his face.

"Now," the wyvern continued, "if everyone is quite through with all this flippity-floppity business, I shall take my leave."

"Wait," Ragna said. "You *wanted* the prince to end up in your body, didn't you?"

The wyvern gave her a sideways look.

"It was a test that confirmed the boy's evil nature. I must admit I was concerned for Chauncey, though. He spent too many hours at the mercy of this form's seductive power. He came through like a champion, but it was probably unfair of me to swap bodies with him, even for a short time. For that, I do apologize, my boy."

"It's all right," Chauncey said. "At least you found out what it's like being humanoid."

"Can you fly with that punctured wing?" Ragna inquired.

Herald grinned. "My dear, I've flown with much worse injuries than this." He turned his serpentine gaze on the other gnome. "And *you*, Rooter Regal . . ."

"Yes?' the trader-gnome asked apprehensively.

"Behave yourself, or I shall eat you next."

The wyvern punctuated his threat with a puff of black smoke.

"You can begin," he continued, "by conducting Ragna home and using your . . . *expertise* to see she and her siblings are well cared for."

"Yes, sir."

"Now," Herald continued, "as you all have ruined my planned theatrical exit, I shall have to settle for a less dramatic one." He paused. "By the way, if any of you happen to be passing by a certain dragon's lair someday, feel free to pay a visit. I solemnly promise not to let my appetite get the better of me."

"You bet," said Prince Chauncey with a smile.

"Oh! And one last thing."

"What's that?"

Herald closed a great talon over Vicarius the sword, and with the beating of his splendid purple wings, vaulted himself into the air.

"I'll be taking *this* with me."

Everyone turned to look at Ragna Riggle.

"Good riddance," she laughed.

DR. SCOTT SIMERLEIN

ONE OF SCOTT'S earliest writing escapades was conspiring with his mother, week after week, to use all twenty of his elementary school spelling words in a single grammatically correct mega-sentence. His teachers never recovered.

At Palmer College of Chiropractic, Scott created a comic strip for the college newspaper and compiled those strips into his first book, *Smi, the First Tri Guy and Other Chiropractic Cartoons.* Scott was also known for playing the university mascot, a purple wyvern named Torque.

After graduating valedictorian, he headed up the Word Crafters writers group in LaPorte, Indiana. In 2013, Scott was named LaPorte County Poet Laureate, a distinction he continues to hold.

Scott enjoys ~~hoarding~~ . . . (ahem) . . . *collecting* Snoopy memorabilia. He is co-author of *The Got It! Guide to Peanuts Hallmark Ornaments*.

As a Purdue University Northwest anatomy professor, Scott writes and produces comedic anatomy song videos for his Simersong Siblings YouTube channel:

www.youtube.com/channel/UCFVd6OQ45vuzUqv_z4gyzKw

Now an exciting new chapter begins with *Switch Blade*. Scott is sincerely grateful to Hydra Publications, the Word Crafters, and his mom, Mary Lu.

Author's note: Chauncey, the main character of *Switch Blade,* exhibits symptoms of Duchenne's muscular dystrophy. Hence, his surname, du Shayne.

KING'S ROAD

G. DEAN MANUEL

THE CLASH of steel against steel rang out in the cold winter morning. William stared into the dead eyes of his opponent, a darkling ravager, and could feel not an ounce of warmth. The creature was a thing filled with shadows, bound by ancient, evil sorcery to the will of the Dark Lord. The darkling looked vaguely humanoid in shape, with thick, shaggy hide and beady, red eyes. They were perversions of nature, the combination of man and beast through sorcery. It was even said among his people that these darklings had been around since the Dark Lord had first come to these lands, perverting and enslaving man and beast alike to his campaign. Not even death released them from their servitude.

He parried the clumsy thrust of the darkling to his side and riposted. His grandfather's sword slid through the darkling easily. It crumpled to the ground. William smiled when the other three darklings surrounding him backed away a step. He had become separated from his small company of soldiers in the heat of battle, could hear them trying to get to him, but was unconcerned. He was a true prince of his people and was well acquainted with the art of combat.

The darklings struck from either side. William side-stepped to the right, away from the third, knocking one blade into the other. Again his blade flashed and another darkling fell.

Behind him, his men had rallied against their opponents, and were making their way to their prince's side. The prince briefly considered offering mercy but knew he could not. While some darklings were intelligent, they were completely loyal to the Dark Lord. William grimaced at the thought of the Dark Lord. He had been menacing their small northern kingdom for many generations.

The bigger darkling saw that the prince's guard would be upon them soon, so swung his heavy sword in a last ditch attempt. The prince waited until momentum would not allow the darkling to do anything besides finish the blow then dodged to the side, keeping the bigger darkling between himself and the remaining one. The brutish blade struck the ground hard enough to bury it slightly on the frozen earth.

William buried his sword almost to the hilt into the creature's side. The two rubies, the eyes of the Gryphon, sparkled. The darkling was consumed by the magic of the blade, falling to the earth a pile of ash. The last darkling gave a little yelp and, not wishing to share his companion's fate, ran.

"My prince, are you alright?" asked an out of breath guardsman.

"Perfectly fine, Joffrey." The prince watched the fleeing darkling. "Just a bit of morning exercise. Are out of breath, my friend?"

"A bit, my prince. Rushed over to make sure you were fine. Should we pursue that one?"

"Hmmmm... I need to have a talk to your commander regarding your fitness regimen." William glanced once more at the retreating darkling. "No, let that one go. Let him tell the others of his ilk that my grandfather's sword has been reforged. Let them fear. Let the Dark Lord himself know that the time of his reckoning will soon be at hand."

"Aye, milord." Joffrey looked down at the pile of ashes at their feet and made the sign of the Warden. "The men saw, sir. They saw and it gave them hope."

"They aren't the only ones that have found hope." William looked over to Joffrey. "I could use hope. I mean, darklings this far south upon the King's Road? Things have fallen further than I had feared."

"Aye, my prince, things grow darker and darker every day. The Dark Lord and his minions become ever bolder."

"If I had every doubted my path, this has made it clear. The threat of the Dark Lord must be met." The prince shook himself from his grim thoughts. "That is not now, though. Those are concerns for soon but not today. Let us make haste, I wish to make Magra's inn before nightfall. Tonight, I will have something warmer in my belly than hard tack."

As Joffrey went to relay orders to the men, William stood, looking down the King's Road. It stretched off into the distance and he knew that there would many miles traveled until he reached his destination.

WAVING a bony hand over the viewing pool, the heavily shrouded man grimaced as the image faded from its depths. He shuffled over to a table laden with alchemical equipment, his bones cracking and creaking all the way.

"That little bastard will ruin everything. I've waited too long, endured too much, and planned too well for some whelp to upset things now! If his stupid jackass of a father wasn't so inept, everything would be fine! Now look what he's making me do! Now I have to tell my lord, and he's not going to be happy. Nope, not happy at all. Probably make me clean up this mess," he muttered, his eyes going in and out of focus.

Once at the table, the old man's fingers flew across its contents, all the while still mumbling to himself. Quickly, he gathered fennel, anise, and mugwort. He crushed the herbs within a mortar with practiced ease. He added three drops of distilled marsh water. Bringing the paste to his nose, he inhaled deeply. Thoughtfully, he grabbed some rowan wood and threw it in the mix. Continuing his crushing, he grabbed a lead flask and uncorked it with what remained of his teeth. With a look of intense concentration, he carefully let one drop of dragon's blood fall into the mixture. It gave a satisfying hiss. An insane smile lit the old man's face as he poured the concoction into the alembic, a long-necked glass container used for distillation of magical potions.

A few minutes later, his concoction made its way up the neck of the alembic, dripping slowly into its flask. Reaching into a pouch, he clutched an eagle talon in his left hand and extended his right towards the flask. Arcane words spewed from his mouth, causing sigils to glow on the outside of the flask with a sickly, green light. A slow smile spread as the light unfurled to a pure emerald. The potion was ready.

Grabbing the flask, he took down its contents in one gulp before it could lose any potency. He screamed as the potion coursed through his body, blazing through his veins with emerald fire. He floated perilously close to unconsciousness as the world faded to blackness around him.

"Master?" the man rasped. He felt, more than saw, movement within the darkness that enveloped him. Two red eyes blazed in the darkness, fixing their stare upon the old man. He shuddered.

WILLIAM MADE his way down the hall, the heels of his well-oiled boots beating out a cadence against the stones. He had grown to a man's height, just cresting six feet, and his body showed the rewards of years of hard labor; arms and legs like small tree trunks, heavy with corded muscle. Little scars crisscrossed his body, each a payment for the skill with the blade he wore easily upon his hip. Armor peeked from underneath his silken tunic, the tiny links of the chains speaking of exquisite craftsmanship. A green cloak spread across his back with a coat-of-arms; a gryphon running rampant clutching a sword in its fore claws and a rose in its beak. As the two guards at the end of the hallway snapped to attention at his approach, he flipped an unruly lock of hair from his eyes. His curly red mane fell to just below his shoulders, free from tie or bind.

"Prince William, we were given strict orders that the king was not to be disturbed. His Majesty said he would be… wrestling with important matters of state," one of the guards said, unable to meet his prince's steady gaze.

"Announce me," William said, his green eyes flashing dangerously as the guard looked ready to object. "Announce me," he repeated, enunciating each word carefully.

"Yes, my prince," the guard said, bowing so deeply his forehead almost touched the floor. The guard quickly slipped through the door.

William listened as he was announced and his father began to curse loudly. He heard a woman's voice arguing with the king. It was almost a full minute before the guard returned, still unable to meet William's eyes.

"He will see you now, my prince."

William strode through the door, stopping in the center of the hall, standing before the great throne. His father stretched languidly across the seat of power. The king's robe was undone, showing an expanse of sickly, pale flesh. Years of comfort and ease was evident in the softness of his hands and the rounded curve of his belly. A double chin hung loosely as he languished, turning his head to regard his son. His chubby fingers found their way around a full wine goblet and he tipped it back without care. Red wine ran down his chin, rolling down his chest and cutting a path to his groin. Prince William sketched a quick bow, holding it far less than was respectful, though the king took no notice, waving indolently to his son. With an air of studied boredom, he asked, "And to what do I owe this unexpected pleasure?"

"I came to report on the progress at the northern front. I thought that I would deliver the report to you in person," William stated tersely.

"What, did the battle become too scary for William?" his father mocked, "Or did you bore of the soldier's life, finally? I honestly don't see why you find it so appealing. Too much of your grandfather in you, I suppose."

"Thank you, Father, that was a most gracious compliment," William said, feigning ignorance of the king's acid glare. "No, I have not bored of the soldier's life. I thought it has been too long since we have had a chance to see one another."

"Through no fault of my own," the king sniffed with indignation. "You are the one who is always leaving to be somewhere else. Helping out farmers and what-not." The king made a lazy, dismissive gesture with his hand as he took another large draught from his wine goblet.

"Aye, father, helping farmers and what-not," the prince replied, forcing a smile, the momentary darkening of his eyes going unnoticed by the king, "But I am here, and I would spend a few happy moments with you before we are forced to move on to other matters."

"Is that all you have for this old man, just a few meager moments to spare," he lamented, to William's surprise.

"I wish, with all my heart, there was more time to spare for you and me, but these are dark times. Things have been set into motion that will not be so easily turned aside," William sighed as he plucked at the hilt of his sword.

The king looked to his son, his eyes narrowed in surprise. He watched as William made his way to a seat and dragged it closer to the throne. William sat down stiffly, his shoulders slumped forward as if in defeat. *Does he know???* the king thought worriedly.

William looked up and saw his father's concerned expression. He made a half-hearted attempt at a smile and said, "What was it like when you first became king?"

"That's an odd question. Why do you wish to know?" the king asked, trying to keep his expression neutral. He was almost sure William could hear the thumping of his heart.

"I don't know, I just..." William looked flustered— almost distraught, "I just..." He took a deep, calming breath. "I just want something that connects us." He shrugged. "Something that makes us father and son. It is no secret we are two very different people. I want to know if you felt the same things I am feeling, now that my majority is close."

The king's eyes softened. Looking down upon his son, confused and lost, he found himself wanting, for the first time, to comfort this young man who was so much a stranger to him. Looking kindly to his son, the king resolved the boy should know his father and said, "I was afraid. And excited. I was confused, that much is sure." He chuckled ruefully, his eyes staring off into the dreamy space before him. "I was going to rule this kingdom with a fair and just hand. All would speak my name with adoration and respect. I was going to be everything a great king was. Just like my..." The dreamy look disappeared, replaced by a haunted expression, tinged by fear. Looking to William once more, he was struck by how closely he resembled his grandfather.

William pressed forward in his seat, his body a mass of tensed muscles. "Then what happened, father? How did it come to this?" William paused, his breath bated in anticipation, hoping he had not pushed too far. This was it, what he truly wanted to know.

The king cast his eyes downward. His voice rose, barely above a whisper, each word dripping with regret. "Your mother. When my father died, she lifted me from the morass. I found my life mired in." His eyes became unfocused, staring back down the years to the past. "All the dreams I had of the great king I would be came crashing against the reality of actually being the king. I would wake up in a cold sweat that I had made some terrible mistake that would lead my people to catastrophe.

"I was a wreck, afraid to make the simplest of decisions, lest it led unto disaster." A small smile played across his lips. "She came... she came and believed in me." He looked up, his eyes lit with a fierce love that had long been absent. "She told me that I could do it and I was able to. And then... and then..." He inhaled a strangled breath. "Then you were born and everything seemed perfect. It *was* perfect. The kingdom was well: our borders well protected and our people well fed. Then, when you were barely four winters old, your mother came down with the wasting sickness."

He looked up to the prince once more, his face drawn tight with grief. "Others had come down with it. A full quarter of the kingdom was struck down with it. We had physicians, clerics, even wizards coming and going from the palace for a full year. It was the longest year of my life. They had performed every rite, cast every spell, and used every trick of medicine over my wife's disease-ridden body. And I sat powerless." Tears began to run free. "*Me*! The most powerful man in the kingdom and I had to watch my queen die a slow, torturous, year-long death. Oh, she was brave. More brave than I have ever been. Every time you or I visited her room she had a smile ready and waiting for us."

The king stopped, unable to continue. Tears streaked each man's cheeks as they were both trapped by the mournful reminiscence. Minutes passed as prince and king tried to dam the grief that threatened to wash them away. Looking upon his son, the king realized they had more in common than he once thought. They had her.

"Do you remember her, my son?" His voice cracked as he choked back sobs. "I mean how she was before the sickness took her?"

William shook his head, breathing deeply to calm himself, and said, "Not much. What I do remember has been muddled by time. The only true memory I have of her before the illness is of her singing a lullaby to me because I had woken up in the middle of the night with terrors."

The king nodded, lost in his own memory. After a few moments he said, "She would have been very proud of you, my son." His face darkened for a moment. "And she would have had some not so kind words for me in regards to my character. But you have asked a question that has too long remained unanswered. You see, when your mother died, I was devastated. Lost in grief. But what truly killed the man I once was did not happen until about three months after your mother's death. They found the cure." The king's eyes hardened to twin pieces of granite. "Not three scant months after I had buried my beloved, they found the cure. An extract made from Lorelei's Bells. Those damn things grow everywhere! Hell, there were probably some growing not twenty feet away from her the whole year before she died." His hand slapped the arm of the throne with bruising force. "That is the reason I fell. I couldn't cope. How could life be so cruel and meaningless? So I grew gills and took to the bottle. Alcohol let me forget. But I couldn't have you around; you were too much of a reminder. You would make me remember..." his voice trailed off.

"Remember what? Mother?" William probed.

Father looked to son, smiling sadly and said, "Oh, no. Not of her. You were my reminder of how I failed her." His smile faded, replaced with a guilty expression. "You see, when she was dying, right before the end, she made me promise to be strong for you, William. I promised to raise you to be a great king that was worthy of one day leading this country. But I couldn't do it without her, so I left you in more capable hands and lost myself to darkness. They seem to have done a fine job in my stead."

The king's gaze roamed over William, actually seeing him for the first time. His eyes stopped, fixating upon the sword belted to William's side. "I know that sword," he moaned, looking sharply at his son. "That is my father's sword!" The words were an accusation.

William sighed. "Yes, it is, father," the prince said, avoiding his father's eyes.

"But it was broken so long ago. I thought it was lost after your mother's death." The king's voice was pensive.

"It was taken by Sir Silas, Duke of Attlebury, for safe-keeping. Kept for the day the blade could be reforged," William said, still not meeting his father's eyes.

"And with it you would administer the Test. When I failed to be worthy of the blade and by extension the crown, the Gryphon would strike me down." The king did not need to look at William to know his words were true. He stood, a look of consternation crossing his face, and said, "If that which has been broken has been remade, you have reached your majority. You are sixteen now."

"I turned sixteen yesterday, father," William said in a small voice.

"What a poor fool I have been," the king said, falling back heavily upon his throne. Putting his head in his hands, he said, "And poorer father still. I thought you would not reach your majority for another month." A fierce determination sparked within his eyes. "Call the court. I would do this Test before them so there is no doubt of your worthiness to rule."

"No, father," said William, rushing to the side of the throne, "I only did this because I thought you were some cold-hearted villain. That you were a despot. You are just a man who lost his way in the woods. I can help you find your way back. I can save you!"

The king smiled at his son and said, "My dear William, you already have. These are dark times, my son, the people need you to guide them through it. I am... I am the problem."

"But you do not have to die for me to do it." The prince looked to his father, pleading with his eyes.

"Lad, do not grieve for me. I have made many mistakes in my life; this will not be one of them. Will, the people must see that you are worthy where I was not. No matter what your heart says about me now, remember I have brought this country to the brink of ruin. There are things you don't know." The king laid his hand gently upon his son's head.

"But where am I to find the strength to guide these men through darkness? What if I, too, am not worthy?" William asked, his voice sounding child-like.

Raising William's chin, the king tapped his chest. "Inside of you. Just remember: no matter what, I believe in you. And just because I am gone, does not mean I have stopped. Now go, I would be a king one last time before I die." He headed off to his chambers, calling for his manservant along the way.

William sat at the foot of the throne in silence for a moment. Wiping his tears away, he got to his feet. Once more heel struck stone with a determined step. His father would not die in vain.

THE KING SAT in front of his mirror, his image within telling the tale of his guilt. He examined himself; disgusting rolls of fat ensconcing bones made brittle by years of leisure. He was ashamed. He knew his people starved to provide him the means by which he had affected his transformation into this behemoth of gluttony.

"Olivia, what have I become?" His voice was nothing more than a hoarse whisper. He looked past himself in the mirror to his manservant, Jacob, who stood silent in the corner. "Why do you serve me?"

"Milord?" Jacob replied, clearly confused.

"You must have been so proud, at one time. Bragged to your friends. The king's manservant. But years have proven me no king," Jacob's master said, tears threatening to flow once more. "I have almost brought doom upon us all."

Jacob stood silent, clearly at a loss for what to do. He sighed in relief as the king's eyes shifted once more to his reflection. Clearly his lord was distraught, but Jacob did not know any words that would act as balm. Mostly because the king's words rang with truth.

"I will see you believe in me once more, Olivia." He turned towards his servant, "And I would have you proud to be in my service, Jacob. Call the court; tell them their king requests their presence tomorrow at mid-morning. I will be a true king once more before the morrow meets its end."

All the strange talk merely deepened Jacob's confusion, who simply bowed and said, "As you say, milord."

"Jacob, one more thing before you go. This is for you." The king handed him a package bearing his royal seal. "Do not open it until after the noon bells have tolled."

"Yes, milord," Jacob said, concern written upon his face. He bowed once more and headed off to complete the tasks he had been charged with.

Turning back to the mirror, the king said, "Olivia, my queen, my love, give me the strength to do what I must do. Give me the will to be who I once was, to remember the man I should be. May the path that lies before me lead me to you, once more." Looking at the mirror he watched as a single tear sped down the paths of his face.

PRINCE WILLIAM WALKED into the room, startling its occupants. The two looked up from the maps spread before them. One was tall and lanky, with a hawk nose and angular features. The other was short and stocky, looking like nothing more than a bull standing on two legs.

"Ye a'maist made me soil maself, laddie!" the shorter one said, his thick brogue making the words difficult to understand.

"Is it done, my prince?" asked the taller of the two.

"No, Silas, it is not," William responded.

"'N' how come th' hell nae!?!" the bull man yelled.

"My father wishes to do it tomorrow, in front of the court," the prince said, preparing himself for the coming storm.

"Whit kind o' dunderheided bugger are ye, Willie? Dae

ye think yer da is just gonnae lay down an die? Surprise wis our best bet," Angus said, very nearly foaming at the mouth.

"I will have to concur with my stalwart companion's uncouth, and somewhat disrespectful, assessment of the situation, Prince William," Silas said, putting an emphasis on the prince's name.

"You two weren't there! I believe my father wishes redemption. Would you have me deny him that chance?" William looked from Silas to Angus and back again.

The angry look softened on Angus' face. "Nay, laddie, if 'twas mah da, ah would've given him a chance, too," Angus said, glancing meaningfully at Silas

"I apologize, my prince. You are wise to give the old king a chance to redeem himself in the eyes of God, at the very least," Silas said, pulling a handkerchief from his pocket to cover his mouth as he coughed.

William nodded distractedly. For a moment he said nothing, locked in an inner struggle, then looked to each man in turn and said, "But we would be fools not to be prepared for any trickery on his part. No matter how much I want this to be so, we cannot be caught off guard."

"Glad tae hear ye say it, laddie. Now yer thinking lik' a king," Angus said, clapping William on the back.

The prince looked at each man with red-rimmed eyes and said, "Is that what it means to be king? Never able to trust those around you? Always looking over your shoulder, waiting for the moment the assassin's blade reaches out of the shadows? If that's what it is, I don't think I want to be king…"

"Laddie, life is far from fair. I'll nae tell ye it is. Some o' us hae harder paths tae tread. Bit yer fowk need ye, laddie. A shadow descends fae th' north 'n' if'n ye don't fin' a wey tae dae whit needs daein', then we're doomed," Angus said softly.

Silas coughed and turned aside his head as the prince started sobbing into Angus' shoulder. He had almost forgotten they were dealing with a boy barely past his majority. A boy who would soon bear the weight of a nation upon his shoulders.

After a few minutes his sobbing ceased. William took three calming breaths in quick succession and dried the tears from his eyes. Looking up at Silas and Angus, he said, "Go now, make whatever preparations that need to be made. I will take tonight to mourn my father." He looked from one to the other, a hard edge creeping into his gaze. "For tomorrow he dies by my hand, one way or another."

Prince William spent most of the night trying to find sleep that would not come. He felt as if he was perched on the edge of a great battle that had yet to begin. His stomach was tied in knots, his hands sweated profusely. Realizing sleep would not find him, he tried to remember the good times his father and he had shared. Not finding many, he replayed the day's conversation over and over in his head.

Would his father go through with it? Could one conversation, however meaningful, make a man change? As much as William hoped, the practical side of him said no. A plague of doubts began to eat away at him. Is this the path he should take? Was he worthy of being king? Did he want to be on the right path if it meant his father's death? Like little demons, each question gnawed at William's resolve. He tumbled into darkness that pressed in at all sides. Just as William was about to let himself be taken, give himself over to cool oblivion, a voice broke the dead silence that wrapped around the cacophony of his mind.

"Hush, little William, don't say a word…" The ghostly

voice was followed by a golden face that radiated so brightly the shadows fled. She looked down at William and smiled.

Mother.

This time, as William fell into darkness, it was warm and inviting.

THE COURT WAS abuzz with gossip, made all the more electric by the appearance of the old gentry, many of whom had not shown their faces in court for over a decade. Most of the newer lords—fops and dandies to the man—scoffed at the dress and manners of the old lords. The words 'peasant lords' came up in more than one quietly held conversation. The old nobility, for their part, took no notice of these young upstart lords, deeming them beneath their collective regard.

A line could have been drawn down the center of the great hall, demarcating old from new. At the center of the field of battle, situated between the warring factions, were the youngest of the old gentry. First and second sons who had been sent to court in their fathers' stead. They bridged the gap between old and new. Like their fathers, they wore swords belted at their sides and armor that peeked underneath their tunics but, like the newer lords, their tunics were cut in the latest fashions and were made of silken threads woven through with gold.

When William walked in, he saw his father's amused expression as he watched the verbal jousting of the venerable Lord Cahill and the young and rash Lord Barkus. William's gaze swept the room, amazed at how quickly Silas and Angus had spread the news. Nodding to many of the older lords, many of whom had fostered him at their keeps, he made his way through the crowd.

"My liege, when did we start allowing mongrels within the throne rooms? We should have someone fetch the Master of the Hounds to round up these stray dogs," Lord Barkus said, his dry, raspy voice grating to the ear. His grin was ear to ear as he turned to accept his companions' praise.

"Stray dogs!" Lord Cahill roared, his deep baritone shaking the very rafters. "You would do well to watch that tongue, you sniveling, witless worm! Before someone sees fit to remove it from your mouth!"

"Are you threatening me, barbarian!?!" Lord Barkus rejoined, so shocked at the affront that he almost gasped himself into unconsciousness.

"Threaten?!? Oh, no, not threaten," Lord Cahill said, a huge grin splitting his face. "I don't threaten flies, you land-less twit! I merely promise them cold, crushing death, then give them *cold… crushing… death.*"

Lord Barkus' voice reached a fevered pitch as he whined, "Milord, I demand this man be removed from the hall immedia-"

Lord Barkus' request was drowned out by the laughter of Lord Cahill and several of the other old gentry. "You demand?" Lord Cahill's voice rose above the din. "You demand nothing, you simpering pansy! Go home with your tail between your legs and polish your 'title'! At least, in my day, we had the balls to demand satisfaction from the one who wronged us. My son has a child of barely two winters that has bigger testes than you. I don't know who to feel sorrier for; you or your wife. You have to live with 'em, she has to act like they please her."

Laughter exploded around Lord Cahill. Lord Barkus looked around the great hall in horror as its many occupants pointed and laughed at him. He appeared to be about to break down in tears as he made a beeline to the door.

"Stop, Lord Barkus. Don't leave quite yet. I think that will be quite enough, Lord Cahill," the king said, still wearing a bored expression. He scanned the great hall, his gaze fixing upon William. For a moment, the veil of his expression slid back, revealing the turmoil that raged beneath the surface. The moment passed, and the mask slid back into place and the king once more looked around, amused. "My son, the prince, is here. Tell us, William, what tales of far off places do you bring to us?"

"I come bearing terrible news, father. A shadow moves to the north that endangers our kingdom," William said.

"Is that so?" the king asked, making a clucking noise with his tongue. "That is horrible news indeed. Is there any other business to be brought before the court?"

"Yes, my liege, as you know, the winter solstice revel will be happening soon, and we still have not decided whether it should be a masquerade or not," one of the faceless dandies said from within the crowd of new gentry.

"I had nearly forgotten we had not come to a decision as of yet," the king said. "I do believe we shall declare it as a masquerade."

"A party!?! You speak about a party when our nation stands upon the brink of war? Your Majesty, something must be done!" Lord Cahill exclaimed vehemently.

"Why, Lord Cahill, do you bother our royal personage with such petty trivialities? I employ generals who are very well equipped to handle such small matters. This leaves your king free to handle important matters of state, such as the winter revel," the king said, speaking to Cahill as if he were a child to be scolded.

His words caused an uproar among the old gentry. Each raised their voice, adding to a maddening cacophony, each one a denouncement of the king's dismissal of the war. The hands of the royal guards strayed close to swords as the old lords began to work themselves into a frenzied mob. The king looked around, a bored expression seated upon his brow. Just as it was about to explode into violence, a resounding crash caught everyone's attention.

"There will be order in this hall," Lord Silas said to the now silent room. He stood in front of Lord Angus, who still held the upper half of the chair he had smashed. "You will comport yourselves as rightful lords of this land or you will be removed from this hall!"

"Thank you, Lord Silas. At least one of my retainers remains loyal enough to his liege not to threaten him with violence," the king stated, giving everyone a stern look.

William stepped forward in the silence that followed. "Father," he said, "I have one more piece of news. My birthingday is two days gone, so I am now past my majority."

The hall erupted into the chaos of scraping chairs, raised voices, and shocked gasps. Through it all, the king sat with a slightly perplexed expression once more upon his face. Calmly, he stood and grabbed a wine goblet from the table next to him. Raising it in the air, he proclaimed loud enough to be heard over the din, "Then a toast! To my son, William, may this day mark the transformation of boy into man, of a prince into a king! Know that I have always been, and shall always be, proud to call you my son."

The great hall sat in stunned silence, the disparate groups united in one dumbfounded expression. Then, slowly, the nobility gathered their wits and toasted their prince, some more enthused than others. William ran over his father's words in his head, torn by his duty to a kingdom he had served his whole life and a burgeoning love for a father he never knew existed.

"Are there no words you wish to share with these, *your*

loyal retainers?" the king asked, lazily gesturing to the crowd. William looked up at the emphasis upon the word *your*. Nodding to his father, he took a deep breath and approached the throne.

"Father, my lords, my ladies. Our king has summoned us here today because news of my birthingday..." William's words drifted off, looking over the assembled faces. He was lost for a moment until a look from his father snapped him back to reality. He shook his head, clearing out the cobwebs, and finished, "But I have come for a more serious matter."

William pulled back his cloak, revealing the sword sheathed at his side. The assemblage gasped as they laid eyes upon the beautifully wrought hilt formed in the image of a gryphon ascendant. "This sword is the birthright of my family. Broken during the reign of my grandfather, shattered in the defense of the castle against Morgul invaders. Once more, these same invaders threaten our lands, and this sword must once more be called in defense of our land! What was broken has now been made whole!"

The older gentry cheered as the prince drew the sword into the air. Many of the younger nobles looked on in confusion. The others looked on in wonder having been raised on tales of the sword and its heroic wielders. William pointed the sword at his father, looking down the fuller of the blade and said, "I invoke my right, as heir to the throne, one who has passed his majority, to call for the test of the Gryphon."

The hall erupted into chaos once more. Lord Cahill's voice raised itself above the din of the crowd. "Quiet! Quiet!" he shouted, "This is not a common tavern taproom! This is the hall of kings! And today we bear witness to this kingdom's most sacred of rites!" Every man's voice died in his throat. "That's better. You've asked for the test of the Gryphon, where a king proves to his court his worthiness to lead us. To fail in the test is to die, you understand this, Prince William?"

William carefully controlled his emotions, fighting hard to keep his expression neutral. For a moment, he found himself six winters old once more, wishing nothing more than for his father to hold him. Unlike when he was younger, his father would probably do it now. But there was no time and there never would be again. Looking up from his ruminations, he nodded towards Lord Cahill and said, "I understand."

Everyone appeared to move in a blur of motion as the prince stood rooted to the spot, only seeing his father. Around him, attendants were setting the stage for the Test. As the minutes passed, William searched his father's face looking for some sign of hesitation, some sign his father regretted his decision. The king looked almost oblivious to the events around him but William knew the truth. The prince wished he had met this man long before it came to this.

All too soon, everything was in readiness. Lord Cahill looked towards William and said, "My prince, if you would place the sword within its holder we may begin with the Test."

William looked from the king to where Lord Cahill gestured. The sword's holder was a beautiful statue of a gryphon, made out of silver and platinum with eyes of plum-size rubies. The beak of the statue was open with a recess to fit the sword. William stepped forward and slid the sword home. He stood frozen for a moment, hand still upon the hilt, his resolve beginning to give way. He looked up at his father and his face hardened. He slipped away from the gryphon, his hand moving stonily from the hilt, and took a position behind the statue. As soon as his hand moved away from the hilt, the gryphon's beak slammed shut. William winced.

"Oh, this is so *very* interesting," started the recovered

Lord Barkus. There were titters from the part of the hall containing the new gentry.

"Laddie, if'n ye dinnae find yer upper lip firmly attached tae yer bottom lip, ye'll be fetchin' a healer tae hulp remove mah boot fae yer arse!" Angus growled at the dandy.

Lord Barkus blanched but, before he could respond, Lord Silas said, "The next person that speaks who is not the King, Prince William, or myself, will be forcibly removed from these proceedings." Lord Silas gave a signal. More guards entered the room and surrounded the court, halberds at the ready. When he was assured of everyone's silence, he continued, "Now, my liege, there has been a challenge to your rule. Prince William of the house of Tarlon. How do you answer?"

The king chuckled mirthlessly. "What else can I say? I agree."

"Does my liege wish time to prepare?"

"How does one truly prepare?" the king asked soberly. "No, no time. I have no need, I've surrounded myself with dandies and whores. Who do I have to say goodbye to?"

This brought a discontented wave of murmurs from the assemblage. Lord Silas quieted everyone with a look before any momentum was gained. "As you say, my liege," Lord Silas said solemnly. "If you would step before the gryphon statue."

"I would know what this proves?" Lord Barkus said in a loud, shrill voice. When guards started moving towards his position, his voice pitched up an octave and he said, "I think I have the right to know!"

Lord Silas raised a hand and the guards went back to their positions. "You are right, of course, Lord Barkus. You have a right to know what this is all about. Let me tell you the story as I know it."

Silas cleared his throat. "Well, this story takes place about three generations ago, in the times of many of our great-great-grandfathers. Lord Albus Tarlon was a young and dashing lord, well liked by the populace. The king at that time was something of a monster. He was hated by the common folk and nobility alike for his stifling taxes and wanton excesses. Lord Tarlon led an army against the king and, after many great battles, was victorious. The kingdom rejoiced, the evil ruler deposed. While many in the kingdom were happy with this turn of events, some asked if we had one bad king, what is to stop it from happening again? So, Lord Tarlon, soon to be King Albus Tarlon the First, consulted with the court wizards. From this, the test of the Gryphon was born, a way to make sure that the kings that would follow would always keep the land and its people their first priority. To make sure only the worthy sat upon the throne, and, begging your pardon, my liege." The king waved a negligent hand to Lord Silas. "A way to depose a ruler that was unfit for the crown."

"How does it work?" cried another of the dandies.

"Within the statue is bound the spirit of a Gryphon. Noble and courageous," the king said, surprising the assemblage. "'Tis our house's coat-of-arms. When you take hold of the sword, he lays judgment upon you. If you do not pass, you die." Turning towards Lord Silas, the king sighed. "Lord Silas, we are done answering questions. I wish to get these proceedings over with."

"As you say, my liege," Lord Silas said, sketching a bow. "If you would take position."

The king stepped into position, rolling the sleeves of his wine-stained robes. "May the heavens look kindly upon me," he whispered under his breath. William and Lord Silas were the only ones who'd heard his utterance.

Before William could do or say anything that would jeopardize the proceedings, Lord Silas said, "Whenever you are ready, my liege, please draw the sword."

"Of course," the king said in an offhand tone. Under his breath, he said, "Goodbye, William. I love you, son." His expression did not change as he spoke his words, and his eyes never left William. Even when his hands crept towards the hilt.

"STOP!" Lord Barkus called, his now booming voice filling the hall. Creeping tendrils of magic crawled across the hall, wrapping all its occupants. Everyone froze in place at his command. "Now, my liege, I must most strenuously object to you doing this. We have obligations that *we* have made. It won't do to have you dead. The Dark Lord will have this land, and we will make sure of it."

"But you, on the other hand, Prince William," Lord Barkus continued, turning towards the paralyzed prince, "and the rest of the assembled lords, well, you all can die horrible deaths and we will attribute it to the Gryphon. Yes, that will do nicely. I am sure that my Dark Lord will reward me most handsomely for such a feat."

The dandy lord didn't see the Gryphon's eyes spark angrily at the mention of the Dark Lord. Nor was he paying attention when it released the sword, pushing it into the waiting hands of the king. Looking down, dumbfounded, at the sword in his hand, the king didn't know what to do.

Save your son, a deep thrumming voice echoed inside the king's head. The voice was filled with such terrible, eldritch majesty, he was stunned for a moment. Then he gathered himself and set his bulky mass in motion.

"Lord Barkus!" the king yelled. Lord Barkus stopped, dagger poised above William, his face betraying his surprise. The traitorous lord turned toward the sound of the voice. The king thrust awkwardly with the sword, having not wielded a blade since his youth. He was able to sink it to the hilt in the dandy lord's chest, albeit clumsily. "Don't touch my son, you bastard!"

Lord Barkus slid off the blade, clutching his chest wound. He fell to the ground with a loud thump. The king spat on him.

You have done well, the voice again echoed, *but you know you are not worthy. You know what must be done.*

William's father nodded to himself and strode purposefully towards the statue and slid the bloody blade home. He looked to his son, still in the grips of the mystical paralysis and said, "I love you, William. Never forget that." The king grabbed the blade and burned from the inside out.

His eyes never left William.

Minutes passed before William fell free of the enchantment holding him. He fell to the ground next to the remains of his father. The king was nothing but a pile of ash. William sobbed quietly, ash running through his fingers.

Lord Silas grabbed the boy gently by the shoulders. "My prince, I know you wish to mourn but now it is not the time for grief. The king is dead and the throne is empty. You must complete the test of the Gryphon and prove yourself worthy to lead."

"He saved me, Silas. Then he died for me, for us! I should honor him," the prince argued.

"Aye, that is fur sure, laddie," Angus said, his voice uncharacteristically somber. "'N' th' best wey ye kin dae it, is by completing th' test. Git up laddie, honor yer faither."

William looked up at the two lords and, for a moment, his eyes burned with hate. He hated these men for taking him down this road, for forcing the death of his father for the good of the nation. Then he stood, hands covered in his father's ashes, and grimly gripped the hilt of the sword, waiting for the burning he wished would come. Instead, the beak unlocked and he withdrew the sword from the statue. He looked at the blade sullenly then slammed it back into its scabbard. A cheer went up amongst the crowd.

William looked up to the assembled lords and took a deep breath. "Convene the war council. Danger comes down the King's road from the North. Evil abounds in our land, and it is time it was rooted out!"

William fell back onto the throne, suddenly feeling very heavy.

THE NOON BELLS TOLLED across the city. Jacob sat, looking down at the package his king had given him. In the larger scheme of things, he had been forgotten. He thought it best. With no slight amount of trepidation, he unwrapped the bundle. A simple note was within along with two bank notes:

DEAR JACOB,

You have served me loyally for many years. I hope that you will continue that journey just a little bit further. There are many that my rule has hurt. I wish to remedy that which I have done. Contained within are two bank notes. Payment I received from Lord Barkus to align myself with an evil man. Hopefully, William will be able to fix that.

One bank note is for you and your family. I wish you to have the best in life. The second is for you to assist the people of this nation.

To be clear, my name is not to be attached to any of this. Remove the funds and do what you think best. Feed the poor. Set up orphanages. Whatever you think will help my people. I don't really have the right to say that,

*do I? I never treated them as 'my people.' Ease their
suffering. I know the majority of it I caused. And the rest,
I did nothing about. So, do the best you can by our
people.*

Thank you for your service,
Martin of the House Tarlon

JACOB'S TEARS stained the page. He stood and wrapped
his cloak about him against the chill. He walked out of the
castle and never once looked back.

The old man stepped gingerly into the inner sanctum of
his Master. He hated being here, in a place that reeked of
death. Not that, as a rule, he hated death or the stench of it but
here, in this place, it was a promise of things to come. He
rounded the corner and dropped to his knees upon catching
sight of his Lord.

Seeing was a sort of a misnomer. What the old man
beheld was an emptiness in the room. His Darkling Lord was
more of an absence within the room, an immense absence. He
currently surrounded the spirit of Lord Barkus, holding him
within coils of void.

"You have failed me, worm," the Dark Lord said, his
voice *shivered* through the old man's bones. "Service to me
doesn't finish after death."

The old man watched as Lord Barkus' spirit was forced
into a waiting suit of armor, the inside of the suit lined with
specially enchanted hooks that spanned two planes of existence. Lord Barkus threw back his head and howled in pain,
but no sound passed his ghostly lips. The greybeard sighed in
relief when Lord Barkus was finally fully ensconced within
the armor.

"What is it, Phineas?" the Darkness asked.

"The Gryphon stymied my attempts to get the old king's soul, Master."

"The Gryphon, the Gryphon, *the Gryphon*! How I loathe him. I will rend him until he is obliterated from existence. Until every single reference to his name is eradicated." The Darkling Lord's ire shook the room with its force. "I tire of everyone's failures! Can *none* of my servants succeed at the tasks given to them?"

Phineas threw himself prostrate upon the rough, hewn floor of the chamber. "Master, I beg your forbearance! It was the Gryphon that was at fault!"

"Oh, dear Phineas, you shall have my forbearance. I shall not kill you. You might regret that in the days to come," the Dark One said and motioned to the guards at the door, "Take him to the Chamber of the Wurm. Tell them I will call when I want him released."

The guards, humanoids twisted by the Dark Lord, immediately grabbed Phineas as he pleaded to no avail. By the time they'd reached the door, he was sobbing.

"Worry not, Phineas, you will have a chance to serve me once more."

William stared out over the battlements, his gaze following the King's Road north towards the mountains. He heard the light footfalls of Lord Silas coming up from behind him, and without turning said, "He's out there, Lord Silas."

"Who, my pri—king?"

William glanced at Silas and smirked. "It feels odd to say, doesn't it?" Lord Silas merely shrugged. "He's out there, the Dark Lord."

"He's always been out there, King William."

"But his threat has never been more present." William turned away from the parapet and locked gazes with Silas. "We must root out the corruption. It won't have ended with

Barkus. And once we have cleaned our house, we march. We march to save the very soul of our people."

King William Tarlon the First let his eyes follow the King's Road. He let out a heavy sigh. The King's Road was not an easy road to follow, even his eyes were getting tired, and he knew that he still had many miles to go before he could rest.

G. DEAN MANUEL

G Dean Manuel is a multi-genre writer who enjoys testing the limits of his ability. He has written everything from Weird West to Dramatic Fiction.

He hails from the tiny country of the Philippines but currently resides in Olathe, Kansas. There were many states, an earthquake, a couple of tornadoes, and even a talking dog between point A and B, but he survived. (Don't ask about the talking dog, his name is Clarence and he still owes G Dean twenty bucks.)

Besides writing, G Dean is an avid gamer, a lover of all things fruit and vegetable, and a prolific reader. He is also a closet cinephile and out of the closet logophile. Besides fiction, G Dean also tries his hand at poetry from time to time. Some of his poems may even be good!

You are still wondering about the talking dog, aren't you? It is quite a tale but I don't have enough room here to tell you…

You can usually find him on line on his blog (https://writersloungeblog.blogspot.com/), Facebook (@Deantheblogger), or Twitter (@courtjester). You can always reach out at fbwriterslounge@gmail.com

THE ARTEFACT

ROSS BAXTER

JUD BROUGHT his horse to a stop and tried to orientate himself. The small clearing looked like any number of others they had passed through in the previous few hours, and with the absence of any defining landmark he was struggling to find his way back to the ruins.

"I thought you said you knew the way?" said Mosta, a thin-faced man riding a bay mare behind him.

Jud ignored him, thoughtfully rubbing the dark stubble on his chin with his leather-gloved hand. He had stumbled upon the ruins two weeks previously whilst looking for lead-ore deposits. Substantial and rambling, the alluring remains promised much in the way of useful materials for his trade, although he knew better than to investigate on his own. In this part of Hallamdor only a fool would venture alone and lightly armed into the maze of tumbling walls and dark passageways that he had spied. Despite the capital being a long three-day ride away, he had immediately returned to Mercaster to recruit assistance; splitting any loot three ways far more appealing than being dead with it all. But now Jud seemed completely unable to relocate the huge abandoned manor, his notes seemingly lacking in the required detail.

"Perhaps we should retrace our tracks again?" suggested Silja, pulling her huge black stallion to a halt beside him.

"I don't know," Jud muttered, angry at himself for getting lost. "We've already circled around twice; it should be around here."

All three scanned the dense foliage that pressed in around the clearing, each wearily trying to find some clue or sign. It had been a hard ride from the comforts of Mercaster, and none of them wanted to return empty handed. Fortunately for Jud, both his companions were pragmatic enough not to blame him too much.

The three riders were there for the same reasons, but all were looking for different things. Jud was a skilled artificer, a specialist in the crafting of intricate mechanisms such as time keeping devices and technical apparatus. As such he was there to find any of the rarer metals and alloys or any usable remains of crafted machinery. The towering and dark-skinned Silja was looking for any weaponry she could re-craft. A skilled and powerful warrior, she had once led Mercaster's Provost Guard, but since retiring early she now made a good living fashioning weapons for the nobility. Taller, broader and more heavily muscled than her companions, she still looked every bit the fighter of great repute. In contrast to the warrior, the third rider, Mosta, was pale, slight and thin-boned. More of a collector than a dealer, he was an authority on ancient texts and manuscripts, and always eager to search for more. Each of the three knew the potential rewards which could be found in any long-forgotten ruins, but each also knew the ever-present dangers.

"Hark!" hissed Silja, holding up her gauntleted hand for silence.

Apart from the sound of a distant crow, both Jud and Mosta could hear nothing.

"This way," she whispered, quickly dismounting from her towering mount.

Jud and Mosta alighted and followed the warrior, cautiously leading their horses towards a space in the trees at the far end of the glade. The ground underfoot was damp and spongy from the near-constant drizzle, with stunted shrubs which snagged and tugged at their boots. Then, as they squeezed through the trees, they all felt the ground suddenly firm up, as if there were a hard surface beneath the moss and rotting leaves.

"Finally," Jud whispered under his breath, relieved at seeing Silja had found an overgrown track which had once been wide and paved.

They moved silently in single file along the forgotten trail, each careful to avoid the mossy overhanging branches and frequent patches of thorny brambles. After a few minutes Silja stopped and moved her horse to the left to allow Jud and Mosta to draw alongside. Ahead stood a derelict gatehouse, and behind it grey stone towers loomed menacingly in the mist.

"Well done!" whispered Jud, clapping Silja on her broad leather-clad shoulder. "What did you hear which betrayed its location?"

"That," said Silja, pointing to a warped wooden door on the gatehouse which hung open on creaking rusted hinges. "And we don't have to whisper; no-one has been here for a long time."

Jud nodded, ever thankful that Silja had agreed to accompany them. Her highly-tuned instincts gave her an uncanny ability to perceive the hidden, equipping her with a sort of sixth-sense. Such talent, when combined with her considerable martial prowess, made Silja the best sort of companion.

"So, let's make a start then," said Mosta.

"We still need to be very careful," Silja warned. "I sense something unnatural about this place. We should hobble the horses here by the gatehouse and proceed on foot. Once in the ruins we must stick together at all times."

Both Jud and Mosta knew better than to argue and quickly secured their mounts. They then fell in behind the warrior and followed in cautious silence. Silja walked slowly forward, scanning the bushes and ramshackle buildings of which the gatehouse was the largest. The three passed under the weathered stone arch, side-stepping the heavy ruined gates which hung broken and useless. In the dreary afternoon light the surroundings appeared monotone and lifeless, the dark greens and browns of the overgrown vegetation seeming to merge seamlessly into the dark matte stonework of the crumbling gatehouse.

"How long do you think the place has been abandoned?" Jud asked.

"Hard to tell," Mosta shrugged. "When you told me about it I searched the manuscripts and maps but could find nothing cast-iron. There are a number of possibilities, though. One is that the ruins are those of the lost stronghold of the Leroux Bandit Clan, which was put to the torch nearly two hundred years ago by Lord Highsmith. Otherwise, it may be the remains of some long-forgotten baronial retreat, abandoned during the purges of the peninsular wars. It could even be the fabled Elvaston Manor, but I very much doubt that."

The mention of Elvaston Manor sent an involuntary shiver through Jud; stories about the Elvaston family were what adults used to frighten children He still vividly remembered the tales his own mother told him, always full of dark magic, sinister heresy, and lingering death.

"I didn't think Elvaston Manor was actually a real place?" remarked Silja.

"Oh, yes, it most definitely was," Mosta answered. "The Elvaston family were merchants who plied the waters of the western sea, amassing a vast fortune by supplying virtually all the royal houses in the land with curiosities from the then unexplored far continent. But some of the more abnormal and peculiar things they found they kept for themselves, and eventually their ships catered only for the increasingly bizarre whims of the family. The later generations became reclusive and eccentric, retiring to Elvaston Manor. The business collapsed some years later and the family line supposedly died out. Most of the stories relate to the unnatural fetishes of the last of the Elvastons, and their dabbling in the dark arts in the manor. But, despite the attraction of a good story, I think the profusion of weird legends and tall tales told about the place are mainly fantasy. Nothing has actually been heard of the Elvastons for over a hundred years."

"Still, I hope this place is not Elvaston Manor," Jud muttered, thinking of his dead mother.

Mosta made to answer but was silenced by Silja. The warrior swiftly drew the large sword she kept secured across her back. Jud's cutlass and Mosta's slim rapier seemed tiny and pitiable in comparison, but they drew them anyway. They followed Silja's gaze to a ramshackle outbuilding to the right of the track ahead, scanning the open door and dark glass-less windows. In this part of Hallamdor the danger could be anything; rogues, bears, pit-badgers, firedrakes, or a dozen other unsavory predators, all eager to make a meal of them.

"What?" whispered Mosta.

"There," Silja answered, as eight dark shapes suddenly

flashed out of the doorway bounding towards them, closing the gap at lightning speed.

Jud immediately recognized the snaggle-toothed maws and malevolent yellow eyes of the bounding polrats, stepping to one side to give himself space to fight. He had faced such dog-sized rodents before and braced himself for the vicious onslaught. The first lunged straight at him and he despatched it with a single slash of his cutlass before spinning to hack at another which circled behind him. His cutlass cut only air as the second snarling polrat dodged and lithely snaked left. He whirled and saw yet another, this one lunging low at him and biting hard into his lower calf. With a yelp he swung the cutlass down hard, neatly separating the polrat's head from its scrabbling body. He turned again to meet the next attack but saw Silja's long sword split it cleanly in half.

Just two of the huge rodents remained, both backing away from Mosta who stood ready to strike. With incredible speed and agility Silja unstrapped her light bow and fired two quill arrows in rapid succession, each finding their target with deadly precision.

"Thanks," breathed Mosta, glancing quickly around to see all the assailants were accounted for.

"I think that one likes you," grinned Silja, pointing her bow towards the polrat's severed head, which still gripped Jud's leg in a deathly clench.

Jud nodded stoically, struggling to prise the bloody jaws apart with his cutlass. The polrat had bitten into the thick leather pads which topped his boots, but luckily none of the needle-sharp teeth had gone through. He twisted the cutlass again to break open the jaws, not wishing to touch the matted greasy fur of his now dead assailant. With a sharp snap the jaws broke and he knocked the head to the floor before kicking it hard into the undergrowth.

The three companions paused a moment to catch their breath and clean their weapons. Silja also retrieved the two quill arrows from the spitted polrats; never one to waste any weaponry. Once finished, they quickly moved off, Jud and Mosta again following in Silja's broad wake.

As he walked, Jud silently surveyed the surrounding vegetation; it seemed strangely more exotic than the usual shrubs and thorns of Hallamdor. Some plants were even completely unknown to him, probably the clinging remnants of old overgrown imported gardens he thought.

Ahead loomed a large building; imposing, dark, and unwelcoming. Battered twin towers rose on either side to frame a stark central structure with slab-like walls completely bereft of any aesthetic qualities. Clusters of outbuildings flanked the main house, all built from the same dark basaltic rock.

"Where do we start?" Jud asked Silja.

"We're all looking for different things," Silja answered, turning to face her two comrades. "Mosta is here for valuable manuscripts and books, Jud for rare alloys and finely-crafted devices, and myself for exotic metals and expensive blades to re-craft. But this place has an aurora I've never encountered so strongly before; part malice, part belligerence, all tainted. We can't split up and we have only two hours of daylight left. I suggest we enter the main building and search the central rooms together, gathering anything we deem valuable. By sunset we need to be on our mounts riding back to Mercaster."

Jud and Mosta nodded their agreement. Though neither was attuned like Silja, both felt the same sense of unease and menace which pervaded the whole place and even seemed to seep from the very ground on which they stood.

Silja moved forward, picking a course through the

tangle of brambles and fallen masonry towards the wide steps which led up to the imposing main entrance. The studded oaken doors were closed, the wood discoloured and swollen with moisture and rot. Silja forced her hand into the uneven space between the doors and pulled. Slowly the gap widened as the lock crumbled into rust and hinges grudgingly gave way to her warrior's strength. She pulled hard on the right-hand door and it creaked open wide enough for them to gingerly pass through into the gloom beyond.

Inside, the entrance opened into a wide hall, dimly lit by light filtering down from the small windows placed high in the thick stone walls. Most had lost their glass, and dark puddles of stagnant rainwater pooled on the stone flooring under them. Piles of debris and broken roof beams littered the hall, the majority seeming to have come from the floors above through the partly-collapsed ceiling. Looking upwards through the yawning hole they could see small patches of grey light beyond missing roof tiles two or three stories higher.

Once their eyes adjusted to the murky interior they moved slowly forward, warily scanning the crumbling architecture whilst looking for anything of use or value. They stepped lightly over spoilt tapestries, mildewed linen, and clothes spilling from smashed cabinets and drawers fallen from the floors above, and around broken furniture and floorboards. The place appeared untouched since being abandoned, with only the harsh hand of decay having played a role in the chaos around them. A strange smell pervaded the hall; heavy and pungent, something which Jud thought he knew but just could not place.

"There's a body," whispered Mosta, pointing to the left.

The three walked slowly over, checking for traps and gaps

in the floor. The corpse lay on its back and had been dead many months, although something appeared odd about it.

"Look at the eyes," said Mosta. "They're still there. Dried and desiccated, but still there. Nothing has taken them, though the eyes are always the first thing to be eaten by critters, birds, or maggots."

"Have you noticed that there are no cobwebs in here either?" mused Jud. "Plenty of dust and debris, but no sign of any life at all."

"The body looks like that of an adventurer," murmured Silja. "Young, maybe in his twenties. But his sword is undrawn and still sheathed in its scabbard. There's no sign of what killed him; no marks, tears, or rips in his clothing."

"Well, the building seems to be in a less damaged state further in," Jud offered, hoping he sounded optimistic. "I'm sure we'll find better pickings there."

The others both nodded and they continued through the ruined hall towards a dim corridor at the far side. Apart from the soft sound of their cautious footsteps on the rubble-strewn flooring, the place was in absolute silence. Silja reached the wide passage first and swiftly drew the smaller of her two swords. Jud and Mosta followed by drawing their own blades, though neither knew what she sensed. After a pause to let her eyes adjust to the thickening gloom the warrior moved forward into the wide corridor, pausing to look into the rooms at either side. The first doorway revealed a large kitchen with assorted pots and utensils scattered on various ranges and tables. Next came the kitchen storeroom filled with shelving full of crockery on one side and racks full of food boxes on the other. Large sacks of rice and flour, grey and moldy, sat on a low central table. Strangely, none of the sacks seemed to have been disturbed by scavenging vermin or insects.

"This is more like it!" Silja announced, stepping lightly through the next doorway.

Jud and Mosta followed, seeing a room which appeared to be some sort of common room for soldiery. From the racks of rusty weaponry and hangers of mildewed leather, Jud guessed it to be the place where the guards once ate and relaxed between duties. He then saw the faded emblem painted on the far wall.

"Damn," he sighed. "It is Elvaston Manor."

Silja and Mosta followed his stare, both recognizing the peeling crest so synonymous with the dark legends which dominated so many of Hallamdor's stories for so many years. The Elvaston name conjured up different connotations for each of the three, none of them good.

Silja returned her gaze to the room's contents. She quickly scanned the antique armaments, her expert eyes appraising the quality of craftsmanship and metal beneath the tarnish and corrosion.

"This one alone makes my trip worthwhile!" she grinned, withdrawing a lustrous light colored two-handed sword from the rack. "A fantastic piece, forged from a single crystal of topaz by a master weapon-smith; it's worth a small fortune."

"Topaz?" questioned Jud. "I know it's a hard mineral, but surely it would be too brittle to be of any use in battle?"

"This is imperial topaz; the mineral is cooled and drawn over decades in a subterranean foundry, by two or three generations of weapon-smiths. The resulting single crystal is incredibly strong, and remarkably expensive."

Mosta regarded the axe with suspicion. "But why would a weapon of that value be left here when this place was abandoned?"

"I don't know," Silja replied, staring in admiration at the fine semi-transparent blade, her thoughts taken with the exquisite craftsmanship. "But with this sword I have every-thing I came for. Now, let's get something for you both and be gone from this place."

Jud nodded and turned, not wanting to spend any more time than he had to in the grim ruins.

The next three rooms contained nothing of value or inter-est, and the corridor led them to a collapsed staircase and another passage which led off left and right.

Silja paused and then moved to the right. "I smell some-thing for Mosta."

The passage ended abruptly at a large closed door. After placing the topaz sword carefully on the ground, Silja tried the heavy wooden door. Although not locked, the damp wood had badly warped, and it held solid until Silja's third shoul-der-barge. Inside it was pitch black.

"A library!" exclaimed Mosta, smelling the damp parch-ment wafting from the darkness.

Jud was the first to get a torch lit and with caution ventured through the doorway. Inside was a large rectangular room, wooden shelving covering all four windowless walls from floor to ceiling. The racks were crammed with books, manuscripts and scrolls of every description, some of which spilled into jumbled piles on the floor where shelves had collapsed. Four heavy reading tables with chairs occupied the centre of the room; their surfaces covered with a clutter of dusty books and yellowy mildewed papers. Jud took another step but froze suddenly, seeing a figure seated at the nearest table.

"It's quite dead," Silja reassured him, moving towards the figure with her own torch.

Despite the dampness of the room the corpse appeared dry and desiccated, it's blotched and mottled skin pulled tight over high cheekbones. Brown teeth grinned through ruined lips and eyeless sockets seemed to stare at them. Skeletal fingers still grasped an open book, as if their owner were still reading.

"Much older than the last corpse," Silja mused. "I'd say this one's been dead a hundred years."

"This is amazing," Mosta gasped, mesmerized by the thousands of texts and manuscripts illuminated by his flickering torch.

"Then grab what you need and we'll move on," said Silja flatly.

"It's going to take me hours to go through this lot," Mosta pleaded.

"It'll be sunset soon," Silja replied. "We don't have time."

"I'll stay here whilst you and Jud search the rest of the corridor, that will give me time to find something of value," said Mosta.

"No-one should be alone in this place," retorted Silja. "The Elvaston taint is so strong I can actually taste it."

"You're not my mother!" Mosta shot back angrily. "The corridor is only fifty yards long, find something for Jud and then come back. I won't leave the library and I'll shout if I need you."

Silja simply shrugged and shook her head. Jud moved back into the corridor, glad to be away from the grinning cadaver and eager to find something of value for himself. The open doors of the next three rooms yielded nothing of interest, but the forth was closed. As Jud moved closer to the door he was suddenly overcome by acute nausea, his stomach gripped as if in an iron vice. He stumbled backwards, the feeling decreasing with ever step. Silja stepped forward and Jud could hear her dry retch as she reached the door. After trying the handle, she quickly retreated back towards him.

"A protective spell?" Jud asked.

"Aye," Silja agreed. "It's lost some of its potency over the years, but someone was very keen to prevent access to this room."

Jud smiled; protective spells usually always guarded items of high value. He took a deep breath and shoulder-barged the door. The door did not budge an inch, and Jud bounced backwards from it, vomiting over his boots as the protective spell hit him hard.

"Men!" Silja tutted in jest, trying not to laugh too hard.

As Jud tried to regain his composure the warrior put down her torch and grasped her new two-handed sword in both hands. At first she simply held it, making a few light sweeps to gauge its balance. She then suddenly pirouetted around, swinging the heavy weapon in two rapid arcs before planting the heavy crystal blade squarely into the crack between the door and its frame. She then danced three steps backwards out of the nauseating range of the spell, leaving the weapon embedded.

"That's no way to treat a fine sword," Jud slurred, wiping vomit from his chin. "I thought you said it was worth a kings' ransom?"

"The reason for the huge value is because it's virtually indestructible," she answered. "As I said before, the single crystal bestows an almost magical strength."

She moved to the side of the door and with a grace and agility belaying her size she high-kicked the hilt of the crystal sword three times in rapid succession. Wooden splinters flew in all directions, and she finished the display with a fourth kick placed expertly in the centre of the shattered door. Jud could only stare in admiration as she retreated, heavy sword in hand, stifling a series of dry-retches.

The door swung inwards on groaning hinges, releasing waves of the stomach-churning spell into the corridor. Jud quickly re-lit his torch and threw it spear-like into the darkness of the protected room. The flames revealed a square and windowless space, completely empty apart from what appeared to be a heavy stone alter built into the far wall and an ornate wooden box which sat on the grey floor-stones in the centre of the room.

"Looks like we're not spoilt for choice of booty," Jud reflected.

"True," muttered Silja, "but the protective spell is still far too strong for us to enter the room."

"Don't worry," said Jud, taking off his light pack and withdrawing a coil of thin rope, "I'll show you what us men can do!".

He quickly uncoiled the rope, pleased to finally get a chance to prove his worth in front of the skillful and consummate warrior. Once uncoiled, he fashioned one end of the rope around to make a lasso, cleverly knotting the twine to give it strength and weight. After a pause to judge the distance, he pitched the noose forward into the room, managing to loop it around the box on his first attempt. The box felt heavy as he pulled the line tight, taking care not to let it slip underneath.

"Pull slowly," Silja urged, "the spell may actually be centered on the casket and not the room."

Jud nodded and slowly drew the box towards them, thankful that the overpowering sense of nausea did not increase as it neared. He shook the rope off and peered down at the small chest, excited by the quality of the workmanship and by the fine materials. The darkly polished wood appeared pristine, completely unmarked by the damp and dust of the ruins. Delicate lettering covered all the surfaces, expertly scribed in a language Jud had never before seen. But the most exciting thing was the intricate lock which sat in the centre of the lid. Even in the dim light of the corridor he could clearly make out the shine of contrasting precious metals and a mechanism both elaborate and outlandishly exotic in design.

"Stand back!" Silja warned, gripping the topaz broadsword tightly in her gauntleted hands.

"What?" gasped Jud.

"We've no time to figure out how the lock works," she said darkly. "I'll open it with the sword."

"No!" Jud yelled. "The lock alone is worth my journey. Whatever's inside is just a bonus."

Silja nodded her understanding. "Hopefully Mosta has found something in the Library by now. Let's collect him and get out of here."

Jud stowed his rope and grasped the box. It felt oddly warm and surprisingly heavy for its size, but all he could think about as he heaved it upwards was the magnificent locking mechanism.

Silja turned and marched down the corridor towards the open door of the library. She stopped suddenly on the threshold and deftly gripped her sword with both hands again. Jud gently put the box down and grabbed his own weapon, warily stepping close behind the warrior. The room was empty. Mosta's torch still flickered where it was propped against one of the tables, but he was gone. Silja and Jud quickly searched the room, pulling at the shelves and checking under the tables. Then Jud realized something else was missing.

"Silja!" he hissed. "The corpse is gone!"

The wooden chair was empty, dark stains marking the old wood where the body had sat. Everything else looked the same as when they had left not long before.

"He couldn't have gone past us," Jud reasoned. "The staircase is impassable so he must have gone back in the direction of the entrance hall. Maybe he found what he needed and went outside to get some air?"

"I don't think so," said Silja flatly, examining the walls and corners of the room.

"Mosta!" Jud shouted, the echoes of his voice answered only by silence.

"We need to go," Silja urged. "Now."

"But we can't just leave him?" argued Jud.

"There's nothing we can do for him now," she said. "We need to leave. Trust me on this."

For the first time in all the years he had known the warrior, he saw a look of genuine fear on Silja's face. He needed no further explanation and immediately made towards the door.

As they raced out into the hall they saw two figures stood by the main doorway.

"Mosta!" shouted Jud with relief. "Thank the stars!"

"Steady," cautioned Silja, gripping Jud's arm. "Look again."

Jud slowed his pace, squinting in the darkness towards the figures blocking the doorway. Both had drawn swords, and although the smaller of the two did appear to be Mosta, something was definitely wrong. Then he saw; Mosta had been disembowelled, a dark bloody cavity yawning where his stomach and intestines had been. Yet still he stood with drawn rapier, shoulder to shoulder with the hapless dead adventurer they had found earlier.

"Follow me!" Silja commanded, charging at the two figures with the topaz sword raised.

Jud followed, holding the heavy box in one hand and his stubby cutlass in the other. As Silja neared the animated corpses parted and moved forwards. She engaged the nearest, the dead adventurer, swinging her sword in a vicious arc. But the cadaver moved with a deceiving speed, deftly dodging the blow at the last second and jabbing its tarnished blade towards Silja's unguarded flank. Silja swerved expertly, and the blade skidded off her plated tunic. She took a couple of steps backwards, quickly re-appraising her attacker. Jud reached her and put down his box, nervously watching Mosta, who waited by the door with lifeless eyes burning into him.

Silja maintained her position, goading the dead adventurer to attack. The corpse made a couple of feints which the skilled warrior easily avoided, then suddenly leapt forward with unnatural speed, his rusted sword a blur. Silja stepped left and then forwards, thrusting the two-handed sword up between them. The cadaver's whirling sword struck the topaz sword on the crystal blade and ran the length to the hilt, sparks marking its progress. Silja twisted her weapon sharply, trapping the cadaver's sword between the guard and the blade. With a heavy tug she jerked the weapon out of the corpse's hand, sending it clattering away. As her opponent hesitated she swept the great sword upwards, cleanly taking off his sword arm at the shoulder. The blow had little effect, and the dead adventurer immediately came back at Silja with just the flailing fist of its left arm. This time she barged straight into the corpse, her weight and speed knocking it sprawling backwards to crash heavily to the ground. In a flash she was by her floundering assailant, her sword slashing through its scrawny neck to part the head from the torso. Mosta's corpse took this as the cue to charge Jud, with its slim rapier flashing.

"Mosta, it's me, Jud!" he yelled, bringing his cutlass up in defense.

If the corpse heard, it made no sign. Instead it flung himself at Jud, the rapier skittering off the cutlass with bright orange sparks. The blood drenched body swung again at Jud, forcing him backwards with a vicious onslaught. Jud parried each of the blows, waiting for his chance, but the thrusts and swipes kept coming without pause. He found himself backed against the wall, the stench of blood, bile, and excrement from the corpse almost as overpowering as the swordsmanship. Knowing he had few options he swung onto the offence, using his strength and the heavy steel of the cutlass to blunt Mosta's attack. As their weapons clashed again the thin blade of the rapier shattered, and Jud drove the curved blade deep into the corpse's chest whilst grabbing hold of its sword-arm with his left. The effect of what should have been a fatal blow seemed minimal, and instead of collapsing backwards the corpse pushed back, trying to bite him. Jud tried to retrieve his blade but it was wedged fast between the vertebrae of Mosta's spine, and all he could do was restrain the sword arm and try to avoid the snapping teeth. As he pushed back again something flashed by his cheek and he saw a quill arrow bury itself deep into Mosta's dead right eye. The strength suddenly left the animated corpse and it flopped down lifeless onto the ground.

"Out! now!" yelled Silja, carrying her own weapons as well as Jud's box.

Jud dashed panting through the open doorway after the tall warrior, running as fast as he could but still not catching her despite the weight she carried. They skidded through the abandoned outbuildings and into the trees where the three horses stood nervously hobbled.

"I'll take the gear, you bring Mosta's mount!" Silja commanded.

Too out of breath to answer, Jud simply obeyed and snapped off both hobbling ropes before leaping up on his frightened horse. Within seconds they were both galloping at full pelt through the trees towards safety.

AFTER GETTING the box back to his workshop in Mercaster, it took Jud four days to figure out how the lock actually worked. It then took another three for him to open it without damaging the fine mechanism inside. As an artificer who prided himself in his technical ability to build complicated pieces, including the best locks in Mercaster, it was the most interesting and informative week he had spent in years.

When he finally got to look inside the box he found an even greater challenge. The object within had a spherical base the size of a medium watermelon, upon which sat an inverted cone, wide and open at the top and funneling down a point on the surface of the cerulean metallic sphere. It was formed from what appeared to be a molybdenum and corundum alloy, a pairing which Jud had previously thought impossible to combine. By tapping on it he knew the sphere was thick but hollow, but he could find no access or any way to tell what was inside it. The funnel and sphere were covered with a swirling engraved text, the language and characters completely different in nature to that on the box, and just as equally unreadable. But the strangest thing was the constant warmth of the sphere, a low heat which emanated without any detectable source of sustenance, the temperature remaining constant no matter the temperature of the surrounding air.

Eventually, Jud had to admit defeat. Despite all the hard work and his best efforts, he was at a complete loss, with absolutely no idea what the strange artefact was. He could not even guess at its origin, age, or function. Without any visible access, he was unable to see inside without breaking the sphere and probably ruining it, and all he could do was to transcribe the strange text onto parchment and try and find a scholar able to translate it.

After a few days of indecision, he finally took the transcript to Mosta's apprentice, Tremeta. Although not the most learned scholar in the city, he did feel a sense of responsibility for her. When he and Silja had first returned to Mercaster they had gone to see Tremeta straight away. The girl had been shocked and scared by the news of what had happened with Mosta, and unsure of what she should do next. Jud and Silja had calmed and persuaded her to continue with the business; Mosta having no kin and her being almost at the end of her training. Although hesitant, Tremeta had agreed to keep the business running, having no-one else in Mercaster to work for and having a number of unfinished jobs to do for various customers. Now, a couple of weeks later, he was pleased to see her well, busy, and hard at work. On seeing the mysterious text she was a little perplexed, having never encountered anything like it. She gladly promised to try and translate it, but warned it would not be easy and would likely take some time.

Happy that she and the business were faring well, he left the parchment with her and returned to his workshop. He was in no real rush for the translation, and as days turned into weeks his attention was drawn to other projects. As he endeavored to reduce his backlog of outstanding commissions he soon put the mysterious artefact to the back of his mind, placing it on one of the top shelves of his workshop alongside his unsold constructions.

JUD WAS STRUGGLING with the mechanism of a new timepiece when he heard a loud banging on his workshop door. He sighed, carefully placing the tiny cogs in the correct order on his worktable. It had been a busy few weeks; the new fashion for astronomical timepieces amongst the local nobility kept him fully occupied.

The banging continued as he unlocked the workshop door. In the narrow street outside stood an expensively clad young woman, flanked by two hulking minders. Jud did not recognize her, but from her age and make-up he guessed her to be a mistress of one of the Mercaster barons.

"Good afternoon," smiled Jud. "How can I be of assistance?"

"I'm looking for a gift for my love, for the Festival of Light," she announced. "I know he has bought things from here before."

"Please come in," said Jud, opening the door wide and beckoning the three inside. "Most of my work is for specific commissions, but I do have some finished items which may be of interest."

He led them into the workshop annex where most of his unsold items were on display. The majority were stargazing mechanisms, left over from the previous fashion amongst the Hallamdor nobility, along with a few intricate locks and a couple of finely tooled pocket knives.

"Do you have any timepieces?" the woman asked.

Jud sighed. "Timepieces are very popular at the moment. I only make them to order, and with the Festival only two days away I'm afraid I wouldn't have time to make even the simplest one. But if you tell me who your love is, I may be able to come up with something based on what I've made for him or her in the past?"

"It's Baron Samedi," the woman announced proudly.

Jud nodded sagely, trying to disguise his sadness for the young woman. He knew Samedi to be a particularly cruel and twisted individual, seemingly set on squandering the good legacy of his forebears on a host of hedonistic enterprises.

"I'm afraid I probably don't have anything that would interest the Baron," Jud apologized. "Perhaps you should visit Silja the weapon-smith; she has plenty which might take his fancy."

Samedi's mistress nodded and made to leave, but then she stopped and pointed to the top shelf of the workshop's racking. "What's that?"

Jud turned to follow her eyes, seeing only the mysterious artefact from the ruins of Elvaston Manor.

"Oh," Jud said in surprise. "That's just something I'm working on. I don't think it's anything the Baron would be interested in."

"It's not for him, it's for me," she admonished him. "Let me see it!"

Jud shrugged and lifted it down to the counter. As always, it felt warm to the touch.

"What an interesting vase," she mused. "What does this writing mean?"

"I'm not quite sure," Jud replied. "It's an antique, and I don't know the full history behind it, or even its original purpose."

"Well, it will look wonderful in my bedchamber, filled with flowers," she enthused. "How much do you want for it?"

"I'm afraid it's not for sale, my lady," Jud whispered.

"The Baron will look very dimly on you if you refuse to sell something to me," she warned. "I'll give you two hundred crowns for it."

Jud hesitated; he had no desire to upset the unstable Baron Samedi, and two hundred was a substantial sum of money for something which had no obvious use or function. In addition, Mosta's apprentice had so far failed to come up with any sort of translation, despite having been working on the transcript for months. Perhaps it was time to cut his losses and make a sale.

"Two hundred will be fine," he nodded, reaching up and wiping the dust from it. "Would you like it wrapped?"

AFTER A FINAL POLISH with a silk cloth, Jud regarded his latest timepiece with pride. The work was his most complicated to date, and he had managed to exceed his own high expectations. It put him in a good mood, and with it being the Eve of the Festival of Light he decided to finish early; he thought he at least deserved a few hours off before a night in his favorite alehouses.

As he started to lock up the workshop he saw Mosta's apprentice running towards him down the narrow street.

"Jud!" she shouted gaily. "I've finally got the translation!"

Jud turned the heavy keys back in the opposite direction and re-opened the door.

"I was just about to buy myself my first mead of the festival," he said with a smile as he held the door open.

Tremeta entered, a leather satchel gripped tightly in her hand. Although barely nineteen, the apprentice was doing well since the disappearance of Mosta. She continued to run the shop, and business seemed to be good. Jud opened the shuttered window and beckoned her over to the workbench.

"You won't believe what you found in the Elvaston ruins!" Tremeta panted, still out of breath from her run. "I really struggled with the text, but two weeks ago someone brought me an ancient scroll written with a similar patois. It was a poem, and by luck I discovered Mosta had a later version of the same poem written in classic text. By comparing the two I eventually managed to translate the script on the artefact."

"And?" Jud interrupted.

"It's incredible; the artefact is actually a soul jar!"

Jud frowned, trying to recall what a soul jar was.

"A soul jar is one of the key elements in the dark art of Necromancy, created by the most sinister of magics. It's a sort of vessel used by a Necromancer to draw spirit life-force from the living; it then stores the essence up to be fed from later. The mage would use it by cutting out the organs of still living victims and placing them in the top receptacle for the soul jar to leach from. As long as the Necromancer has a steady supply of victims, they can virtually live forever by tapping the stored life-force in the soul jar."

"Nasty," said Jud, his frown deepening. "So, what exactly is inside the chamber?"

"I'm not quite sure, but I don't recommend you open it to find out," Tremeta replied. "Soul jars are incredibly rare, and in terms of value they're priceless. There are many dark mages who would literally give anything to get their hands on a soul jar. You can name your price!"

Jud shook his head sadly.

"What?" asked Tremeta.

"I'm afraid I sold it yesterday," muttered Jud. "For two hundred crowns."

"What?" Tremeta gasped, her face reddening. "Tell me you're joking!"

"I'm afraid not," Jud offered, his face pale. "I offered you ten percentage of the sale value for the translation, which means I owe you twenty crowns."

"But you could have bought half of Mercaster with what you could have got!" wailed Tremeta. "Who did you sell it to?"

"To Baron Samedi's new mistress. As a flower vase."

"A flower vase?" gasped Tremeta.

"She said it would look nice in her bedchamber," Jud answered. He tried to stifle a smile, despite the scale of the loss he could still see the funny side.

Tremeta sighed; she knew the stories about Samedi and realized the chances of getting the soul jar back were very slim. "I put together a list of the potential buyers and had even picked the island I was going to buy with my ten percent."

"Well, let me buy you a drink at the tavern instead," suggested Jud stoically. "You look like you need one."

Tremeta nodded, and with a white-face followed the artificer back towards the workshop door. Jud opened the door just as Samedi's mistress got there. This time she was accompanied by a hulking brute of a man.

"There you are!" she shouted angrily at the surprised Jud. "That flower vase you sold me was a fake. Any flowers placed in it whither and shrivel within minutes, it must contain some sort of poison!"

"Oh," said Jud. "Have you got the vase with you?"

"It's here," she hissed, beckoning the brute forwards. "I want my two hundred crowns back!"

Jud looked at the soul jar grasped in one of the man's huge hands. It appeared intact.

"I'll be happy to refund your money," said Jud, holding out his hand towards the thug for the soul jar.

"Give her the money first, you cretin!" growled the henchman, obviously unhappy to be on an errand when he could be drinking or brawling in one of Mercaster's hostelries.

Jud looked the man up and down. He looked like most of the thugs employed by Samedi: large, stupid, and brutish.

Although not usually one to turn the other cheek to an insult from such a dolt, Jud decided to let it go. "If you'd be so good as to wait a moment, I'll get the money."

"You'd better be quick," said the thug menacingly. "You wouldn't want to upset us."

"Of course," nodded Jud, retrieving the bag of crowns from a locked drawer under his workbench. "Here it is."

Jud returned to Samedi's mistress and offered her the bag. "I'm sorry the vase was no good. Please accept my sincere apologies."

The woman grabbed the bag, and then a malevolent look crossed her face. "What about payment for my time that you've wasted? Maybe one of your timepieces for my love would be an adequate compensation, unless you want my man here to take it out of your face?"

Jud regarded her for a moment, never surprised by the greed and avarice such people often showed. He reached into a drawer and withdrew one of his early and clumsy attempts at a prototype timepiece and handed it to her. "This one here is an exquisite example, one I'm sure it will be to the Baron's taste."

Samedi's mistress eyed it suspiciously. "Is it valuable?"

"Of course," Jud lied. "Valuable and exclusive."

"Consider yourself lucky," she sneered, pocketing the timepiece and then turning to the thug. "Give him the stupid vase."

The ruffian held it out, looking sullen at not having the opportunity to get physical. As Jud reached for it the thug let it drop with a sick smile. As quick as a flash, Tremeta shot forward and caught it before it hit the ground. She then took a step backwards, the soul jar firm in her grip.

"Why, you little sneak!" shouted the man, pulling a wicked looking blade from his belt.

"Madame," said Jud politely. "Hopefully I've recompensed you enough for the vase. There really is no need for anyone to get hurt, and I'm sure the Baron would prefer to have you back by his side early on this festival night?"

"I'm no longer with the Baron," she spat. "I grew tired of him, I've left him for someone else."

Jud regarded her with sad contempt, knowing that no mistress of Samedi's ever got the luxury of leaving him. He wondered how long she would live before Samedi tracked her down and killed her. "Well, I'm sure the Baron will be feeling quite aggrieved, which is never pleasant. Perhaps you should go and be with your new love, which hopefully for you is a long way from Mercaster."

"Do think I'm scared of him?" she hissed. "I left his bed, and Haggath here left his barracks as well so we could make a new life together. Haggath was his most skilled bodyguard; we've nothing to fear."

Jud's contempt quickly subsided into pity. He doubted the thug was even a bodyguard, never mind Baron's most skilled one. Neither would have a chance once Samedi tracked them down.

"Please, take the money and the timepiece, and get as far away from Samedi as fast as you can," implored Jud with sincerity.

"Maybe you've something else in this place we might want?" leered Haggath the thug, making a play of scanning the shelves.

As soon as Haggath's eyes were off her, Tremeta darted forward, and with a gravity-defying high-kick booted the knife out of the thug's hand. He whirled in surprise only to be caught by second kick to the crotch, which dropped him like a sack of potatoes to the hard stone floor. By then Jud had his own weapon drawn, but saw he had little need of it with the thug gasping for breath and Samedi's ex-mistress wide eyed in stunned surprise.

"Take the money, the timepiece, and your goon, and get out of here, or I'll drag you both to the Baron myself!" Jud hissed.

Samedi's ex-mistress helped the thug to his feet and they quickly left without another word. Jud smiled at Tremeta with new respect.

"Nicely done," he said.

"Looks like the soul jar still works," whispered Tremeta in wonder as she watched the two depart. "If it can leach the life out of flowers then I'm sure it can take the spirit from anything, and I know at least three buyers who will pay a king's ransom for it!"

"Well, I reckon we deserve a different type of spirit just now," grinned Jud. "Let's go to the tavern and raise a toast to the Elvastons!"

ROSS BAXTER

After thirty years at sea, Ross Baxter now concentrates on writing speculative fiction, mainly sci-fi and horror. His varied work has been published in print by several publishing houses in the US, the UK, and Australia. Married to a Norwegian and with two Anglo-Viking kids, he now lives in Derby, England.

Links to Ross's works can be found at @rossbaxter1 or via Amazon.

UNDER LOCKE AND KEY

JAY ERICKSON

"I LOVE THIS PLAGUE!"

Gwendolyn heard a glass tinkle against another, and she imagined Adjutor Spirell toasting her master, the bloated and balding Thedwin, with whatever alcohol Thedwin fed him this time.

"People are dying," came the nasally response Gwendolyn was used to hearing.

"And demand is up because of it!" the adjutor exclaimed. Gwendolyn closed her eyes. She could see it now: the alcohol sloshing out of the glass and splattering against the worn oak bar top, Thedwin's bored expression at hearing this same outburst again and again, reaching under the counter for the rag that was already there and waiting to be used.

Gwendolyn reached out and dipped her stick into the fire, turning it slowly so that the end blackened, then reddened under the heat. Right before it ignited, she pulled it back with the tip now smoldering and giving off a slight cedar scent. She continued sketching under the table as she always did when it got late and the only people left in the Parched Goat were the Rondure Dimmet cartel. This evening she was drawing a rose.

It just wasn't safe for a twelve-winter-old girl who was beginning to blossom into womanhood to wander around with those drunken mutts. Yet, there she was. Spirell wasn't a bad sort. He never leered at her like his thugs, the servitors. He never wanted… that. No. He eyed her in a calculating way, evaluating her worth to him, knowing that at some point he'd cash in.

Gwendolyn thought about it. She decided maybe that was worse than the servitors. At least she knew what *they* wanted. With the cartel boss, she couldn't be sure.

"What's got ye in this fine tizzy now, Ser?" she heard Thedwin ask. She knew he didn't care, he never cared about anything but his business. He hardly cared for her at all. She was just cheap labor, only requiring a moldy pallet to sleep upon and whatever scraps were left at the end of the night. But Thedwin would ask Spirell anyway. Hells, it was the only way he made any coin anymore on account of the Red Tears. The plague had driven everyone away. If she focused hard enough on her drawing she could even go nose blind to the burning bodies piled in the streets.

Fen-Thane was a doomed village, it was only a matter of time. Located a half day's walk from the Malten border and two days from the capitol of Halsbren, Fen-Thane was smack dab in the middle of nowhere and it was dying fast.

It was how the Rondure Dimmet took over the village without anyone blinking an eye. Soon there wouldn't be enough labor left living for the Rondure Dimmet to use for smuggling and they would abandon them to their fate and prey on the next weakening town until all Halsbren was drown in their own tears of blood.

"The end of the plague," Adjutor Spirell replied, only a little more morose. "The end."

"Ye expect us all to die soon then, eh?" Thedwin asked, and then finished with a "Ha!" laughing at his own bitter joke.

"No, you fool, a cure is coming," Spirell said angrily.

That got Gwendolyn's attention. She stopped scratching at the table and began to listen more intently.

"Aye, I'm supposed to believe that?" Thedwin said, thinking they were still bantering. "Defiler's got room in the hells for all of us sinners. Maker is the only one that can cure us and he sure as hells doesn't have his sights on us."

"Spriggans don't believe in the Maker and they survived just fine." Spirell pointed out.

Thedwin scoffed. "They're a race of rodents, the lot of them. T'was probably the carriers of the Tears, the filthy vermin."

Now it was Spirell's turn to laugh, Thedwin was rarely worked up about anything. "Tell us how you really feel about the littlefolk then?" Thedwin harrumphed, and Gwendolyn could just imagine him folding his thick, pasty arms over his pendulous abdomen.

She heard Spirell begin to whisper to Thedwin. Intent on learning all she could, Gwendolyn began to crawl out of her safe spot under the table as she strained to hear what the cartel boss was saying.

"…emissary is coming," she caught, followed by, "… my people intercepted a message for King Edgar's vizier himself. Said to look for the one with the rune-etched sword … the key to the cure."

Gwendolyn could see her master now, who was shaking his head in disbelief. "That's so vague. Everyone has swords, even fancy ones."

Spirell reached up and grabbed the back of Thedwin's thin hair to pull him closer. Gwendolyn had to move around the table completely to hear what he said next. "Then how's this? The emissary will arrive in five days' time–that's what the missive said. That was two days ago, and it's two days to Halsbren Proper from here. Where do you think they're heading to first?"

"Here?" Thedwin said, wide-eyed.

Gwendolyn could see the back of Spirell's head as he nodded. "And I expect you to be the most cordial of hosts to our spriggan emissary, regardless of your feelings for the race."

Thedwin nodded, and Spirell released the tight grip he had on the barkeep's head. Angry red flesh glowed from Thedwin's neck.

Spirell turned and made eye contact with Gwendolyn, who was too riveted to move. Did the spriggans really have a cure to the madness that had surrounded Gwendolyn for her entire life? It was all she could remember. It was how she lost her parents, her brother, everyone, and wound up less than a slave to Thedwin just waiting for when it was going to take her, too.

"I thought you were happy about the plague." Thedwin stammered. "Now you want the cure?"

Spirell's smile was devilish as he winked a knowing wink to Gwendolyn. He turned back to face the fat tavern keeper. "If I hold the sword, I hold the cure. If I hold the cure, then Halsbren belongs to the Rondure Dimmet." His smile grew wider. "It will belong to me."

II

Gwendolyn waited eagerly the next day, hoping earnestly to see this spriggan.

"Why a sword?" she heard Thedwin mumble periodically throughout the day. "Why not a scroll? Or a vial? Or like a case? I thought the important types always walked around with cases?"

Spirell, who had also lingered all day with his hung-over thugs, spat back, "Because every traveler has a sword for protection, even a spriggan. It's a sure-fire way to ensure it makes it to Halsbren Proper unnoticed. Who robs an already armed man just for the thing they're armed with? But a case of some kind would draw attention to them."

Thedwin only grunted in acquiescence.

The day drew into night, and the men began to pinch and prod at Gwendolyn as they always did. As usual she had to bat away their advances until either Thedwin or Spirell put a stop to it. This time though, instead of stopping them, Spirell remarked, "She is blossoming quite nicely."

Thedwin nodded. "Aye, been saving her for the right one."

"Really?" Spirell asked, and Gwendolyn still found herself listening to them as she swept the tavern floor.

"I figured since today was gonna be a day of big change, with you getting the sword and all, I'd go all out. Reached out to him first thing this morning." Thedwin's next words turned the blood in her veins to ice. "Comes tonight, he does."

Gwendolyn heard Spirell make a lude remark about Thedwin's appropriate 'word' choice, and the two began laughing together. They were laughing, and Gwendolyn felt hollow. She knew Thedwin was going to barter her virginity off one day. She just thought that she would be older, more... prepared.

Gwendolyn took a step away from the two men so they

couldn't see her eyes begin to water. Initially she was excited for the day, because it meant that she would see the spriggan who was going to save them all. Now she was terrified of what the night would bring.

It came all too quickly.

As dusk fell, so too did the overwhelming feeling of doom. Servitors laughed and jeered at her, as if they knew what was in store for her. Perhaps they knew that after her virtue was sullied, Thedwin wouldn't hold them back any longer. She'd be fair game. Gwendolyn's stomach tightened in revulsion at the thought. Unable to contain her fears she rushed to the privy outside and promptly vomited into the rank hole.

She just wanted to stay in there, to hide, but Gwendolyn knew she could not. Thedwin would find her. She even briefly thought about sticking her hands deep into the privy and covering herself in the waste of others, just so she would be too foul to touch... but she knew all he would do then is bathe and perfume her, and she might very well give herself the Red Tears for her troubles.

Fitting really. The plague wouldn't even have the good decency to kill her off first. Gwendolyn sighed and gathered her courage, fighting against the tears that threatened to spill out. It had to happen at some point. She always knew it would, Thedwin didn't keep her around all this time just to sweep.

She took a deep breath and turned back to the Parched Goat. She would meet the new obstacle, head held high. As she walked back into the tavern through the double doors, thunder peeled across the sky behind her in ominous warning.

IT WAS LATE when her fate arrived. The tavern was full. Fuller than it had been in months. Perhaps word spread through the Rondure Dimmet that their fortunes were changing. It was like everyone in town–hells, all the humans within a few miles–were packed within the Parched Goat, waiting out the dreadful storm that swept in.

Gwendolyn noted a stranger with a large bulldog and an unusually shaped staff, thicker in the middle and tapered at the ends, with strange metal bands that encased those ends. The sight of it, and the woman who held it, gave her pause. The woman was in her mid-winters, perhaps early thirties, but life clearly had been hard on the battered woman. Rigid scars, thick and ropey, lined the right side of her face. They jutted from the bandana she wore at her temple just right of her grey eye and traveled all the way down over her cheek to the strong ridge of her jawline. She sat at the bar drinking whatever swill it was Thedwin was offering tonight. It was little surprise that none of the men approached her. There was a coldness about her, and because of her deformity, many would call her–ugly. The bulldog, a white and brown bundle of muscles and fur, lay contentedly at the base of her stool, his golden eyes watching.

Spirell sat next to the stranger, sharing in her silence. Gwendolyn could see the crime boss growing more and more dissatisfied as the night lumbered on. The spriggan had yet to be reported. "Blasted rain," Spirell grumped.

Gwendolyn thought too that maybe, just maybe the hard rains outside might delay her "evening" as well. But when the doors opened, and Gwendolyn watched Thedwin's crooked mouth twist into a wide smile, she knew that the time had finally come.

She felt her insides plummet as she turned to face the doors. A thick, muscular man with dark skin entered, a smile, equally as vicious as Thedwin's, growing on his ruggedly handsome, clean-shaven face. He was perhaps as old as the woman at the bar, give or take a few winters. Grey had begun to tug at the temples of his black curly hair, and lines of age were beginning to crease his face. His eyes glittered at her like onyx chips.

Four equally large, dark-skinned men, all much younger, entered behind the broad man.

"Maltenese?" Spirell said next to her, surprised. "But the blockade? He would risk plague and exile for a piece?"

"Not just any Maltenese," Thedwin retorted, and Gwendolyn could tell he was happy that he surprised the cartel leader. "That's Deprin Nix."

III

"DEPRIN NIX." The words sounded like spit coming from Spirell. "You can't be serious."

The Maltenese were still far enough away that Gwendolyn knew Spirell couldn't be heard through the din of the unusually active tavern.

Thedwin shrugged. "The pay's worth it. It'll pay off the cost she imposed on me this last decade, and the next few winters to come!"

Spirell snorted, "She's cost you nothing, you cheap lout. Deprin takes pleasure in hurting girls… in breaking them."

"He pays well enough," Thedwin said, as if closing the matter.

Spirell looked at Gwendolyn, but there was no pity in his eyes for her, only a calculation, an assessment of her worth. It had lowered. "Shame," was all he said as he turned back towards his drink and away from the approaching men.

Gwendolyn stood frozen as Deprin approached her. She knew she should run. She should bolt away like a terrified hare and go somewhere, anywhere, away from the man. But where could she go? She had no where.

"This is her, I assume," a deep resonant voice rolled from Deprin's full lips.

"'Tis," Thedwin replied.

"She is… exquisite. Like a moonblossom on the verge of expanding its beautiful petals for the first time," he said soothingly. Seductively. "I will take the greatest of pleasure in helping you…" He paused, his eyes searching her, making her feel filthy. "Bloom."

Deprin tossed a heavy satchel of coin at Thedwin, his eyes never leaving hers. Her whole body shook with terror. With revulsion. She did not want this. She did not.

Distantly she heard the clamor of the coins as Thedwin missed his catch and they scattered to the ground behind the bar. "Enjoy yourselves, my friends," Deprin said to his comrades. "This is sure to take me a very long time."

Gwendolyn could only watch as his large hand came up to caress her face. Long dark fingers with thick knuckles and tapered nails reached up to feel her skin, and his touch was coarse, like ragged stone. He brushed a tear from her cheek as they began to silently tumble from her eyes. "This will be magical for us, love," he said quietly.

His other hand came up and cupped her face. He pulled her to him, bending low. She could see his thick lips puckering up. She bit back the revulsion as he bore down on her. His breath, stinking of spoiled wine and cinnamon, was hot on her face. She closed her eyes and tensed under the assault.

Instead of feeling the roughness of his face upon her,

instead of the wetness of his lips against hers, she felt him suddenly still. Gwendolyn dared to look. Her gaze was met not with Deprin's eyes, but that of his chin thrust out and high. Her eyes trailed down and she could see the long, polished shaft of white wood barring his way.

"The young woman objects."

Gwendolyn blinked in surprise at the voice. It was distinctly feminine, but there was something about it, a richness, deep and full of timbre, like silk sliding over her skin. She followed her gaze down the length of the staff to the source of the voice–the scarred stranger.

She held the staff up with her left arm. The sleeve had fallen back, and Gwendolyn could see strong, sinewy muscle beneath an intertwining web of reds and greens. It was a tattoo.

It was *THE* tattoo, Gwendolyn realized.

The stranger bore the stigma of the "tainted." The mark of the Jasian Enclave, an interconnecting weave of two colors that looked much like a thorny entanglement, or in this case a web. The red symbolized her impurity and also stood for blood, while green marked her as a disease, symbolizing putrescence. The religious powerhouse that was the Jasian Enclave was felt everywhere, especially in the battered little town of Fen-Thane.

The Jasian Enclave believed that women could only bear intimacy with a man if–and only if–they were wedded together. Should she bear a child without first being wed, then she was cast as an exile and her flesh etched with a permanent stigma. The Enclave felt that the archetype she represented, that of giving herself to a man out of wedlock, was somehow a contagion and could be communicated to others, much like the plague ravaging them. Therefore, under the laws of the Enclave, she was to keep that arm always exposed so all could see that she was impure, "tainted."

The significance of that tattoo was lost on no one.

"Whore," Deprin barked as the stranger guided him away from Gwendolyn by the throat.

She stood gracefully and kept backing him up until they were a good distance from the bar. Gwendolyn watched as Spirell turned around and eyed the display casually, his drink still in hand.

The other Maltenese stopped what they were doing and began to encircle the cloaked woman, who seemed almost diminutive compared to their massive bulk. "No different than what you seek to make her," the stranger pointed out.

She guided him to the center of the tavern until only the silver metal tip was underneath Deprin's chin. The other four men around her began to draw blades.

Thedwin opened his mouth to object, but Gwendolyn watched Spirell raise his hand, silencing the barkeep. Clearly the adjutor wanted to watch it all play out.

"What makes you think you can deny me what I purchased?" the Maltenese hissed.

"No one should ever be bartered like a commodity. Not child, not man or woman, and not race," she added.

"Well that's going to put him in a tizzy," Spirell whispered to Gwendolyn. "Maltenese barter in slave labor, particularly gnomes."

Spirell was correct. Deprin exploded into a monologue of racial superiority and supremacy over women. He tore into the stranger for her sinful debaucheries and to Gwendolyn's surprise, the stranger let the whole degradation of her character play out, all while the men with swords closed around her like a snake coiling around its prey.

"I'm going to bleed you, whore, just because I can,

because it is my *right* as a man," Deprin finished. "I'd offer to give you one last ride, but I don't want to soil myself."

Gwendolyn's eyes snapped from the stranger to Deprin as he slapped the staff out of the way and moved in for the kill. He reached for the long dagger sheathed at his hip, but the stranger was fast. With a lunge, the ball end of her staff smashed into Deprin's hand, disarming him. He howled in rage, and then chaos erupted all around her.

The stranger, being smaller than the men around her, wasn't still like Gwendolyn might have thought with such a long staff. She was a blur. She moved laterally, forcing the fighters to gather to the center and pivot to keep her in sight.

"Oh, that's smart," Spirell remarked as he pointed for Gwendolyn. "Look at their feet. When weight is transferred to their lead foot like that they can't transfer their weight into their blows. She's rendered their size useless to them. And as for their range, well… she has the staff, the perfect outfighter."

Though she was untrained, Gwendolyn saw that Spirell's knowledge of fighting was spot on. The stranger kept moving on the men, making all their constant turning cumbersome. At some point the stranger managed to circle around one of the men to a blind angle and then she lunged directly at him, scoring a forceful blow to the back of his head. He crumpled to the filthy wooden floor.

"It's a dangerous game she plays," Spirell added in commentary, "she uses lunges to increase the power of her blows while denying them power in theirs, but…" He looked at her with a twinkle in his eyes. "They still got swords. It only takes one good hit, no strength needed, on her throat, inner thigh, belly, then she's done for. Swords are like venomous snakes—they just need one good bite."

She continued to jog and pivot, and often followed in the

direction her prey was moving, overlapping the men upon one and other. It was a game of reactions and attrition. She was faster than them and never minded giving up ground. She baited them, drawing strikes out of them, and evading.

Deprin picked up his long dagger and lunged at her, his teeth bared like a wild animal. She parried and dodged away, still moving.

"Won't be long now," Spirell said, and Gwendolyn wondered if the comment was meant for the stranger, or perhaps for her own fate when Deprin had won the brawl. But then, she saw what Spirell meant. Those men were built to overpower and dominate quickly. They weren't built for prolonged battles. Soon enough they began to slow down, becoming unfocused, less keen to take the stranger on. Two men eventually gambled and lashed out at her, and she caught both of them behind the head in a double tap strike, dumping them to the floor with their comrade. With three down, only Deprin and one ally remained. They were labored and bruised from her ripostes, and yet the stranger looked barely winded, though Gwendolyn saw her face covered in a sheen of clammy sweat.

Another circle, another lunge, another thug downed.

Finally, it was just Deprin and the stranger.

"Coward!" Deprin yelled at her. "Fight me face to face like a man!"

Gwendolyn saw the woman smile at the corner of her mouth. "You've made it very clear already. I am no man."

Deprin roared and struck at her like a mamba. The stranger gracefully pivoted away in a spin, bringing the metal end of her staff around and driving it into Deprin's kidney. He cried out, dropping to his knees, but the stranger offered no mercy. She slammed the staff in quick succession into his back, thighs, buttocks, and neck until she drove him completely to the ground. And without so much as a victory flourish, she thrust the staff down upon the base of his skull. Deprin fell very, very still at her feet.

The stranger looked up and whistled. Completely forgotten, the bulldog hopped to his feet and trotted beside her. She turned to walk for the door.

All around her, Rondure Dimmet began to shift and stand up, drawing cudgels and other instruments of violence from sheaths and hooks at their belts.

Spirell, however, was clapping. "Marvelous milady. Simply marvelous."

The stranger regarded him with the turn of her head, and by proxy of standing next to him, Gwendolyn as well. The look there in the stranger's grey eyes was... confusing. It seemed like... longing. Gwendolyn saw Spirell nod to his servitors, and the men sheathed their weapons and went back to waiting for the spriggan. He held his hand out towards the bar. "Please, milady, do me the courtesy of letting me buy you a drink."

The stranger looked down at the bulldog who merely opened its mouth and panted in a happy gesture, the stubby tail wagging at her. She sighed and walked back to the bar.

"Most excellent," he said with a laugh. "Thedwin, another of whatever Miss...?"

The stranger looked up at him from under the strange headband that held her black hair back. "Locke. Lydia Locke."

"Yes, another for Miss Locke and myself please!" Spirell called jovially.

Thedwin spit on the floor. "She just cost me dearly, and now you want me to pour her a drink?" he told Spirell outraged.

"Yes, and you'll give her a room for this evening, too, if

she wants it," Spirell said flatly, leaving no room for argument.

Thedwin grumbled as he eyed both Spirell and Lydia maliciously. He fixed their drinks and gave Lydia a key, which she slid under the folds of her cloak. Spirell engaged her in small talk about fighting, and Gwendolyn saw it as an opportunity to finally slip away. She was no stranger to violence, and especially not death, but this was the first time she was the focus of it.

Carefully, she tried to retreat from the main chamber when Thedwin yelled, "Ye ain't going nowhere yet, Gwen!"

Gwendolyn froze and slowly pivoted back around. Thedwin continued, "I've got a contract to honor with Nix. It's yer job to care for him," Thedwin glowered at Locke, "especially when he wakes up."

Gwendolyn watched as Lydia Locke tightened at those words. She turned away from Spirell's gesticulating and whispered something to Thedwin. Gwendolyn couldn't hear a word as far away as she was, but the bulbous man seemed aghast, he shook his head no, and said something that must have been none too pleasant.

She watched as Lydia slid her hand into the folds of her cloak again and produced a coin purse. She dumped the contents on the table and Thedwin's eyes bulged. As he nodded dumbly, Spirell began to laugh.

Lydia Locke stood up and walked towards Gwendolyn, those grey eyes full of determination. Behind her, the bulldog followed in tow. When she reached Gwendolyn the scarred woman simply said, "Follow me." She turned and walked out the doors.

Gwendolyn looked back towards the tavern and an angry Thedwin giving her a shooing motion with his hands. But it was Spirell's eyes that now chilled her. His evaluation of her had clearly gone up. She was more valuable in those cold eyes then Gwendolyn had ever seen in the past. Warily, Gwendolyn turned and followed the stranger, Lydia Locke.

IV

"FETCH WATER TO FILL THE TUB," Lydia Locke commanded of a confused Gwendolyn.

Gwendolyn gave a small curtsy. "Y-yes milady," she stammered as she took hold of the water bucket to fill the tub.

She made multiple trips back and forth to the well, through the soaking rain, and she noted that each time she returned, Lydia was wearing less and less. When she came back with a bucket full of water for the last time, she was drenched to her very bones, and the stranger was wearing little more than a light robe draped over her smallclothes, and the low-sitting headband that held her hair back.

Gwendolyn tried not to stare at the woman as she sprinkled strange pebbles into the water, but it was difficult. Lydia was corded with muscle, and much like her face, her copper-toned body was emblazoned with stark white scars.

Gwendolyn's eyes drifted upward and saw Lydia watching her. Her face flushed as she looked away. "I'm sorry."

"Don't be," the woman answered her. "Each adornment on my body is a lesson. I am not ashamed of them."

Gwendolyn turned to face the woman old enough to be her mother. "You're not?"

Lydia shook her head no. "Everything I am is written upon my body. Each battle," she said as she traced the scars on her ribs. "Each contest of my life has left its mark upon me. Some visible, others not so much."

Gwendolyn noted that aside from scars, the woman also had the visible signs of child-bearing on her stomach and hips. Gwendolyn knew she was staring once again, and Lydia added, "I was a mother, once." She reverently rested her hand over the stretch marks on her belly.

"And the tattoo?" Gwendolyn asked.

Lydia looked at Gwendolyn with no remorse in her eyes. "Marked by ignorance and hypocrisy. I was in need back then. I suffered and was ignored. I regret my choice, but I do not regret what followed." Gwendolyn was surprised to see Lydia's storm-grey eyes watery with emotion. "The bath is ready. Get in."

Gwendolyn's eyes went wide. "Me?"

Lydia nodded. "There are plenty of bubbles, I will see nothing, I promise."

Gwendolyn looked down at the water and to her surprise, it was full of pink bubbles. She gasped, "How is this possible?"

"The littlefolk are great alchemists. Crafters from automatons to tinctures. I have met a few in my time. Now in the water you go," Lydia ordered, and she turned around.

Gwendolyn stripped off her wet clothes, leery that a stranger asked her to get in the bath, but knowing her options at this point were to either do as Lydia–the woman who defended her virtue–asked of her, or return to the tavern and serve the needs of Deprin for the evening, she did as she was bade, shuddering at the thought.

Gwendolyn slid one foot into the water and was delighted to feel the bubbles tickling her skin. She relished in the feel of her own bathwater. Normally she was forced to use the old bathwater of others because Thedwin didn't want her wasting his resources.

When she was covered to her neck in the water, she felt the presence of Lydia behind her, just outside the tub. Gwendolyn started when Lydia reached out with a brush and began to gently work the knots out of her hair. She was surprised at the soft and gentle nature of the woman who had just thoroughly beaten five men. "Why are you doing this?"

"Because it is unfair, what they ask of you," Lydia responded. "Tonight, you are a child. Tomorrow… I cannot say what tomorrow will bring you, my dear."

Lydia began to hum to her then as she wet the brush in the water to loosen the tighter kinks out of Gwendolyn's hair. Gwendolyn closed her eyes, leaning back, and she breathed in the fragrant oils coming from the bubbling waters. She felt cleansed inside and out, refreshed by the scents. She had never known a bath could do anything other than remove dirt.

In time she opened her eyes and looked to her side. There she saw the bulldog resting peacefully next to a brass-hilted sword decorated in an array of crisscrossing scratches. "What is his name?"

"Crux," the woman answered her.

"Crux," Gwendolyn repeated. "It's a funny name."

"Yes," Lydia agreed. "It kind of is."

At the use of his name, Crux looked up and wagged his little stub tail. Gwendolyn laughed, and after a moment he put his head back down and rested a paw over the sword. Gwendolyn took note of it. "Why didn't you use your sword in the fight?"

"I was never trained to use a sword," Lydia answered. "Where I came from, women aren't allowed to wield swords."

"Really?"

Gwendolyn felt Lydia nod. "My father was a Purist, a kind of warrior priest. I am from a small town in Gurgen called Sentinel's Barrow. Since I wasn't allowed to use a sword, he trained me how to use the staff to defend myself."

"You had a good dad," Gwendolyn said with a smile. "I was only a baby when my pa died. Red Tears."

"I did have a good father," Lydia agreed. "Like you, I lost my father young. He was killed in action when I was not much older than you. My mother, she took his death very hard, as did I. She became addicted to haze to deal with the pain of loss."

Gwendolyn knew what haze was. It was a smoking drug and many of the Rondure Dimmet took part in the vile stuff. Hells, they *made* it, and sold it at a tidy profit.

"I dealt with the pain a different way, yet no less destructive," Locke murmured. "In the absence of my father, I sought to fill the void of a strong man in my life. I made very stupid decisions with them in a desire to feel wanted, loved, but that sense of closeness was never the same. It was only a matter of time before one man impregnated me. He left me alone with a child, and a mark on my arm for it." Gwendolyn stared ahead at the wall, imagining what Lydia Locke's life must've been like. Locke's voice grew distant. "My mother overdosed on haze a month before her grandchild was even born."

"What happened?" Gwendolyn asked.

She heard Locke take a deep breath, "I had committed a crime according to the Jasian Enclave. With Mother gone, the estate was seized by the church. I was alone and homeless with an infant child, my only treasure being my father's bō staff. I sought solace for my child and I with the Order of the Sacred Fist, a monastery north of here, well past the Wilds. It was a long trek for an infant child, but I saw no other way before me. Unfortunately, the Red Tears had just broken out along the main trade roads. My daughter… was one of the first casualties of the plague." Gwendolyn turned to look at the woman, at her grey gaze lost in memory. "I think a large part of me died that day, in my arms," she said in a whisper, mainly for herself.

When Locke turned back to look at Gwendolyn, the girl could see the woman's cheeks were wet. "Though I was only a mother for less than a single winter, it was one of the most important, most cherished, winters of my life." She cleared her throat. "Turn back around, I'm almost done."

Gwendolyn turned, and Locke resumed brushing her hair. "You said that your daughter was only a baby at the start of the Red Tears?"

"Yes," Locke answered. "If she were alive today, she'd be your age." Gwendolyn felt Locke pull the brush away. "I think she'd look a lot like you, actually."

"Is that why you helped me back there?" Gwendolyn asked. "Because I remind you of her?"

"Hmm?" Locke replied, before realizing the question and shaking her head. "No, of course not. I helped because it was necessary, and because what they wanted to do was abhorrent. No child should ever be forced to go through what that monster wanted to put you through. If I could stop it, even for a single day, then I had to try."

"But why?" Gwendolyn asked. "Why risk it for me? Clearly you're someone important. I'm just… nothing."

Gwendolyn felt her chin lifted by Locke's gentle hand. She was forced to look deep into the warrior's grey eyes. "You are not nothing. You are someone. Someone special. Never let these people ever tell you otherwise."

She nodded to the tattoo woven across her flesh, that tapestry of sin in the eyes of the Jasian Enclave. "This says that I am nothing to some people, but I know deep within myself who I am, what I am, and who I will become. I refuse to be called nothing. I am someone. I am not someone you would call important. Sure, I think it would be nice to be important. But I think it's more important to be nice. Lives are too short and too ill spent to be wasted on the frivolity of titles and ranks. If we do not live for one another, what is the point of living at all?"

Gwendolyn tried to absorb those words as Locke helped her from the water and wrapped a towel around her. "I have some spare clothes that you can have. They might be a little large for you, but where I'm going I won't need them." Locke smiled a sad smile to Gwendolyn. "Tonight I want you to sleep on the bed. I will take the floor."

"But…" Gwendolyn objected.

Locke gently stroked Gwendolyn's brushed hair. "Crux will keep me warm. He's been doing that a lot lately."

Again, Gwendolyn saw the muscular dog wag his stumpy tail.

Locke took a heavy blanket and pulled it next to the bull-dog. She gently placed her hand against the sword. Strangely, Gwendolyn watched as Crux did the same with his paw.

Gwendolyn climbed up on the bed. It would be the first time she slept in a bed. As she lay there, she began to silently weep. Not because she was sad, but because it was the best night of her entire life.

V

"UNBELIEVABLE!" Spirell harrumphed as he lay against the

bar top stirring his drink with his finger. "Nothing. Not a damn thing, not a single spriggan found on the trade road."

Beneath the table Gwendolyn sat merrily, humming the same tune that Lydia Locke hummed the evening before. Her burned stick was a blur as she concentrated hard on her latest masterpiece.

Locke and Crux had left sometime before Gwendolyn awoke, and Thedwin hollered at her for sleeping upon the bed. He ranted that he was going to have to burn the bedding now just to get her filth off it. She didn't care. She was happy, Locke had given her a new outlook on life, and she wasn't going to let Thedwin bring it down.

Even better, Deprin Nix apparently left sometime in the morning as well. Apparently, Locke had had a "talk" with him before she left. He wanted nothing to do with Gwendolyn now. She hummed along, mostly oblivious to Spirell's mopping.

"Maybe tonight, we'll see the spriggan," Thedwin mused.

"Didn't you just hear me, idiot? No spriggans were found on the trade road. That means no emissary tonight either. Someone else must've either beat me to them, or they are already in Halsbren Proper, which means the king will have the cure!" In anger, Spirell backhanded the drink off the bar, and glass smashed against the wall.

Normally, Gwendolyn would rush to clean it up, but not today. She needed to get this done. She held the stick in the fire, turning the tip cherry red and biting on the edge of her tongue, she concentrated. She had to draw it exactly right. There were no second chances.

"Gwen, clean that up," Thedwin ordered.

"Uh-huh." She was almost done with that last line, and...

"Clean that up now, you useless waif!" Thedwin growled.

She grunted. The glass could wait. Spirell and two of his

servitors were the only ones in here, and it wasn't like someone was going to get cut on that broken glass.

"What are you doing?" Spirell demanded, right next to her ear. Gwendolyn nearly jumped out of her skin. "And what were you humming? It sounded like an Enclave hymn."

"N...nothing," Gwendolyn stammered. "I'll clean up that drink." She scurried to get away from him.

She quickly grabbed her broom and began to sweep up the glass, watching from the corner of her eye as Spirell sat on the floor and continued examining her work. "Thedwin, have you ever seen this?" He asked with a chuckle. "She really is quite good–hold up, what's this?"

She swept the glass briskly into a pile, when Spirell stood up quickly and over turned the table, she jumped with a start and her heart raced in her chest. "What is this?" he demanded, pointing at the sketch she had most recently worked on.

He stormed over to her, grabbed her by the arm, hard, and yanked her back to the table. "What is this?"

Gwendolyn couldn't look into his angry eyes. "Just... just a sketch, milord. That's all."

Spirell traced his finger along the lines Gwendolyn had drawn, long straight lines that came together in a point. "That's not just a sketch. Where did you see this? Where did you see this sword?"

Thedwin was coming around the bar now. Gwendolyn looked to him for help, but Spirell's grip on her was like iron. "I... I don't remember." She mumbled. "Maybe one of the men last night?"

"No." His voice was dark, deep with hostile intent. "This design–it's made by the littlefolk." He traced the hilt and cross guard.

"Looks like a plain sword to me. Ye sure it wasn't the dagger Deprin Nix was using?" Thedwin asked.

"I know my weapons, I'm a smuggler, you moronic twit," Spirell spat. "These marks on the hilt. They're spriggish."

"Spriggish?" Gwendolyn said, now equally surprised.

Adjutor Spirell nodded, his eyes blazing with intensity. "Now I ask again, where did you see this sword?"

"I... I..." But the words wouldn't come out. She knew where she had seen the blade of course, but the marks were spriggish? Then she understood. She looked to Spirell just as he pieced it together as well.

"By the Defiler's teats." He looked up at Thedwin. "Ready my horses and get me some rope, you fat swine. I know who the emissary of the spriggans is."

VI

THE ROPE BURNED Gwendolyn's skin as the horse jostled her roughly around. She twisted and writhed but it only seemed to make the binding tighter. Her mouth was gagged in a filthy bar rag soaked in whatever swill Thedwin had cleaned up that morning. The alcohol and the up and down motion made her light-headed...

They caught up with their quarry at sundown. She had just made a small camp for herself, and she was sitting, resting against a boulder, the hood of her cloak pulled over her head.

Gwendolyn looked around. They were in the highlands. On the horizon, in the dying light she could see the outline of a castle, high up on a large hill. A day away, at least.

Her eyes fell upon the woman sitting against the stone. She was tired, and weary, her strength seemingly sapped from the exertion of travel. She seemed little like the warrior in the tavern the night before, or the mother in the inn. Now, she appeared more like a lonely pauper. And yet, she didn't seem to be the slightest bit surprised at their arrival.

Spirell hopped off his horse with practiced ease. He reached over and plucked Gwendolyn off like she weighed no more than a sack of potatoes. As she struggled to stay upright while bound, she looked up, hopeful to the woman who had stood up for her just one night before.

Locke forced herself to her feet with the aid of the staff. Crux stood beside her, squatting low to the ground, his lips pulled back into a snarl revealing long, sharp teeth. His golden eyes sparkled as he growled.

"Well hello, Lady Locke," Spirell said jovially. "You seem a little worse for the wear. Did you not sleep well last night?"

"Why is Gwendolyn bound?" Locke demanded.

Spirell held his head high. "Ah yes, that. Tis only a small formality. I'll happily unbind her and give her over to you for a small fee. An amicable exchange if you'd like?"

Though the hood obscured most of her face, Gwendolyn could see her narrowing her eyes. She began to pace towards them.

"I want the sword of the spriggans, emissary," Spirell said. Locke froze. The cartel leader laughed heartily. "They really are to be commended. We were looking for a spriggan, this emissary. Who do they send? A human, from Gurgen no less! Clever people to get someone who can blend in with the yokels."

"I'm here to help your people," Locke told him.

"I know. I read the missive. You carry the cure to the Red

Tears. I. Want. That. Sword," Spirell demanded. And to punctuate his desire he drew a dagger and held it to Gwendolyn's throat. She shook in fear.

"The cure will save thousands. What could you possibly do with the sword?"

"Become rich off it of course," Spirell said as if it were obvious. "There is a vacuum of law in this land because of the plague. The Rondure Dimmet has thrived. I have thrived. If an end is to come of it, then it might as well be with a grand flourish! There is nothing the king would not pay for the cure. No amount is too small if it means his life! Why, this plague is the greatest thing that's ever happened to this backwater nation!"

Locke shook her head. "I doubt those infected would agree."

"True," Spirell acquiesced. "But I doubt their voice really matters at this moment, does it?"

Gwendolyn watched as Spirell's men began to flank around Locke and Crux. As they did, the little dog twisted and barked, growling at those who came too close. They moved in a tight circle, covering one another to guard against the beast.

"Come, come Locke, it does not need to be like this," Spirell remarked as Lydia hefted her staff and stood in a combat stance. "I like you. Like what you did to Deprin Nix. You just got caught up on the wrong side of this whole thing. Just give up the sword. There's no reason anyone has to get hurt. I mean, would you really sacrifice this girl, who you worked so hard at saving last night?"

The warrior woman paused in step for a fraction of a second. Gwendolyn shook her head no. She could feel the blade warm at her neck. Her own movements against the weapon made her throat feel wet, from sweat or blood, she didn't know.

Locke reached under her cloak and from behind her back she drew the spriggan's sword. It looked remarkably small in her hands. Gwendolyn could clearly see the crisscross patterns etched across the hilt and down the steel blade.

Spirell sighed in exaltation. "Toss it here, Locke, and I'll release the girl."

Locke didn't move, and Spirell sighed again, this time in exasperation. He drew the knife tighter, making Gwendolyn yelp as she felt the blade bite her skin. Hot warmth ran down her neck, leaking out a trail of her lifeblood.

"That was a mistake," Locke said in a low voice.

Spirell grinned. "Why, are you going to kill me for it? Drop the sword and kick it here. I'm done with these games, woman."

"It was a mistake, because if you weren't infected already, you surely are now." In a swift motion, Locke threw the sword to Spirell's feet and reached up, pulling back her hood. Her hair tumbled out to frame her face as she ripped off the bandana that had previously held it back.

"By the Maker…" Spirell whispered.

The veins across Locke's head stood out black and engorged in the firelight. Gwendolyn could already see them beginning to split by her eye-brows. Locke's once grey eyes were full and red from burst capillaries, tears of blood beginning to ooze out of the corners by her crow's feet.

She was in the advanced stages of the Red Tears. The final stages.

"You… you've doomed your own people," Spirell stuttered. The blade pulled away from her neck and Gwendolyn fell forward. She stumbled and turned to look at the fear in Spirell's eyes. Her blood glistened on his hand where he held the knife, but a moment later, he pulled out a handkerchief to wipe the blade clear with shaking hands. When done, he tossed the rag into the fire.

Gwendolyn looked as the servitors began to back away from the three of them by the fire. Terrified, Spirell wrapped his cloak around his hand and picked up the blade. He wrapped it completely and then retreated to his horse.

Mounting the horse, he turned away, and then looked back to the both of them. "I'm sorry, Gwendolyn, I have no use for you now." He turned and galloped away, his servitors scrambling to mount up and follow their fleeing leader.

Within minutes, they disappeared from the horizon. Locke made a groan, and when Gwendolyn looked back, the woman had collapsed back on the ground in a sitting position once more, red tears flowing down her face.

Gwendolyn sat across from her, tears like diamonds glittering in the firelight on her face as well. "You are dying."

Locke nodded. "For some time now. I've lasted longer than most with the Red Tears." Crux came up to her, and she drew her long copper fingers through his white fur.

"Will I be infected now?"

Lydia Locke shook her head and smiled. "No."

"How come?" Gwendolyn questioned. "I spent the night in your room. You touched my hair." She grabbed her loose-fitting clothes in emphasis. "You gave me your clothes."

"I also gave you a bath," Locke said, and Gwendolyn could see more strength leave her with those simple words.

"Yes," Gwendolyn answered, and then she understood. "It was in the bubbles?"

Locke gave her a small nod. "Something like that." She then looked to Gwendolyn seriously. "You must finish what I started. The spriggans thought I could make it, but..."

"I don't understand. Why didn't you take the cure yourself?" Gwendolyn said through her tears. "Why did you give it to me?"

"When I saw you, when I saw your situation, I realized that I could do more with my last days then just deliver a cure. That I could do more than save lives. What good is saving a life if your will is crushed? I was offered the chance to save a little girl's very spirit. I was offered one last chance to be a mother, to do the things I've dreamed of doing for my own daughter for so long. I never had the chance to give her a bath, or to run a brush through her hair. To sing to her, and tell her that everything thing was going to be all right. I didn't save you, Gwendolyn. You saved me…"

"And now you're dying." Gwendolyn snapped at her. Her voice was thick with emotion, heavy with pain.

Again, she was rewarded with a weak smile. "I was already dying. Those baths have sustained me for weeks. That was my last dose. The one needed to carry me the two days it would take to reach Halsbren Proper. Truth is, when I approached the spriggans about the cure, I was already too far along. The blood in my brain was already too polluted by the Red Tears."

Gwendolyn could feel the water running down her face, she didn't even try and staunch the flow of her tears. "And so, what? You're just going to give up?"

At that, Locke managed a small laugh. It seemed so small, so pained. "I've wanted to give up so many times in my life. When my pa passed, I was ready to die. I loved that man so… But then I watched my mother give up. I watched how his death destroyed her, broke her very spirit. And then I felt the quickening in my own womb… I knew, for the sake of my unborn child, that I could not give up. Not then."

Locke's tears of red mingled with tears of love, creating sparkling rubies against her face. "Even when her life was cut short, and I felt my whole world crumble all around me, I could not lie down. As much as I wanted nothing more than to leave this world and join my family, it wasn't my time. Oh, how I wished it were so! For winters I lingered, living this half-life, and then I saw you... in the tavern, surrounded by unspeakable horrors, and I knew why I had kept fighting for as long as I have. So yes, I think I am finally ready for my last sunset." Locke stared at the sky as the rays grew from gold, to pink, and finally purple. "It has never looked more beautiful..."

"But Spirell took the sword. You need it to complete the mission? You are the emissary." Gwendolyn looked at her, pleading. "The whole nation is counting on you."

Locke's eyes fell to her canine companion and smiled once more. "And now that task must fall to you."

"Me? I can't fight like you. How can I hope to get the sword from Spirell in time?" Gwendolyn asked.

When no answer was forthcoming, she looked up to Locke in a panic. Her eyes were closed, the tears running down her face now black in the growing twilight. The warrior looked tranquil as she squeezed the scruff of Crux's neck weakly. Gwendolyn knew Lydia had found acceptance, some sense of serenity—of peace.

Gwendolyn took a deep breath and wiped the tears from her face. Locke saved her, in more ways than one. She would do this, for her. At least, she had to try. "Explain it to me. If you can..."

Locke opened her eyes. Once more her grey orbs sparkled with cunning. A smile crept along the corner of her mouth. Even in death, Lydia Locke had one last card to play.

VII

SPIRELL RODE hard to the Rondure Dimmet headquarters in Fen-Thane, the sword secure on his lap. He had it! He had the cure! And soon he would be rich beyond his wildest dreams!

He dismounted in a hop, not even waiting for his steed to stop its gait. He ran past his servitors as they saluted him and entered into the chamber where his most prized alchemists were hard at work making haze. He slapped the sword down in front of the gnome, startling the littlefolk.

"Quickly, you can read spriggish, yes?" Spirell demanded.

"Of course I can read it," the gnome fired back indignantly.

"Good. I need you to translate this composition and make the cure to the Red Tears. Quickly," Spirell said in haste as he unwrapped the sword.

He held out the etched blade for his gnome alchemist to study. The gnome nodded, mumbled a bit to himself, and then turned the weapon over. A confused expression dotted the gnome's oversized features. He flipped the weapon back over and studied the length of the blade.

"Well?" Spirell demanded.

"Well, what?" the gnome fired back. "There's no composition. It's a signature."

"Signature?" Spirell shook his head, "That's not right. Look at all of those markings, it's clearly something else."

"Have you ever seen a spriggan sign something?" the gnome said, holding up the sword. "I'm telling you that's all this is, their signature. A craftsman's autograph, trademark, whatever you want to call it. There are no formulae here, unless it is in the name Cavvius Keell, because that's what it says."

Sweat soaked Spirell's collar and his hands felt clammy. "No, no, no. That can't be right. The missive said the cure was the sword. It was the sword!" He slammed his hands on the table making the gnome jump. "Look! Look!" Spirell added. "I'll show you!"

Spirell rummaged through his pockets until he found the folded missive. He pointed to the line and showed it to the gnome, "There, eh! See?"

The gnome looked down and read the line out loud, "Look for the one with the rune-etched sword. It is the key to the cure."

As the gnome recited the words to Spirell, he nodded at their recognition, but then he froze, his eyes going wide. Look for the one *with* the rune-etched sword. *It* is the key to the cure.

"No," he mumbled. "No, no, no, no, no!" he roared. "It's not here!"

"Adjutor," the gnome said to him quietly.

Spirell spun on the diminutive man, fury in his eyes. In the gnome's hand was a small reflecting glass. Spirell was confused for a moment until he saw his reflection in the glass. A thick black vein was beginning to run down his temple towards his right eye.

Slowly, the gnome began to back away from him. "I'm sorry, adjutor."

Spirell collapsed to the floor, looking at his reflection in the glass, as one of the capillaries ruptured in his right eye. He began to laugh as a pink-hued tear rolled down his cheek.

GWENDOLYN WALKED INTO HALSBREN PROPER, staff

in hand, with Crux at her side. In her head, Locke's final words carried her forward.

"Before you were even born, the Red Tears gripped your nation. So many have died too it. Halsbren is a shadow of what it once was because of this plague. But it hasn't just affected us. It ravaged the spriggans too, demolishing the littlefolks numbers until their alchemists worked up a cure that saved their people."

Gwendolyn climbed up the long steps to the castle above. The guards barred her entry, but she held up a missive that Locke had given her, the woman's voice echoing in her head.

"The risk was too high for spriggans to send the cure into plague infected lands. No spriggan could hope to make it and survive, even with the bath, and the cure. Red Tears move too quickly through their system. Where it would kill a human in a week, sometimes more, it would kill a spriggan in a day. So, they came up with an alternate solution, a different means with which to transport their cure…"

She was escorted to a central chamber with plush red carpets and tapestries of the like and richness she had never seen before. A short, slightly plump older man dressed in black robes trimmed with gold approached her. He was clean-shaven, his short-cropped dark hair peppered with grey. Still, there was a kindness in his brown eyes. She held out the missive to him.

Lydia's tale never abated, continuing in her mind. "You see, spriggans are master effigists, creators of subservient automatons and constructs, and one of their most amazing inventions is the effigy, hence their title."

The man introduced himself as Vizier Aznor. He was the very one that Lydia Locke had been tasked to deliver the cure to.

"To my understanding, no other construct has the capability of looking as close to a real creature as a spriggan's effigy, though arguably, no one has a spriggan's knowledge or ability to build things like that either," Lydia had told her. "Rarer still are the Anamnesis. Within that effigy is a collection of knowledge, history, and lore from the greatest spriggan minds. An Anamnesis has its own capability to adapt and learn from its surroundings. It causes people to think that they are living, breathing beings."

Gwendolyn shared the knowledge she had learned from Lydia's final moments with the Vizier. He took it in stride, never once laughing or mocking her. And when she was done, he looked down into her companion's strange golden eyes.

"Good afternoon, Vizier," Crux the bulldog said in a clear, human-sounding voice. "We have a great deal of work to do."

Lydia Locke was not the emissary for the spriggans... she was the guide.

HOURS LATER, Gwendolyn sat on the parapet of the castle watching the sun set. She felt the man known as Vizier Aznor approach her from behind. Placing his hands on the stone ledge, he looked out at the dying day.

"I am to ask, what are your plans, young Gwendolyn? It seems you have an open road ahead of you."

Gwendolyn said nothing as she looked upon the horizon, her thumb gently caressing the smooth white wood of Locke's staff.

"You are a hero now," the Vizier continued, "You helped save a nation. I would think you could ask for anything if you wanted to."

"I want Lydia Locke to be remembered," Gwendolyn said at last.

"And nothing more? I'm sure the king would grant you riches beyond imagining. You are a very important person– you are a voice of the people."

Gwendolyn smiled as she thought of the last words Lydia Locke said to her before the woman closed her eyes forever. "It's nice to be important," she told the Vizier as she looked up at him, "but it's far more important to be nice."

Vizier Aznor smiled a warm smile and put his hand on her shoulder. "So, you desire nothing at all?"

Gwendolyn looked as the sun fell once more beneath the horizon another day gone. "I do have one request."

"Yes?"

She looked up into his dark eyes. "I'd like my name to be Gwendolyn Locke."

JAY ERICKSON

JAY ERICKSON grew up in the Midwest before joining the United States Air Force at the age of nineteen. An avid reader since childhood, he holds a deep love for all things fantasy and science fiction, and writing has always been his true passion.

In 2015, he took that passion further, joining the Halsbren Publishing team. His most recent full-length novels include *Pariah* and *Recreant,* part of the Blood Wizard Chronicles series, and he is also the author of several novellas including the *Stormwind* series. In 2017, Jay entered the gaming world with the release of *The Wild Tide*, a full adventure module, and has recently contributed short stories to several other anthologies, including *Missing Pieces VII* and *VIII* published by Old School Publishing.

Jay currently resides in Northwest Indiana with his wife, two children, and his old English "bulldogge." To read more about him and his work, please visit http://www.authorjayerickson.com.

RANSOM FOR A PRINCE

LIAM HOGAN

THE BATTLE WAS OVER.

I hung my head and stared at the mud, concentrating on the tang of sweat, the echoes of blood and metal. *This* was what defeat tasted like. A taste I would not forget.

At least there was a silver lining; my liege, Prince Douglas, was alive. Captured, injured, but alive. Like me he had been shorn of his sword and his helm; at least he had not been forced to kneel in the dirt with the remnants of his Royal Guard.

The ground rumbled as a half-dozen battle horses approached the riverbank. There was a rattle of armor as the men-at-arms who stood watch over us drew to attention. Glancing up I saw a black boar silhouetted against the grey clouds: the pennant of King Ulfred, the day's victor.

This too I would remember.

"So, the reports are true," a voice boomed from the saddle. "You have captured the Prince."

He did not sound pleased.

Douglas struggled to his feet, one arm held stiffly. He had taken a fall and was lucky to be merely bruised. We'd been making our retreat, the tide of the battle all too clear. But that avenue had been cut off when the Prince's mount stumbled in the treacherous mud. Even then, we might have made it across the river to safety, had a motley gang of Ulfred's mercenaries not chanced across us and had they not been armed with heavy crossbows. We'd had little choice but to surrender.

"King Ulfred," Douglas acknowledged.

"Douglas." The reply was curt as Ulfred scanned his men. "Who is in charge here?" he demanded.

A stocky man stood forward. "I, Sire." He looked ill at ease, reluctant to be thrust into King's Ulfred's imperious gaze.

"Your report, Blaxley?"

"Ah... we came upon Prince Douglas and his Guard by the ford yonder, your Majesty. The Prince was unmounted, his horse lame. Two of his men were attempting to get him onto one of the other horses. The third was guarding their position and would not yield until we promised the Prince fair surrender."

Blaxley paused and licked his lips, looking to his men for support. None of them cared to meet his glance. "Um... given the Prince might be mounted and across the ford at any moment, Sire, we, ah, we accepted."

"Did you indeed? How many of you are there in your squad, Blaxley?"

"Twelve, Sire."

"Twelve? A full dozen? Not a single casualty on this glorious day? Almost as if you and your men had been loitering on the fringes of the action, eh, Blaxley?"

There was a moment's silence as the unfortunate Blaxley bowed his head before Ulfred continued: "And which of this trio of guards stood off twelve brave men, armed as they were with such fine crossbows?"

"The Lady, Sire," Blaxley gestured towards me.

"The Lady!" Ulfred snorted.

"We did not know she was-"

But the King snapped up his hand, commanding the man to silence. He nodded to the rest of his knights and as one they dismounted. The King followed a moment later, handing over the reins of his black charger. He crossed and stood before me, peering down with curiosity.

"What is your name?" he demanded.

"Lady Estelle, your Majesty," I replied.

"I have not heard of a woman fighting, let alone a *Lady*," he said.

"Women have always fought, King Ulfred. The rarity is that I am trained to do so."

"Not just an idle amusement for your Prince, then?"

"Not an amusement, no."

He rubbed his fingers across a short beard flecked with grey. "Do you compete?"

"Compete, Sire?" I raised an eyebrow.

"In tourneys."

"No, Sire. I am a member of the Royal Guard. I find myself too busy to play at war."

"Play!" the King laughed. "You hear that, Sir Lyndon. She calls it 'play'."

"I hear," one of his Knights growled in reply.

King Ulfred waved a hand. "Sir Lyndon used to have a lovely baritone. But he can't sing so well, not anymore. Not since he 'played' at war. Show the good Lady your neck, Sir Lyndon."

The Knight levered off his helm, tilting his chin up and away from us. The scar was long and ugly, stretching from somewhere beneath his chainmail collar all the way to his chin. A miracle he had survived such an injury. As it was, the wound was livid, the skin rippled, one corner of his mouth tugged into a permanent sneer.

I shrugged. "I am not sure if you are arguing for or against me, Sire."

"Ha! You certainly have spirit. But what are we to do with you, Lady Estelle? You are not covered by the normal laws of chivalry, of ransom and safe conduct. I am not even sure if you should be considered a combatant, your ability with the sword untested."

"It was enough to dissuade your men-at-arms," I observed.

"Indeed. And yet a sword and a suit of armour, even one as tailored as yours, do not a combatant make. Blaxley!"

"Yes, Sire?"

"Which is her sword?"

The man-at-arms handed the King my blade.

"Hmm. Light. Barely two and a half pounds? Well balanced. Used, obviously, though not wildly. It has been re-edged at least once. Unadorned. A *practical* weapon."

"Would your sword pass a similar inspection, Sire?" I asked. I had already glimpsed his ornately engraved and gem-encrusted pommel.

His look darkened. "Have a care, Lady. If I draw to show you my blade I shall not be re-sheathing without first letting it taste blood." He stood a moment in thought. "While you are tall and long limbed for a Lady, you are far more slender than any of my Knights, or even those under Blaxley's incompetent command. I doubt you could hold your own against a single one of us, let alone a dozen."

I eyed him shrewdly. "If the Prince had fallen on the far side of the ford, Sire, the offer of surrender would not have been made. I trust I would have bought him enough time to make good his retreat."

"Well now," he drawled, a smile playing across his thin lips. "That's an interesting challenge. Perhaps we should put it to the test?"

I frowned, glancing towards my liege. "Douglas has already given his surrender."

"That he has. Which I shall reluctantly accept and demand appropriate ransom." He yawned theatrically. "Such a lengthy and tedious process. One which leaves his nation without its much loved heir to the throne while his father, King Harold, lies on what will surely be his death bed. A shame, I think, to have the Dukes and Barons squabble over the honor of paying the debt; all the while waiting for the inevitable changing of the guard and wondering what course of action truly benefits them most.

"Or... we can see if *Fortuna Belli* favors you as well as you suggest. The Prince and his two guards will cross the ford with their horses and we will then give chase, with only you to slow us down. Let us see just how long you can buy him."

"And if you catch up with him?" I asked.

"Then I guess he is recaptured. Especially as he and his guards will be departing without their weapons."

"King Ulfred!" Douglas took a step forward and was held firm by the men-at-arms. "I protest."

"Douglas," the King looked over his shoulder, watching as the Prince attempted to shrug the men off. "You are in no position to dictate terms."

"Sire," I shook my head. "Nor is it my position to decide this matter. Please, let me talk to my Prince."

Ulfred nodded and the men-at-arms clanked away. "You have five minutes."

Prince Douglas sat back on the wall with a haste that worried me. Just how bad had his fall been? Might he have cracked a rib? Would he be able to ride?

I glanced over to the King. As he stood with his Knights, chatting away, his eyes lingered on the Prince. Perhaps trying to find answer to the same questions I had.

"I do not trust him," I said, voice lowered.

"Nor should you. Plainly he wants me dead and was displeased I was captured alive."

"Dead? Surely he has won-"

"We may have lost this battle, Lady Estelle, but it was closer than perhaps it appears. With a lesser force we tied up his forces, exposed his frailties. Worse, we dared stand against him. Perhaps next time our allies will make good their promises. Whereas my death might discourage further attempts to limit his conquests."

"Then we cannot trust his bargain."

"Assuredly. And yet we can trust him no more if I am left in his poisonous grasp. Once out of sight, who knows what tragedy might befall me? This is my only chance to escape. Baron Grimaldi is not far from here, waiting on the news of the day. He may not have joined us on the battlefield, but I can count on him to shelter me while our forces regroup. I should be able to ride that far at least, if you can buy us enough time. But-"

"-But it is a suicide mission?" I pointed out.

Prince Douglas nodded, a pained expression in his weary eyes. "Even if you hold the ford treachery is the best reward you can expect."

"Then I will draw out the process and hope the entertainment of seeing a woman fight stays his hand for as long as possible."

He winced and clutched his chest. "I would not--could

not--ask for what you freely offer. You are the bravest of us. And perhaps if it was just my fate..."

He paused, chewing his lip. "While the King is engaged in this cruel sport, our scattered forces can make good their retreat, can retire in good order. The longer the game is played, the more his attention distracted from the mop-up, the stronger we may be when we ride out to meet him once again. I pray that will make your noble sacrifice all the more worthwhile."

I held out my hand and the Prince seized it, his grip shockingly weak. "I ask only that you make it count, Prince. Make him pay."

His grip tightened. "That I swear to do, Lady Estelle, and soon. Now though we must tread carefully. We must make this bargain a reluctant one."

"Meaning?"

"Meaning we must not appear too willing. We must use the strength of his position to make the terms as advantageous as possible. For both of us."

"Time's up," called out King Ulfred. "Well, Prince?"

"Let me do the talking," Douglas said, and I took up position a half-yard behind and to his side, his faithful servant.

"The Lady Estelle is willing to accept your terms."

King Ulfred grinned. "Good, good-"

"-but I am not."

"Oh?" the smile faded.

"They are not honorable. Would any of your Knights be willing to face even one man-at-arms with a loaded crossbow?"

"Lady Estelle did," Ulfred pointed out. "She faced down twelve."

"Not willingly. The Lady did it out of necessity, not

choice. And she was offering to lay down her weapons, not use them."

"Fine," the King waved a hand. "No crossbows. Satisfied?"

"We are agreed that she defends the far side of the ford, correct?"

"Yes... agreed."

"Against your twelve men-at-arms?"

"Yes, yes, can we get on?"

Douglas pulled a sour face. "It's just that there are more than a dozen of you now. If the Lady defeats twelve of your men, do you swear to allow her to go, unharried, and not to pursue her further?"

The King's eyes narrowed. "I swear. Now, mount up and be off with you!"

"One more thing. Your men will only attack one at a time?"

"You're becoming *tiresome*, Prince. Why on *earth* would they attack only one at a time? There are twelve of them. Be gone!"

It took both the Guards to help the Prince onto my horse, while I murmured softly in the mare's ear, unsure if I would see her again. Finally, all three were mounted. It broke my heart to receive their farewell salutes.

"Take good care," I entreated my comrades. "Of the Prince, and of my horse."

As the trio nosed towards the ford King Ulfred watched, expressionless. They were in the shallow water before he raised a mailed hand and called out: "Those conditions. One *minor* change."

It happened so quickly I thought our gambit had failed, that the King had been toying with us all along. The crossbow was small but at extreme close range. I flinched at the sharp twang as it was released.

There was a gurgle and Blaxley fell to the mud, the short bolt protruding from his neck.

"Oops. Alas, there appear to be only eleven men-at-arms and we did agree twelve... Hmm. I nominate Sir Lyndon to take the remaining place."

"I'm honored, Sire," Lyndon croaked, offering a small bow.

King Ulfred leered. "Now, make your way across the ford, Prince Douglas. I'm sure we'll meet again. Quite soon, I expect."

Prince Douglas sat straighter in his saddle. I shook my head lightly. There was nothing he could do, no protest he could make, only time he could waste. He turned and his men lead him across the ford, disappearing into the trees on the far bank. Almost before I knew it, I was alone.

"Well? What are you waiting for?" King Ulfred said, as I stood surrounded by enemies.

"My helm. My shield. My sword."

"Hah! Cross the ford first Lady Estelle and we will throw them to you. I don't want you standing too close, not armed, anyway. I'm not sure I can trust *you*."

I smiled. "You can't. But you can trust Prince Douglas and I do his bidding."

"Even when it results in your death? Perhaps this is why women should not be allowed to wield a sword. They take it all so very seriously."

"War is serious."

"Is it?" he sneered. "Fortunes are lost and made, lives cut short. And yet it is played to a set of rules no less rigid than those of chess. Do you play chess, Lady Estelle?"

"I do." I could have told him more; that my father taught

me, that I rarely found anyone willing to test themselves against me. Few of the ladies of the Court played and even fewer men were keen to risk embarrassment at my hands.

"A pity you didn't mention it earlier," Ulfred said, "That would have been a more pleasant way to contest this ford."

He was toying with me. Trying to make me regret the whole arrangement before the first clash of swords. Mind games.

"Would you have played yourself, My Lord?" I asked, "Or would you have nominated a champion for that battle as well?"

Again his eyes narrowed, his laugh quickly choked off. "Enough banter. Cross the ford, Lady, and we shall see how well you fare in a *real* contest."

I bowed and backed away, walking with a confidence I didn't feel into the shallow strip of river. The cold water came up to my waist, seeping through the joints and slowing me as I took my place on the far side, standing in a foot of water.

The shallows at the river's edge were an illusion; a narrow platform, perhaps two yards wide, lay beneath the water's surface. To either side the water was once again at waist height, almost to the bank. This was the reason I considered the ford defendable: even if they wanted to they could not attack en masse. Not on foot, anyway. I hoped none of the men arrayed on the other side knew the land as well as I did, or they would be begging the knights the use of their chargers.

"Throw the Lady her sword and helm," Ulfred instructed.

The helm I caught, but the sword fell deliberately short and I was forced back into the depths of the river. Stooping over to retrieve it from its bed of mud and pebbles drenched me even more than the crossing, all to the jeers of those watching.

"And my shield?" I asked from the chilly waters.

"Ah, no," King Ulfred shook his head, regretfully. "I'm afraid your taunts about my sword and my chess playing have cost you your shield, Lady Estelle. The fortunes of war, alas. Besides, we mustn't make it *too* easy for you, must we?"

It wasn't just my lower half that felt the chill. I gritted my teeth, lowered the visor on my helm and retook my position on the shallow bar. "Send you first man over," I called defiantly.

And I will take his shield from him, I neglected to add.

Ulfred turned to Lyndon. "You wish first honor?"

The sneer crept into a crooked smile and the Knight shook his head. "I'll wait my turn. Until she has proven herself. And then I shall prove myself."

Ulfred nodded. "You may not get another chance?"

"Then I will have lost nothing."

King Ulfred walked along the line of the eleven remaining men-at-arms. "Which of you," he asked, "wants the command of this company?"

The tallest and broadest of them shuffled forward. "I, Sire."

"Name?"

"Daniel, Sire. Daniel Feathers."

"Well then, Feathers, the job is yours. Once you have taken care of the Lady over there. Think you can handle that?"

"Aye, Sire," he grinned. "It'd be my pleasure."

I'd already pegged him as my first adversary. Against a light opponent, send your heaviest. A double-hander, a bastard, against a one handed sword.

Stupid.

Prince Douglas did not have me in his Guards because I was the *best* with a sword, he had me because I was *different*.

They should not have sent their heaviest; they should have sent their most experienced.

Though, I thought soberly, perhaps Feathers was that, as well.

I learnt my sword craft from a woman, barely five foot tall and slimmer even than I. Her first lesson had been that if I ever attempted to fight like a man--like the man bulling his way across the stream with puppy-dog enthusiasm--then I would lose, as I had lost to her, time and time again. A light-weight swordsman--or woman--must be agile. My suit of armor was tailored as much to that premise as to the propor-tions of my body. It was a mass of compromises; the joints weaker, but allowing me greater range of movement; the armor thinner, but therefore less of a burden.

It was the reason I needed the shield Feathers had fixed to his back. I'd have preferred a lighter version of that as well, even a buckler gives your opponent things to think about. Though I had no intention to stand and trade blows, a shield would narrow the angles of his attack and allow me to disguise my counters.

I heard his labored breath as he fought against the stream's current and the weight of his armor. Such a giant would tire quickly, especially wielding that heavy weapon of his. The longer I dragged the contest out, the less I would have to fear and the further Prince Douglas would get.

Feathers came to a stop, still knee deep, water streaming from the fan-plates above his greaves, as if suddenly wary that I might pose a greater threat than I appeared. I had not, after all, retreated from his advance. His arms and sides were covered only with chainmail, with a back and breast plate that didn't match strapped across and a front-shoulder plate above. I suspected he had on a thick gambeson to make up the deficit in shielding; my first mission would be to dunk him in the water, to make him heavier and slower still.

He panted for a moment, waiting for me to move, to attack, to commit myself. Stood where I was, with the advantage of the shallow platform beneath my feet, that was the last thing I was going to do.

And then he raised his hand-and-a-half high above his head, as if he were chopping wood, confident of his extra reach.

It would have been too easy to drive my thin sword into the wide open spaces his half-helm and chainmail cowl left, into his cheek and *flick* up towards an eye. Instead, I stooped and lashed out low with my booted foot, slamming the metal against his downstream leg.

He staggered satisfactorily, dropping to one knee as he slipped into the deeper depths either side of the causeway he was on, but he recovered quicker than I expected, throwing up his sword and almost catching me as I spun out of reach. He straightened, grinning evilly.

"Tricksy little c-"

I cut him off with a darting thrust that clattered against his armored side. It was only as he groped for damage that he realized I'd sliced through two of the three straps that cinched his breast and back plates to his barrel chest.

His eyes narrowed, busy trying to work out if it had been a lucky blow. If he had been a smarter man, he would have cut the remaining strap himself. As it was, he swung that sword of his in great arcs, trying to bully me out of position. I gave way, but not backwards. I pivoted until he stood once again on the river bed drop-off. His breast plate swung with every step and in rhythm with that swing I stuck him with the tip of my sword, prodding the gambeson beneath. Not deep enough to cut all the way through, not deep enough to do him injury. Just deep enough to prick him, to goad him on.

I waited my moment and, as he once again overextended, I made as though to strike. He turned to catch the blow on the shield strapped to his back and I slammed my body against it, watching in delight as his back leg buckled and into the depths he tumbled.

There was a holler of laughter from the bank of the river, quickly silenced.

Daniel Feathers struggled up, minus his breast and back plate and, alas, his shield. Shaking water from his face, he took up position solidly on the shallow strip of river bed.

"Playtime's over, bitch," he growled, inching forward, holding his bastard blade half-way along its length, "I'm going to make you sorry."

He still didn't get it, the oaf. His long sword was too easy to avoid even if he used it as a spear. And avoid I had to--if I'd met his blows head on they'd have forced me to my knees. As long as I kept moving, he'd not find a home for the point of that bastard blade. But if I was down on the ground...

In turn, he had no defence against my lighter, sharper sword. The only reason he didn't properly fear it yet was because I'd only pecked at him. He honestly thought his heavy, sagging, soaked-wet gambeson was adequate defence.

I gave him a cut above his brow for calling me names. The blood mixed with the water and ran into his eyes, slowing him further. I was tempted by the gap his poorly fastened gauntlet left at his wrist, knowing a strike there would most likely disarm him entirely. Instead, I rapped my sword against his helm, making the dull metal clang, warning him not to close the gap.

Something long and black spun towards me and I ducked behind my foe, slicing upwards as I did. My sword was nearly dragged from my hand as Daniel Feathers stumbled one final time, a look of astonishment on his bovine face. I'd caught him under the chin, the metal of my sword passing through his unprotected throat and lodging against the bones of his neck.

I let the motion of his fall carry me, felt for the slack and yanked my bloodied blade free as the man-at-arms crashed into the dark, covering waters.

I stared at the men on the river bank arrayed against me, scanning for further threats, wondering who had thrown the halberd. It had not missed by much, glancing off the gravel near my feet and carrying on into deeper water. If it had been a spear and had flown true, instead of the less streamlined axe and spike of a halberd...

"You were taking *too* long," drawled King Ulfred, "thought I'd give you a better weapon to finish the job."

A weapon that had been aimed at me. He probably couldn't see the filthy look I gave him, but he must have guessed.

"Oh come on," he taunted, "at least it wasn't a bolt from a crossbow!"

His entourage laughed and I shook my head, annoyed. Not merely because of the interference, but because the King had pegged me as the winner in the contest, despite my attempts to draw it out, to make it appear evenly matched. No fool then, Ulfred.

He gestured at a pair of men-at-arms who practically ran into the river, only slowing when they hit the depths of the middle. Two against one. But how many men are actually trained to work together on the battlefield? Not many and hopefully not this overly eager duo.

I snatched up the halberd, contemplating for the briefest of moments whether I should chance a return throw at the gloating King. But a miss would mean that all bets were off, the rules of his little game broken. Plus, I would be throwing uphill and a halberd is not designed to be thrown at all, not accurately.

Instead, I jabbed one handed towards the advancing men, halting their progress, as I backed up a foot or so. The leader tapped the spiked point out of the way with his sword, eyes glittering as he watched, waiting. When a metal edge skittered along the wooden pole, I lowered the heavy end as if I had lost control. His companion danced triumphantly in and I stuck him with my sword through the hinged gap at his groin.

My sword and sword-hand occupied, the leader, not fully aware of the plight of his comrade, leapt forward, yelling savagely. I tilted the halberd, hoping he'd run himself onto it, but he grabbed at it instead, wrenching it from my grip and lunging to the side. Off balance, he slid down the hidden underwater bank, cursing as the water ran red from his sliced open hand, cursing even harder as it mingled with the heavier flow of the other man-at-arms, who had fainted clean away, bubbles briefly rising where the waters broke over his helm.

Another curt nod from King Ulfred and two more men splashed into the river, joining the third as he picked himself up. Three against one and I no longer had the halberd.

They tried to rush together; the wounded, now left-handed man lagging behind and finding himself squeezed off the narrow causeway. He halted by his probably-dead colleague and began to drag him to the far bank, grunting with effort. A valiant rescue mission. To rescue himself.

I wondered if he might earn himself a bolt from King Ulfred's pocket crossbow. But either way, he was no longer my concern.

Two against one, again. Even better, they were densely bunched with not enough room to swing both their weapons.

The man on the right, armed with an axe, carried a buckler in his other hand, the dinner-plate sized shield protecting his flank, widening their wall of metal and flesh.

I too had a wall. Lighter, true; but no easier to penetrate. And mine had wicked thorns. By the time this particular bout ended, I swore, I would own that man's buckler.

As they closed in, I watched and judged. They had trained together, these two. Their legs moved in concert, though slowed by the unaccustomed battleground of the river. But they had obviously only been trained as a defensive unit. They had no plan of attack other than to press me back.

Like a snail, lumbering and slow.

I trailed my blade in the water. Flicked up a splash of silver that had them flinching in concert.

Nervous, as well as lumbering. All well and good. I was not, I reminded myself, here to win. I was here to eat up as much time as possible, while Prince Douglas made good his escape. I would play with these two. Use their fear against them.

I danced to the side that held the buckler. The round shield jerked up to protect head and face, obscuring his vision as I slapped my blade across the man's exposed thigh.

He jerked back as though scolded, axe clashing against the other man's quarter-stone sword as they struggled to track me.

As a gap appeared between them I swung sideways, clattering my weapon against the wrist of the swordsman on the left. Not enough to cut; neither blow had penetrated armor or chainmail, but enough to worry them, enough to bruise.

The multi-limbed beast halted its advance. "Stay tight!" barked one head to the other.

They would have been better separating. Coming at me from different angles.

Not that the river allowed them. Once again, I gave thanks for the lack of open ground, for the treacherous narrowness of the ford. On open ground, I wouldn't have stood a chance against so many.

The swordsman reached his free hand to his side, remerging with a dagger, twelve inches long, a solid metal cross guard; a sword in all but length.

I danced back a step as though wary of the new weapon and, as the beast wheeled in response, I reversed my attack. A delicate cut across the inner thigh of the man on the left and then up to clip the edge of the axe man's helm.

I hoped the ringing of metal on metal satisfied the watching royalty.

The sword and the axe swung towards me, one wildly, one a more measured thrust. The wildness of the axe attack a dire warning; the unskilled may accidentally fell the master. Swords and axes are sharp things and the untrained are unpredictable. It would not do to get complacent.

Even as I was thinking the thought there was a blur of metaled limbs, the beast split apart, each man twisting to the outside before striking home towards the middle, sword high, axe low.

A practiced and deadly pincer move, impossible to fend off without a shield.

That was, if I had still been where they struck.

I swayed back to their overextended positions, flicked the dagger from the swordsman's grip, heard him yelp. It was a finely crafted thing, that dagger, and mine now. The spoils of war.

That is, if I survived to collect it from the shallow river bed. The heavy axe bludgeoned back towards me and I only narrowly avoided it, grimly aware of what either poll or bit would do if they made contact. It was time I cut this double-headed beast down to size.

I poked my blade at the helm of the swordsman. Not being in control of the buckler, he was reliant on his partner for protection. After a few more swipes the man with the buckler over-reacted, raising the shield too high, obscuring the sight of the swordsman, fouling his defence. I slipped the point of my sword beneath the round shield, angling down, thrusting hard. Even when the man with the buckler tried to correct his mistake, all it did was push my blade further towards his partner.

The point dug into and through the chainmail over the man's stomach, the resistance easily overcome. A pair of eyes widened within the helm, a face whitened, and the swordsman staggered back.

The axe head swung violently towards me, glancing painfully off my arm. I had thought to play with this half of the beast a while longer, but not when the axe wielder was so enraged.

As he raised the axe for another strike, the shield rode up as well, exposing the gap between his cuirass and his skirted waist.

I sliced into it with the keen edge of my sword and he folded in two, dropping his axe, dropping the shield, hands clutching his red-blossoming midriff.

I nudged him backwards as he tumbled, picked up the buckler and threw the battleaxe into deeper water.

Standing defiant, I faced the King and his diminished cohort.

"It's getting lonely over here," I heckled. "Send me more men to kill."

"Sir Lyndon?" asked the King. The knight rubbed at the scarred flesh around his neck, as if in contemplation.

"Allow me," a voice said, as another man-at-arms stepped forward.

"You think you will fare better than your companions?" Ulfred asked. The newest volunteer was slim, his armor a hodge-podge of different items, but chosen to work together, I could see. Chosen for their lightness and flexibility. Not too dissimilar from my armor, though not custom made as mine was.

A salt and pepper beard poked from his open faced helmet. "Aye, Sire. I think I have the measure of her."

This was the experienced man they should have sent first.

Too experienced to volunteer before now. I readied myself, wary.

He did not bother to rush across the river, did not arrive out of breath. Instead he picked his way across, eyes peering left and right, gauging unseen depths.

"Lady Estelle," he said as he came to stand before me, giving a small incline of his head. A bow.

"You have the advantage over me, Sir," I replied, remaining defiantly upright.

"I trust so. But you mean my name? Francesco Tadino."

"Italian?"

"Indeed."

"I hear they have fine swordsmen over there."

"Some of those fine swordsmen are over here," he replied with another nod.

"Hiding amongst a group of crossbow wielding ruffians?"

"Touché, Madame. But I have ambitions."

"So. A dangerous man."

"ENOUGH!" hollered the King, face suffused by red. "Quit your idle prattle, *women*, and fight, damnit!"

The Italian raised his sword, swiveling his wrist swiftly between tierce and quarte and back. A fencer, then.

No doubt he had once been paid to fight as entertainment, in the courts of Italy. He would be swift and supple.

And predictable, I hoped.

I adopted a position that matched his, as though intending to play by his rules. His left hand fluttered behind him, out of reach. I lowered my hand with the buckler, but not as far as he; just to my waist.

His sword darted forward, lightening fast. I parried it to one side, letting the tip dance off my armored upper arm as I swiped my sword towards his shoulder. He swayed and my shot went wide.

"If we had been fighting as we should, first blood would have been mine, my Lady," he observed.

"If we had been fighting unarmored," I hissed back, "I would not have let your sword make contact."

His sword leapt and danced and I met it and guided it wide while I thought about his comment. Was he unused to fighting in armor? Had he only fought contest bouts, ending at first blood?

Would he know how to fight dirty?

As he swung I met his outstretched arm with my elbow, met the edge of his blade with the flat of mine, pushing it back towards him.

He strained and wheezed and swore something in a foreign language. He was not a big man; we were more evenly matched in strength than he had expected.

I did not prolong the wrestling match. As he shifted to try a different attack I swung my freed arm and punched, the buckler bouncing heavily off his sword hand, bruising his knuckles.

"Ha!" he grunted. "That won't-"

My sword edge slid up his blade, metal screeching in

protest. I flexed my wrist as it neared the hilt and drove the *practical* pommel into his chin.

Separating as he took a step back, I raised the buckler into defensive position, my sword resting along its edge, awaiting his next move.

Spitting blood into the river, he came in low, blade angled down, expecting me to block with the shield. But that would guide the tip of his sword towards my outstretched thigh, as it had done to one half of the axe-sword duo. My teacher was better than that. Again I blocked with the flat of my sword, stepping forward to reduce his angles for the reverse cut.

He frowned. Whirled the sword above his head, steel flashing in the dappled sunlight, changing his stroke mid-flow, the sword still pointing backwards, the edge chopping towards my neck.

I moved it easily aside with the buckler and rattled his helm for his efforts.

He prodded and probed, watching me, waiting. With two attacks already on his half-helm, he would no doubt be expecting a third. He was prepared.

I did not do what he expected.

As he probed the edges of my round shield, as he danced away from my counter thrust, I measured his stride. And as he came in once again, I lunged under his blow, spearing my sword towards his armpit, the extension of his arm exposing the weak spot to the keen point of my sword.

It sank deep. Skewered his ribcage, angled towards his heart. Whether it reached it or not did not matter; the blow was a fatal one.

But I was rewarded by a sharp sting in my side. The Italian's blade had snuck through, sliced along my waist even as I struck home. It hadn't penetrated far, the thrust of a dying man, deflected by the buckler, reduced by the light chain mail just above my faulds.

But it was enough. I had been careless, or he had been lucky, even in death. I did my best not to show I was injured, however slight. Ignoring the lancing pain, I stood erect as the Italian fell face forward into the waters, joining the others I had slain.

"Sir Lyndon," the King said in a peevish tone. "I really must insist."

The Knight nodded grimly. "Aye, Sire. It is time."

I had not realized how tall he was. Six foot at least, perhaps taller. Armed with what appeared to be an estoc--a Knight's sword, all point and no edge, a weapon to be used against a similarly heavily armored foe. I would be careful not to let that point anywhere near my thin armor.

"Come to let me finish the task?" I asked, waving my blood soaked sword at his scarred neck.

"Come to finish yours," he croaked, gesturing to my side, where the chainmail was beginning to darken with red.

And then he swung.

Sword fights are sword on shield, or sword on armor. Or more likely still, shield on shield, armor on armor. A sword is too fragile and too valuable to risk clashing against another, or against the metal rim of a shield. You use your sword in defence to guide your opponents blow to the side, not to meet it. You use the flat, not the edge. Only in mummers' plays do swords clash edge to edge.

Sir Lyndon did not aim for me, for my helmet, for my armored limbs. Not even when I raised my arm too slow, the rip in my skewered side making me gasp as I hauled my sword-arm into the air.

He aimed for my blade, curving his blow so that his dull-edged sword met mine in midair.

And smashed straight through it, the tremor of the tortured metal coursing down my arm, paralyzing my nerves and my muscles, making my side spasm as I looked stupidly at what I was left holding, trying to recognize its new shape.

There was my sword, shorn in two, the fragile tip and a full third of its length gone, the new end a blunt wedge of dull gray metal. Ruined. Useless.

He grinned, waggled his unblemished weapon. "Specially hardened to shatter pretty little swords like yours," he said. And then swung at me again.

There was a moment of silence, of total blackness. Another while I tried to work out why it was so bright, until I realized Lyndon had knocked my helm from my head. A glance down through a shower of stars to where I knelt told me my sword hand was now empty.

A glance backwards showed me why I was still alive. Sir Lyndon was turning slowly, his giant sword held aloft, the sound of cheers from the river bank filtering through the tinny ringing in my ears.

I fumbled in the water, grasping for my shattered blade, for the fallen dagger, knowing I wouldn't find either of them in time, acid rising in my stomach, burning my throat, trying to blink away the shadow that dogged the edges of my vision, the shadow that told me only one of my eyes was working properly. I was at the big Knight's mercy.

When my hand did knock against something, it wasn't my sword, nor the dagger. It was hard, stout, and round, neither blade not hilt, lurking just below the surface. It was the pole of the halberd that had been thrown at me to end the first bout.

The sharp metal point and axe had dragged one end down to the depths where the tip of my sword lay, but the shaft was wooden and floated, pointing my way.

I grasped it and whirled at the advancing Knight, pain in my side ripping through me as I did.

The metal end, the long spike with its rounded axe-blade and curved hook, trailed a sparkle of watery drops as it drew an arc through the air.

Sir Lyndon didn't have time to get out of its way, not fully. Seeing it coming he stepped forward to meet it.

Stepped forward, so that he rather than I got to decide where the axe-head landed.

There was an almighty *crack!* as the wooden shaft, slippery and wet in my hands, smashed down onto his armored shoulder. A splash as the head of the halberd cart-wheeled back into the middle of the stream. A smaller splash as Sir Lyndon staggered to one knee.

It was no victory. I had merely delayed the inevitable. He was already rising as I stared at the shattered, splintered end of the pole.

Unhelmed. Exhausted from my battles. Wounded. One-eyed. Armed with nothing more than a two-foot wooden splinter, against a heavily armored Knight wielding a sword sharper and stronger than any I had ever known.

I was dead.

I lunged forward before he could fully regain his feet, before the momentary daze of my glancing blow receded, and thrust the wooden shard through the narrow gap in his face plate.

There was a breathless silence, punctured by a sickening gurgle, before the mountain of a man measured his great length in the watery grave.

I stumbled back, leaking red from head and from side, the sound of the river distant in my ears. Stumbled and fell.

Across the river bank, King Ulfred peered down, perhaps unsure of what had happened, unsure of the victor.

A sudden burst of noise rolled down the river bank behind me, yells and clashes of metal on metal, swords on shields. The watching eyes from the opposite shore flicked upwards, weapons wagging back and forth.

Despite the six remaining men-at-arms, the four Knights of his guard, Ulfred wavered. He had just lost his champion and with an unknown enemy force hard by, he barked a curt order to the men-at-arms as he mounted his horse, wheeled it around, and galloped away, the other Knights following in his wake.

Lying in the cooling waters of the river, listening to the gurgle and trill of eddies and flows, I awaited my death.

But the men-at-arms ignored the Royal command, backing slowly away, vanishing into the woods on the far side. Was I too distant for their crossbow bolts? Or were they holding them in reserve against an unseen enemy, a force of unknown size and disposition?

As the water climbed as high as my chin, I began to drift.

My head was lifted from the cooling waters. I tried to struggle as someone pulled and tugged, and then there was the face of Douglas, my Prince.

"You... came back?" I croaked in fear. "Ulfred-"

"Ulfred is gone," he half-smiled. "I ran into a small force of our men. Thought we'd best come back and help." He looked around the river strewn with bodies. "But it appears you have left us no-one to fight."

I did my best to grin but my body was wracked by a coughing fit that ripped at the wound in my side. I closed my eyes, welcoming the cold blackness as the soft gurgle of the river ebbed away.

LIAM HOGAN

Liam Hogan is an Oxford Physics graduate and award winning London based writer. His short story "Ana" appears in Best of British Science Fiction 2016 (NewCon Press) and his twisted fantasy collection, "Happy Ending Not Guaranteed," is published by Arachne Press. He hosts the ever popular literary event, Liars' League. Find out more at http://happyendingnotguaranteed.blogspot.co.uk/, or tweet @LiamJHogan

ONLY AN ELF

STUART THAMAN

"IT CAN'T BE DONE," Kimiko said quietly. He looked over the plans once more before rolling the parchment back into its tube. The forge was noisy, and his assistant didn't catch the words.

"It can't be done!" Kimiko said a bit more loudly, making sure his assistant, a lithe elf entirely out of place in the hot, humid forge, could hear. She nodded and took the scroll from Kimiko, then placed it back in a leather pouch on her side. Next to all the dwarves working in the forge, Enessäna looked like a giant, though she just barely reached five and a half feet tall.

Ducking out of the doorway, Enessäna put her long legs to work carrying her toward the castle high on the hill over the forge. The structure was dark and imposing, and she dreaded the task of telling King Ashmir that his sword could not be made. The king, a stout dwarf who had ruled over Stonehelm for several hundred years, had grown angry and violent in his old age. And if there was anything Ashmir hated more than his elven slaves, it was being told that one of his ideas wasn't going to work.

Still, Enessäna made her way quickly up the hill, passing by dwarves on either side who cast curious glances her way. She was marked as a slave, branded by the king himself after her village had been sacked by dwarves, and the X-shaped scar on the side of her neck still throbbed with fresh pain. She'd been a slave for three weeks, and her light blue flesh still needed time to fully heal.

With a fine layer of sweat on her forehead, Enessäna finally reached the base of the dwarven keep. Stonehelm was built in the shape of a helmet, hewn directly from the granite of the side of a towering mountain, and Enessäna had to walk through a low overhang resembling a mouth to reach the inner courtyard. Vigilant dwarves watched her every move from either side.

Inside Stonehelm, the dark granite was lit by sparse torches casting long, flickering shadows on the hard ground. Though Enessäna had only recently been stolen from her home, she knew most of the passages through the keep quite well. Her elven memory held almost every detail of her life—especially the day her family had been slaughtered by marauding dwarves.

King Ashmir's audience hall was located directly in the center of Stonehelm. The chamber was large, filled with wooden barrels of mead and long tables used for the festival feasts the dwarves seemed to enjoy almost every night. When Enessäna arrived, the hall was close to empty. The king stood near his throne, a mug of beer in his hand as was typical, and he was conversing with several other bearded dwarves. The conversation was vivid, and Ashmir kept spilling his drink over the sides of the cup as he gestured.

"King Ashmir," the tall elf began from roughly twenty paces away when the conversation lulled. To go any closer to the king meant a breach of etiquette, and slaves who disregarded custom seldom lived to see another day.

After several more minutes of conversation passed, the king finally looked to Enessäna with disdain in his eyes. "You're not holding a sword in your hands, mongrel," he spat.

Enessäna bowed her head respectfully. "Master Kimiko does not believe the weapon you have requested is possible, sir," she said, her eyes fixed on the polished floorboards beneath her.

She heard the dwarf's footsteps approaching. The king stopped in front of her, and she winced in anticipation.

"Not possible?" Ashmir questioned, his tone showing a bit of restraint.

"No, sir," Enessäna repeated. "Kimiko says he cannot make the sword." She fished out the scroll from her leather pouch and offered it forward.

King Ashmir sighed as he snatched the scroll from her grasp. He looked it over for the briefest of moments, and then his fist collided with Enessäna's hip and sent her sprawling to the ground. Though the dwarf was far shorter than Enessäna, he was certainly stronger.

She wasted no time scurrying away from the king, only stopping momentarily to snatch up the discarded scroll from the ground. Once more outside the inner sanctum of Stonehelm, Enessäna rubbed her side. Her flesh was bruised, tainting her light blue skin an ugly shade of purple. She could feel her hatred of the entire dwarven clan growing with every throb of pain.

"Come here," a voice whispered from somewhere in the darkness down an unknown corridor. Enessäna turned her head sharply, and fresh twinge of pain rattled down her spine from the brand on her neck.

"Here," the voice whispered, and Enessäna knew the accent to be elven. She darted toward the darkness, trusting her instincts and trusting even more in the hope that an elf truly did command the voice she had heard.

"You're new," the tall stranger said. Enessäna looked her over and recognized the curve of the female elf's ears designating her as a member of one of the northern tribes. She couldn't quite place the name of the tribe in her mind, but she had seen elves like the one before her previously.

When she was reasonably certain she was out of earshot of any dwarf, Enessäna finally spoke. "What are you doing?" she questioned with a whisper.

The other elf smiled. She had long hair that shimmered in the darkness like a raven's wing. "I saw you with the king," she said. "You must be more careful."

"What do you mean?" Enessäna asked.

"When you have bad news to deliver, do not go inside. Either wait for Ashmir to be too drunk to know what he hears, or do not tell him at all. It is better to forget a message and be punished for a poor memory than to bring him bad news," she explained.

Enessäna still held the blacksmith's scroll tightly in her hand, and something about the way it felt beneath her grip gave her a bit of resolve. "I won't let him break me," she stated evenly.

The tall elf laughed. "I know," she said, "but it does not matter what you allow and what you do not. Dwarves are cruel by their very nature. King Ashmir *will* break you. Just learn to keep your head down, and you'll survive."

Enessäna held her breath as a loud, mostly drunken dwarf stumbled somewhere nearby, shouting things in a language she did not recognize. When he was gone, she turned back to the corridor, but no elf was there. Enessäna was alone.

THE ELVEN SLAVE quarters were sparse, cold, and unfor-
giving. The walls were made of stone similar to the floor, and
there was no drain cut into the rock, so every time it rained,
Enessäna became quickly soaked. Her thin garments did little
to shelter her from the elements, and no effort she could
muster would still her shaking limbs. She was the only elf in
her cell which had clearly been designed for more than a
dozen occupants, and her solitude brought her another
measure of fear. She assumed the elf she had met in Stonehelm had a room closer to the keep, but she did not know for
certain. The dwarves had a limited supply of slaves, and
Enessäna only glimpsed others of her blue-skinned race on
rare occasions.

Staring at the water accumulating in the bottom of her
cell, Enessäna wondered if she would be able to survive. She
truly believed she was strong enough to survive captivity, but
there were cracks in her mental armor. Some of the cracks
were rather large. To be a slave was to lose her elven identity,
to be reduced to something beneath her prideful heritage.
Then the wind shifted, blowing a fresh blanket of cold
through the cell's metal bars, and Enessäna's thoughts were
once more lost in her misery.

Outside the cell, a pair of young dwarves sat idly in front
of a fire, grumbling against the elements despite their relative
warmth. Enessäna tried to make herself as small as possible.
She had hidden the blacksmith's scroll in a gap between
several loose stones on the wall, though what good it might
possibly do for her she had no idea. The thought of unrolling
it and trying to burn it for warmth crossed her mind more
than once, but she had nothing to create a spark. There she

shivered, cold and afraid, her only hope lying in the dawn that was still ten hours away.

MERCIFULLY, the sun found Enessäna still alive when it broke through the clouds at dawn. An armor-clad dwarf unlocked the elf's cell and departed, leaving the door open for Enessäna to rise and go about her daily tasks. She was thankful for having only been shackled hand and foot once, though the memories of being dragged from her mountainside home still stung her mind. Enessäna knew she was faster than the dwarves, of that she had no doubt, but where would she go? What would she do? She knew enough to survive on her own in the wilderness, but a life of constant fear, of perpetually being hunted, was almost as bad as being a slave.

Wearily, Enessäna clambered to her cold feet and stumbled out into the meager sunlight. She tried to wring out her shirt, but her hands could barely close around the threadbare fabric, so she abandoned the task in favor of finding her daily meal at the forge. Her quarters were not situated far from Kimiko's anvils, and the sight of smoke winding its way into the sky made her grin with the thought of warmth. Inside the building, she hurried to the nearest fire, catching a wayward glance from her owner, but Kimiko did not say anything.

The old dwarven smith watched his charge as she shook some life into her bones, and then he offered her a wedge of aged cheese from a nearby table, which she greedily devoured.

"Thank you," Enessäna said between bites, though she wasn't quite sure she meant it.

"What did our fair king say in response to your news?" Kimiko asked. He took up the piece of iron he had been working and slid it into the coals of his forge, turning his back to the slave in the process.

"He was upset," she replied between bites. "He did not say much."

Kimiko took the iron he was working from the forge and began hammering it, shaking his head and muttering something about the king under his breath. The ringing echoed through the forge, adding to the noisy cacophony. When Enessäna had finished her breakfast, she donned a heavy leather apron and took up her position next to her master, ready to assist the old dwarf with whatever needed doing.

"Why can't you make it?" she asked when Kimiko dipped the iron he was working into a bucket of water, giving her ears a temporary respite from the noise.

The smith eyed her with a curious expression. "There's no metal like the king wants," he said cryptically. "The enchantment he needs is too strong. The weapon would break the first time it was drawn."

"What kind of enchantment is it?" Enessäna asked. "What does it do?"

Kimiko let out a long sigh. "The king wants a sword capable of cutting through solid stone with precision, though I do not know why. The enchantment is most commonly referred to as The Demon's Tooth, and it is incredibly rare. In fact, I have only ever read of such magic—I have never seen it with my own eyes."

Enessäna thought for a long moment, a myriad of ideas flashing through her mind. "You need some sort of metal to make it?" she asked.

"Something stronger than iron and steel," Kimiko said, pointing to his own supplies. "The legends say mountain copper can hold it, a material the smiths of old called Orichalcum, but I'm not convinced such a metal exists."

"Mountain copper," the elf wondered aloud.

"They say it shimmers like blood, some bright red color, and can only be found high up on the mountains where the snow constantly blows." Kimiko took a fresh iron ingot and slid it into the coals. "You don't believe those legends, do you?" he asked with a scoff.

Enessäna didn't know what to think. Elves, by their very nature, were regarded as overly superstitious, and Enessäna was no exception to the stereotype. She held many years of fond memories in her mind, and most of them revolved around the elders of her tribe regaling the younger elves with tales of glorious heroes, legendary conquests, and epic weapons used to kill dragons and demons. She had loved those stories, though their recollection brought the telltale wetness of tears to her eyes when she thought of all those storytellers the dwarves had senselessly slaughtered. The two clans hadn't even been at war...

As a flood of memories came to her all at once, Enessäna drifted toward the back of the forge, away from the fires and the incessant hammering. The elders of her tribe had told stories of such precise weapons. There was a legend every elf learned in their youth, though Enessäna assumed the dwarves had never heard of any heroes with pointed ears. Enessäna, just like every member of her tribe, knew the name and exploits of A'el, the First Elf.

Thousands of years ago, or so the legend went, A'el had wielded a blood-red sword when he had slain a human king in order to release the entire elvish race from bondage. A'el was referred to as the First Elf because he created the first independent elvish tribe. Before him, the tall race had always been slaves. Their histories had known nothing but servitude, though the master had changed frequently through the ages. Now, as Enessäna watched her dwarven captors bustling about the forge, she wondered if she was even still an elf in the eyes of her ancestors—or in A'el's eyes. Sadly, she knew what she was: nothing.

A'el's sword had borne a name, she knew it had, but she couldn't conjure it up from memory, so addled with crippling self-doubt was her mind.

"A'el would not see my ears," she muttered. "A'el would not see *me*. He would only see chains." She slunk back against one of the walls, feeling the cool stone through her thin shirt, a sharp contrast to the heat coming from everywhere else.

"What's that?" Kimiko asked, looking up only briefly from his anvil.

Enessäna shook her head.

"You said something, didn't you?" the smith went on between loud hammer strikes.

"It was nothing," the elf replied, shaking her head. *I am nothing.* She moved back to Kimiko's station and took up her place next to his forge. "I'm surprised you heard me at all."

Qul'sempet, Enessäna remembered in the old language. *The sword's name was Qul'sempet: The One Who Rises.*

The rest of the day went by in somewhat of a blur. Enessäna smiled as she let her mind wander down the old paths of her homeland. She loved the stories of her elders, and getting lost in the ancient legends gave her a few precious hours in which she could convince herself that those story-tellers were still alive—that her entire tribe had not been murdered by dwarven hands.

When night came, the enchanting illusion of A'el's legend was broken by Enessäna's unyielding loneliness. Her chamber was cold, as it always was, and no amount of memories could break through the bleak iron bars at the front of her cell.

"I am no longer an elf," Enessäna said to the wind. "I am only a slave. A slave has no identity."

And so the years passed.

At first, Enessäna had tried to measure the time of her captivity as it slipped by, but her dwarven masters were not keen on keeping accurate calendars. Other elves came and went from Stonehelm, sometimes entire scores of them at once, and Enessäna grew to know a few of the other blue-skinned slaves quite well. Still, she did not consider them to be her kin or even companions. She was a slave, a member of nothing, and her only friend was a tightly bound scroll hidden away in a secret alcove of her sparse prison. Despite the elements, the scroll kept her somewhat warm. Enessäna never admitted it to herself, but the thought of becoming skilled enough to put the plans to use was the only thing keeping her from voluntarily joining her slain tribe in death.

As the years had gone by, Enessäna had done everything she could to remain in the forge as Kimiko's personal servant, and the rest of the dwarves hadn't ever cared. So it was that she had subtly learned the basics of blacksmithing. Kimiko had even personally shown her a few things and given her several menial tasks, but the clever elf had always learned more than she had ever let on.

When she was confident in her abilities, Enessäna finally began to make her key. She waited until she was alone at Kimiko's station, hammering a piece of raw iron into a basic cylinder for some larger project, when she slipped a thin piece of scrap from a fold in her shirt onto the anvil. She had stolen the sliver earlier, and none of the other smiths had noticed it missing—not that any of them had ever kept records of their scraps. As she hammered away, she kept a watchful eye on the nearest dwarves, but it didn't matter. None of them even glanced her way.

Finally, Enessäna knew she had a blank key of generally the right dimensions to fit inside the lock on the outside of her cell. That night, she began the tedious task of filing down the key with the sharp edge of a stone on the side of her cell. It took several weeks before the key fit snugly into the lock, and then Enessäna's escape was at hand.

She waited for the perfect night. Despite the years since her capture, dwarven guards still slept outside her cell, and she had no idea how she would be able to slip past them undetected. Dwarves liked to drink, and her guards were no exception. After another month of icy solitude, a dwarven celebration provided her the perfect opportunity. Sometime after midnight, illuminated by the full moon, her guards retired to their posts in a drunken haze. It didn't take long for them both to fall fast asleep.

Enessäna's lithe arms fit easily through the bars of her cell without even scraping against the iron. She placed the key against the lock and had to stifle a laugh as it moved inside the mechanism. Her filing had worked, and the two primitive tumblers within the lock clicked into place above the cylinder, opening the door with a noisy clank. Had Kimiko, a very talented locksmith, made the mechanism, she knew she would have never escaped. But he hadn't, and so there she stood.

"I am not an elf," she reminded herself. One of the dwarves stirred near his fire, but he merely turned himself over in his drunken sleep.

Enessäna didn't wait a moment longer. She shut her cell door, locked it once more, and then bolted for the nearest trees to hide her flight, the key tucked safely away in her clothing.

It did not take long for Enessäna to find the familiar paths of her former home. Though it had been quite some time since she had seen the towering pines and moss-covered boulders that once marked her tribe's territory, she knew they were landmarks she would never forget for as long as she lived. Something about the close proximity of Stonehelm to her elven home brought a wave of hot anger to Enessäna's mind. The two races had lived less than five miles apart without conflict for as long as she could remember. Yet Enessäna was owned by the dwarves, and all the elves she used to know were dead.

The slender elf stopped once at the place where her own homestead used to stand near the edge of a dense copse of birch trees clinging to the side of the mountain. Then she darted back toward the center of the village with a line of tears running freely down her skin. The center had been where the elders had called home, and there was one building in particular that guided Enessäna's hurried steps.

The home of the elders was partially above ground, but the majority of their residence had been tucked into the side of the steep mountain itself. The outer shell was nothing more than a collection of burnt timbers. The doorway had once been etched with beautiful, swirling designs, though now Enessäna could only barely see their faint outline in the soot.

Inside, the smell of death and fire filled her lungs. Still seated on his wooden throne, the chief elder's corpse was a blackened, putrid mess. The years had taken their toll on his once-proud visage, and vines were beginning to grow up his skeletal legs. Enessäna moved beyond the throne as quickly as she could.

In the back of the room was the entrance to the underground portion of the elders' hall, and the door had since fallen to the ground. With a deep breath to steel her nerves, Enessäna descended the winding, narrow staircase.

Several overgrown rooms lined the sides of the stairs.

Enessäna passed two storehouses, a records room which had been entirely burned, a small chamber filled with broken casks, and a large bedchamber before she arrived at her destination: the place where the elders had kept their secrets. The door to the final chamber had once been stone, but dwarves knew more about the rocks of the world than even the wisest of elves, and it had taken them no time at all to break down the portal during their raid.

Enessäna gingerly stepped over the shattered door to stand amidst the barren, burnt shelves. There wasn't much of anything left. Thankfully, her large, oval eyes were accustomed to the darkness, for the ventilation shafts carved into the roof had collapsed, and no sunlight reached the room at all.

The dwarves had taken almost everything from the chamber. She thought of A'el's legendary sword and knew she was a fool. She didn't even have proof of the elf's existence. In the center of the charred room, Enessäna slumped down and let the reality of her plight fully sink into her mind. The dwarves would pursue her. She wasn't valuable as a slave—there were others who could easily do her job at Stonehelm—but dwarven cruelty was only outdone by dwarven pride. Her escape would be a slight upon their crazed notions of honor, and her capture would be the only thing that could remedy the harm she had wrought. Her capture and torture, and then her death.

"There's nothing here," she whispered to the musty darkness. Though she had spoken to the room, the words stung her soul the most. She knew they were true. She was nothing.

Enessäna knew that elves, superstitious as they were, often created complex, puzzle-like systems to hide their most beloved treasures. Wiping a stream of tears from her cheek, Enessäna stood up from the ground to begin her search anew.

She scoured the stones for signs of something hidden, for any sort of clue, pushing aside rubble and going over every inch of the room in detail.

Only a single object managed to catch her eye. Against the wall farthest from the door stood a battered, scorched crate. She had pushed it aside to investigate the stones where it had stood, and something rattled inside. With curiosity threatening to overtake her doubt, she pulled the burnt crate apart, revealing a handful of small metal discs inside.

Each disc held a specific design, but they had been damaged in the fire, and Enessäna couldn't figure out their purpose in the darkness. Slowly, watching her step in the damaged complex, the elf emerged into the early morning sunlight with the discs in hand. They were silver under the years of grime built up on their faces, and they looked malformed. Whether they had warped in fire or had been poorly made to begin with, Enessäna could not tell. Regardless, the discs captured her attention.

And then the gruff sounds of dwarves riding sure-footed mountain goats began to filter through the trees, and she knew they were after her. Luckily, the search party was still a far way off down the slope of the mountain. Unsure where to go, Enessäna set her feet in the opposite direction of the dwarven voices. She ran down the slope of her former home as quickly as her legs could take her. She realized after a moment that she had gone down the opposite side from the one she had ascended, and it was a face of the mountain she did not know well.

A few small streams crisscrossed the landscape at the bottom of the mountain, and Enessäna stopped at the edge of one to refresh her spirit with cold water. Out of nothing more than her natural inquisitiveness, she took a quick moment to splash some water onto one of the discs and clean it. Even with the dirt and ash gone from the surface, she still had no idea what the pieces had been for or why the dwarves had not stolen them. Perhaps, like her, they had had no idea what they were.

She knew the majority of the coin-like objects was iron, and it had gone soft over the years. But something else inside the metal caught her attention. There was a glinting streak through each medallion, and the light it reflected had a distinctly red hue.

Orichalcum?

Enessäna's heart caught in her throat.

She had seen Kimiko extract metals from stone hundreds of times, but she had no idea how she would do it on her own in the wilderness without any tools. Then the sounds of dwarves caught her attention once more, and she sprinted from the stream, angling her path around the base of the mountain to take her back toward Stonehelm.

Slowly, a plan began to form in Enessäna's mind. It was a ridiculous idea, but it gave her something to strive for—some shred of hope.

When night fell, Enessäna knew she had put a good bit of distance between herself and her stocky pursuers. She was close enough to see light from Stonehelm's fires drifting into the sky when she finally spied a protected hovel behind a thick stand of fir trees. She was hungry, but there was no time to forage for food or attempt to hunt. Her hunger would have to wait.

Rain began to fall sometime after midnight. Just like in her cell, the cold water pooled around Enessäna's body, sending shivers down her spine and setting her teeth to chattering.

In the dark, secluded recesses of Enessäna's mind, a dream began to stir.

A'el, a proud imagining of a beautiful elf clad in shimmering armor with a winged helm upon his head, strode
through the mists of her imagination. He was surrounded only
by darkness, though he swung a brilliant red sword after
every few paces, and Enessäna could hear it striking enemy
combatants, though she could not see them. Blood sprayed
across the elf's sharp features, and Enessäna felt the dream
beginning to ebb back into the empty oblivion from which it
had surfaced.

Desperate, Enessäna tried to urge the dream onward. She
didn't want it to end, but the more she desired, the closer she
reached toward wakefulness. Finally, A'el turned toward her,
his bloody face glimmering in the void of the dream. He held
his brilliant sword easily at his side. "Only an elf—" he said,
and then Enessäna awoke with a start, her heart thrumming
away in her chest at a wild speed.

Unable to wait even a moment longer, Enessäna took off
through the darkness and the rain. Her feet—battered,
calloused, and bloody from years of shoeless slavery—sang
with pain on the uneven forest floor. She didn't care. The pain
was only a reminder of what had been done to her tribe, what
had been done to her, and what she was going to bring down
upon her dwarven captors.

"I'll kill them all," she growled when the first buildings of
Stonehelm came into view. Enessäna ran a hand across her
forehead to flick some of the rain from her skin, though it
didn't do much good.

Standing at the edge of Stonehelm, she wasn't far from
the forge complex where she had worked for so long. Kimiko
made his home nearby, and Enessäna found her feet taking
her in his direction almost of their own accord.

Inside the building, Kimiko wasn't the only dwarf fast
asleep. He had a family, and Enessäna wasn't sure how to get

to her master without rousing the entire dwelling and possibly bringing all of Stonehelm down on her before she even began her night's work.

Against all of the rage swirling through her entire body, Enessäna was forced to wait. She crouched behind a patch of scraggly bushes where she would have a fine view of Kimiko's door. A few moments before dawn, she saw her master emerge.

"Kimiko," she whispered loudly, her eyes darting around in search of any other dwarf who might have overheard.

Turning, Kimiko stopped, though he didn't see the elf.

"Master Kimiko," she said again, rustling some of the branches near her. Thankfully, the master smith discerned her outline behind the haphazard disguise, and he made his way to her with a confused expression on his face.

"I'd been told you had run off," the dwarf said curtly. He wasn't quite forceful with his words, though he was far from friendly.

Enessäna held forth the metal discs and let the pre-dawn light catch the orichalcum veins so they shone red. "I've found the mountain copper, master."

Kimiko's face screwed up even more. "What in the world are you going on about? You're a runaway slave. You'll be killed, and I'll need to find a new assistant. There isn't anything left to discuss."

"The sword!" Enessäna urged, stepping from the underbrush. "Remember the sword! You said you couldn't make it before, but I've found the orichalcum you need to craft it. King Ashmir will want his sword, and you will become the most respected smith in all of Stonehelm!"

Kimiko rubbed his bearded chin for a moment, his face showing nothing but doubt. "I already *am* the most respected smith in all of Stonehelm. I barely even remember the sword you speak of." Shaking his head, he turned to leave.

"Then make the sword for me, master, and let me take it to King Ashmir. Perhaps he will be lenient toward my indiscretion if I present the sword to him, and then you will not need to teach another slave to replace me when I am killed," she pleaded.

"You think Ashmir will spare your life if you give him a sword?" Kimiko scoffed.

Enessäna fell into step next to her dwarven master. "At least let me try," she said. "Please."

"Fine," Kimiko said with a heavy sigh. "Though only because I wish to see the sword. You know as well as I do that King Ashmir will not allow you to live."

ENESSÄNA SPENT the entire day under the watchful gaze of several dwarven soldiers. She was not allowed any food or water, and her stomach rumbled furiously by the time the sun set behind the mountains and Kimiko had finished the sword. She had been granted supervised leave to return to her cell to fetch the plans, though at no point had she been given any privacy even to relieve herself.

The master smith turned the lengthy blade over in his hands with a smile. "You had it right, Enessäna," he said after a moment of silent introspection. "The ore in those coins was mountain copper. If it had been anything else, the enchantment would not have held." He swung the blade slowly through the air several times to test its weight, then finally set it down in a well-oiled cloth on his anvil.

"All the king knows is that you have been found," Kimiko said. His voice betrayed no concern for his slave's life. "He does not know that you have been here all day, nor does he know that I've made his sword. Honestly, I doubt he will even remember having requested it."

"Thank you for allowing me to try," the elf whispered.

Kimiko wrapped the sword and held it out for Enessäna to take. "You've been a decent assistant, though far from the best, Enessäna. I cannot say that your death will bring me any joy, but you brought it down on your own shoulders, and now you have to bear it. I can at least say that I respect your willingness to meet your end having done something worthwhile with your life, however foolish it might have been. Regardless, you're just a slave."

"Again, all I have to offer is my thanks, master," Enessäna replied, her thoughts anywhere but the present. Without thinking, she gave Kimiko a glance she immediately regretted, fearing she had communicated too much. "You'll never know how much it means that you let me try." She turned away quickly from her short master, eager to be off toward the heart of Stonehelm before she accidentally revealed her intentions.

I am only an elf, she repeated as she moved. *I am only an elf.*

Three dwarven guards walked behind Enessäna on her journey into the fortress. Each one of them held a weapon, and they poked and prodded at Enessäna's back as she made her ascent.

At the bottom of the large stone staircase leading to King Ashmir's audience chamber, Enessäna and her retinue of guards stopped. "Wait here," one of the dwarves commanded before taking the steps ahead of them to announce their presence.

Enessäna didn't need to wait to be summoned. She could hear Ashmir's voice booming from his throne room. The rowdy dwarf sounded drunk, and his slurred speech brought a hint of a smile to Enessäna's blue lips. She wrapped her hand around the hilt of the sword.

I am only an elf.

She took the remaining steps two at a time until she reached the door. One armored dwarf held the heavy door for her, a scowl on his face. Enessäna's hand inched toward him, drawing the orichalcum sword imperceptibly closer to tasting dwarven flesh, but she held back.

Not until the king is dead, she reminded herself. *Then I'll kill them all.*

In the back of the audience chamber, Enessäna spied another blue-skinned elf, a slave holding a large wooden cask presumably full of ale. She looked toward the slave, hoping to catch her eye, but the ale-holder's gaze never left the floor.

King Ashmir stumbled from his dais with a frothy ring of foam spread around his mouth and beard. "So you've come back?" he yelled. He ripped a chunk of meat from a spit in his left hand.

"Yes," Enessäna replied, offering a dutiful curtsy. She was still more than ten feet from the belligerent little dwarf.

"And why?" Ashmir sloppily went on. He stumbled backward, and Enessäna took a subtle step toward him at the same time to close the gap, even if only by a little.

"I only left because I wanted to please you," the elf answered.

"To please me?" Ashmir laughed. "You're just a—"

I am only an elf.

"—lowly slave." He turned, beckoning to the elf at the back of the room to bring him more ale.

Enessäna risked another step forward, and one of the dwarven guards along the side of the hall noticed her movement. The soldier began to come forward.

Out of time, Enessäna ripped the sword from its oilcloth and dove forward. The blade sank to the hilt in Ashmir's chest without even the slightest hint of resistance. All Enessäna could do was stand there dumbfounded, stunned that Kimiko's enchantment had been true. The sword could cut *anything*. Then the dwarven king split in two as he fell backward to the ground, and the blade did not waver.

The guard from the side screamed at seeing his king so readily slain and hoisted his axe high above his head, bringing the tip of his blade in line with Enessäna's shoulder. The elf snapped out of her trance at the last possible second and rolled to her left, turning what would have been a fatal blow into one that only rent her arm from shoulder to elbow, throwing a huge spurt of her blood to floor. Enessäna pivoted with a grimace and brought her sword up to block the next attack. The dwarf's axe broke in two on the edge.

Enessäna pushed forward, and the guard's head split to his chin. She pushed the corpse away with a growl, her eyes darting toward the frightened slave, and tried to stem the brutal pain shooting down the right side of her body. "Fight!" she yelled to her blue-skinned kin.

A pair of dwarves closed in on Enessäna from behind, though they were cautious and took their time. Both of the soldiers displayed truly terrified expressions.

"Throw down your weapons," Enessäna commanded.

Both dwarves shook their heads. "You killed the king," one of them muttered in disbelief.

"I'll kill you both," Enessäna reminded them. She held her sword out defensively, but the two guards were far from enthusiastic when it came to attacking her.

One of the guards pointed to Enessäna's ravaged arm. "Not with that, you aren't," he said.

Enessäna knew the dwarf was right. "Perhaps I will not

slay every dwarf in Stonehelm, but the two of you will certainly be counted among the dead." The elf skittered forward and slashed, her damaged body still faster than her squat attackers, and the first dwarf fell with a pained scream.

Enessäna then retreated several steps, and the remaining dwarf lowered his head to charge. When the two collided, Enessäna's only good arm was too high, and she couldn't get her sword turned around quickly enough to stab, so she fell to the ground with a wet, heavy thud. Thankfully, the dwarf's weapon left his hand in the tumble and slid far out of reach near the king's corpse.

With as much strength as she could muster, Enessäna struggled to wrench her body from the ground. She was taller by several feet, and working the forges for so long had given her limbs strength she had never known before, but the dwarf was a well-trained fighter, most likely one of the best of Stonehelm. The guard brought a meaty fist down on Enessäna's chin, sending her head rocketing into the stone floor. A burst of black pain filled the elf's eyes, and she could barely think.

A'el stood, battered and bloodied, in the mist of Enessäna's grasping mind.

I am an elf! she urged with all the will left in her body. The dwarf continued to pummel her, bashing out her teeth and cracking the delicate bones around her eyes.

Prove it, A'el ordered, and then the legendary warrior of old was gone.

Enessäna took another brutal hit that dislodged a significant part of her scalp. Lifting her left arm from the floor, she gritted her teeth and somehow found the strength to level the orichalcum sword. She couldn't swing the weapon, but she didn't need to—she merely rested the blade's edge against the dwarf's back, and the guard was torn asunder.

King Ashmir's audience chamber was silent, though it was far from empty. Armed and armored dwarves stood at every entrance like statues. Enessäna could barely comprehend their presence. She staggered to her feet, her front covered in gore.

"I—"

One of the dwarves at the perimeter threw down his axe and took off his helm. "No one can fight against that…" the guard muttered, his eyes wide.

Several of the other dwarves followed suit, and the whole room was disarmed before long—everyone except Enessäna.

Forcing her ragged body to the nearest dwarf, Enessäna tried to make herself as proud and tall as possible. She towered over the guards, though she could only see from one eye.

"I surrender," the shaking dwarf said. "I won't fight you."

"Fine."

Enessäna brought her shining red sword up from the ground and severed the dwarf's legs from his torso. Holding the blade out to her side, it only took one long stride of her blue legs to leave three more dwarves shattered at her feet. The other surrendered guards began to flee, and she struggled to keep up with them as she swung blindly, knowing that anything she hit would be an enemy.

When the room was finally absent of screams almost all of the dwarven guards were dead, their weapons scattered about the center of the room. A few of them had managed to flee down the front stairs of the audience chamber, and Enessäna could hear them assembling a host of others, whether to surrender or storm the throne she had no idea.

Slowly, the elf made her way to the audience chamber's exit. She held the sword tightly in her left hand, and her entire right arm hung uselessly at her side. She had lost too much blood, and she wasn't sure she'd have the strength for any more killing. Still, the fire of revenge burned deep inside her chest, and she could think of nothing but furthering the dwarven slaughter.

One of the assembled dwarves on the staircase began climbing up toward her, a heavy shield held out before him.

Little good it'll do him, the elf thought.

"Enessäna," the dwarf began. It was Kimiko, outfitted for battle like all the other dwarves in Stonehelm.

Enessäna waited until the older dwarf was just barely within reach of her sword's tip, and then she thrust it forward, catching Kimiko beneath the chin and deftly severing his head from his shoulders.

"The elves are slaves no longer," Enessäna told the gathering of armor and steel before her. "Every slave is to be released at once, and every dwarf in Stonehelm must throw down his arms and come to me."

For a long while, nothing happened. Enessäna stood on the top of the steps watching them, blood still pouring from her wounds. She was growing dangerously light-headed.

Another dwarf dared to approach her. Enessäna turned to him, and the burly warrior dropped his weapon and shield noisily to the stone ground. "I submit," the dwarf said. "We'll release the slaves."

"Good," she gasped, her feet wobbling under her. "Now kneel before me."

The unarmed dwarf did as he was told.

Enessäna took one more step forward and leveled her sword against the dwarf's temple. She pushed the blade against the kneeling dwarf's flesh, and her mind went black.

"Only an elf," she heard A'el telling her from somewhere close by in the swarming darkness.

Her eyes flickered open for a fraction of a second, and she

saw the dwarf still kneeling in front of her, and bright line of blood showed across his partially severed neck, though he was still very much alive. She tried to urge the weapon through the dwarf's throat, but it did not move.

"Only an *elf*," A'el intoned once more. "Not a slave."

Enessäna didn't know what he meant, and confusion brought a fresh wave of anger through her muddled consciousness. "What?" she muttered in the quiet, black realm of near-death.

"Only an elf may wield my sword," the legend explained in her mind.

"I am… blue… my skin," Enessäna struggled.

"No," A'el told her flatly. "You are a slave."

Enessäna felt blood running over her face. She didn't know if she had fallen or been attacked, but she knew it was her own blood that coated her features. "My master's… dead," she whispered.

A'el laughed in the morbid recesses of her mind. "No, your master has merely changed—you now serve the rage which lives inside your heart. You are a slave, and that is how you will die."

On the stone steps leading to the late King Ashmir's audience chamber at the center of Stonehelm, a curious dwarf slowly lifted one of his dead comrades' swords from the ground. He eyed the elf's red blade with suspicion, using the tip of his boot to nudge it out of the way. Then, with solemnity rarely seen among his kin, he remained silent as he plunged the weapon in his hands through the dying elf's chest.

STUART THAMAN

Now the author of almost a dozen novels, Stuart Thaman has enjoyed success in both epic fantasy and psychological horror. His flagship series, The Goblin Wars, has topped multiple bestseller lists in Australia, Canada, and the United States. Aside from The Goblin Wars, he also writes the Chronicles of Estria series, the official novelization of Ral Partha's Chaos Wars miniatures game, and the Umbral Blade series.

You can check out all of Stuart Thaman's works at www.stuartthamanbooks.com, and be sure to follow him on Twitter @stuartthamanbooks and on Facebook at the Stuart Thaman Books page.

Stuart lives in Kentucky with Yoda the Boston terrier and his four cats: Ichabod Crane, Mr. Baghuul, Eleven, and Pennywise. He enjoys rescuing animals, listening to the heaviest metal he can find, and collecting tattoos.

ACKNOWLEDGMENTS

Hydra Publications would like to thank the authors in this collection and everyone who submitted stories for consideration. Hydra Publications would also like to thank you, the reader, for coming along on such a grand journey. Without readers, there would be no writers. If you enjoyed this collection, please consider leaving a review at your favorite book retailer to help more people discover the wonders of epic fantasy.